Book Four:
Redemption Found

By: Alisha Williams

For more information, please address:
alishawilliamsauthor@gmail.com

Book cover design: Alisha Williams

AUTHOR NOTE

Please be advised. This is a reverse harem/why choose romance, meaning the heroine of this story does not have to pick between her love interests.

This book contains explicitly described sexual content and the excessive use of swear words. This book has more of a darker theme than the other books in this series and contains things that may trigger some readers.

DEDICATION

I'd like to dedicate not only this book but this whole series to a very special person to me. Thank you from the bottom of my heart Jessica Pollio-Napoles for everything you do for me and my books. You have been there from not just the first book in this series but my first book ever. You have been one of my biggest cheerleaders and best friends. Thank you for all the hours you spend helping me make the best books I can write. This might be our first finished series together, but it won't be our last. Your amazing girl, don't forget that!

Prologue
Oliver

THE HOUSE IS quiet when I walk through the front door. Emmy and Tyson must still be at Melody's appointment. I really wanted to be there, but I've been absent from the MC life for too long, and I have duties to my club as well as being a boyfriend and a father. It's a lot sometimes, but I wouldn't change it for anything.

Being out of that school and being able to just live our lives with our daughter has been amazing. I'm still having nightmares, but I'm hoping that going to a therapist and having us all behind guarded walls will help with that.

Grabbing a bottle of water out of the fridge, I crack open the top and chug the cold liquid. Today it's fucking hot, and this leather cut does nothing to help with it.

When I'm done, I toss the bottle into the recycling and head upstairs to lock my gun in its case. Emmy knows that Tyson and I are required to have them, but she doesn't like them in the house. We made a decision to compromise, meaning we would lock them up when we were going to be in the house longer than a few minutes. I'm tired, and my head is pounding, so I'm going to go get some sleep before my girls get back.

Just as I reach my room, my phone rings, so I tuck my gun back into its holster. I pull my cell phone out and see the caller ID shows *Firefly*, my contact name for Emmy.

I click accept and answer the phone. "Hey, Firefly. How's our baby girl? I wish I could have been there with you guys."

"Oliver." Her voice sounds panicked, and I'm instantly on alert. "We're at the doctor's office. They have..." Then the line goes silent.

"Emmy?" My voice now urgent. I look at the phone and see the call has been disconnected. "Fuck!" I roar.

"What's going on?" Ben asks, sticking his head out of his bedroom door. He looks half asleep.

"It's Emmy," I say, before turning around and running down the stairs. I need to leave; I need to go to her.

"What about Emmy?" Talon shouts as they both follow.

"Something's wrong," I say, trying to call her back. It goes straight to voicemail. I redial, trying Tyson this time. It just rings and rings.

"For fuck's sake!" I growl, clutching my phone tightly in my hand, ready to throw the fucking thing against the wall. But I don't, just in case one of them tries to get a hold of me again. "I'm going to her. She said she's still at the doctor's office." I start heading towards the door.

"Wait for us. We'll come too," Talon says.

"No time! You're in your fucking boxers." I grab my bike helmet from the side table and throw open the door. I race down the front steps and over to my bike. Just as I turn the key, the engine coming to life, I hear several gunshots coming from the direction of the front gate.

I quickly put my helmet on, push back the kickstand, and take off towards the sounds of gunfire. The shooting gets louder and louder as I get closer. Looking over to my left, I see other members racing towards the gate as well. I'm almost there when a man exits the guard station with his gun raised as he starts shooting blindly and moving to take cover behind a giant boulder. Phantom Reapers start jumping behind cars to take cover while also taking shots at the man. But a few intruders start shooting in my direction, hidden from inside the guard station. Bullets hit the ground in front of me, sending dust flying everywhere. When one hits my tire, I go skidding to the side and end up getting thrown off. I roll a few feet before I force my body to get up and take cover. Running to the nearest tree, I start taking shots too.

One of my men manages to take out the first guy when he pops up from behind the boulder he was using as a shield. As another guy takes a step out of hiding, fucking Harlow drops from the top of the gate, jumping on him like a damn ninja. She knocks him to the ground, pulls out her gun, and shoots him point blank in the head before spinning around to shoot the remaining guy. It all happens in a matter of seconds. The last man drops to the ground, a gaping hole in his head.

Everything is silent. No one moves, not knowing if there's anyone else we have to worry about.

My arm is throbbing, and I know I have road rash covering my entire side, but I don't care. I'm humming with adrenaline, the need to get to Emmy fueling my body.

"All clear," Neo shouts. He takes a step through the guard station, kicking the last man to die in the head just for the fun of it. He looks over at the first guy Harlow killed, and his face lights up as he sees the brain matter scattered all over the ground next to the shattered pieces of his skull. "Nice," he says, high fiving Harlow as she beams up at him like the sun shines out of his ass.

Everyone slowly comes out of their hiding spots.

"Is anyone hurt?" my dad calls out as he stands up from behind a car. Moving away from the tree, I rip off my helmet as I start to limp over to Harlow and Neo.

"It was a fucking distraction," I growl. "It was meant to keep us here so they could fucking kidnap my girlfriend!"

"What?" Harlow asks, her smile slipping into a deadly version of her happy face.

"Before these fuckers started taking shots, I got a call from Emmy. She sounded frantic. She said 'they have', then the line went dead. How much you wanna bet 'they' are the people these cock suckers work for?"

"He's right," Neo says. "There were only about five people outside. I killed them all. Dagger used them as sacrifices so he could get away with whatever he actually planned to do."

"Motherfucker!" my dad roars. "None of the men who I sent as extra back up for Tyson and Emmy are answering their phones."

"She said she was still at the doctor's before we got disconnected."

"Then we gotta go and see what the fuck is up," my dad says, before turning around and calling out to his men, telling them to grab their bikes.

"We'll deal with this," Neo says to me, before looking at Harlow, who is staring at the dead body by her feet, still as a statue. He looks back at me. "I need to keep her within these walls, or she will just storm into Hellhound territory. As fucking amazing as she is at taking out a room full of people, normally they aren't... mobile when she does it.

Three at once, sure, but a whole MC shooting at you... She's Queenie now, and her sister, niece, and best friend were just taken. This very well might be one of the scariest and most deadly states of mind she just entered. I'm going to have to call for backup with this one."

"Backup?" I ask, brows furrowed in confusion.

"Her other lovers. I don't think I can keep her contained long enough to make a solid plan of action."

Bike engines begin revving, and I look over to see my father along with a few men heading over here.

"I'm coming with you," I tell my father. There's no room for argument.

"Of course. But are you sure you're okay?" he asks, looking down at my ripped and bloody jeans.

"I'm fine," I force through gritted teeth. He just nods, and I climb onto the back of his bike. I'm going to have to get mine repaired or replaced before I can ride again.

Neo opens the gate for us, and we take off, speeding down the road. No one gives a flying fuck about the speed limits or cops.

When we get to the doctor's office, there are cops everywhere.

"Fuck," my dad mutters as his bike comes to a stop. I hop off, not wasting any time before searching around; only, I have no fucking idea what the hell I'm looking for.

I see my dad talking to one of the cops. I notice that there's a body in the middle of the parking lot covered with a tarp. I continue to observe my surroundings when my gaze catches on a car. Tyson's car. The trunk is open, and Melody's stroller lies on the ground.

"What's that?" An officer behind me asks. I turn around to see him walking to another cop.

"Looks like some kind of stuffed bunny."

Bunny? I head over to them, snatching the bunny out of the cop's hand.

"Sir, I don't know what you think your-"

"This is my daughter's bunny," I seethe. "Where did you find it?"

He must see how serious I am because he simply nods and then points behind him. “Found it over there, right around where we found the lady on the ground."

“What lady?” I ask, my voice sounding pathetically hopeful. Maybe Emmy just got knocked out, and they took off before getting her.

“She said her name was Amy. The ambulance took her to the hospital,” the officer informs me. Amy. Not Emmy. My heart sinks. At least Amy is okay. Emmy would never forgive herself if anything happened to her.

Looking down at my daughter's favorite thing in the world, I start to shut down. They have them: my soulmate, my heart, and my brother.

It didn't matter what we tried to do to prevent this; they still got them in the end. Ignoring the cops, I start to wander, not really sure where I was going. I just keep walking around the building, needing to get away from the scene.

Leaning back against the brick wall, I stare at Melody's bunny. This is one of the only things that can get her to calm down. Now she's with strangers, in an unfamiliar place. I just hope that Emmy can at least be with her.

A buzzing sound has me looking up. Moving away from the wall, I search for the sound, stopping next to a trash can. Peering in, I see a cell phone vibrating. Not caring about sticking my hand in the trash, I grab the phone.

“Emmy,” I whisper. It’s her phone. The vibration ends, and the screen lights up, showing fifteen missed calls.

Opening her lock screen, I punch in her password. My heart clenches as soon as I see the home screen photo. It’s all of us on grad night; all dressed up for our homemade prom.

Before I know what I’m doing, I’m clicking on her voicemail and playing her unheard messages.

The first few are Talon. One, demanding she pick up, next he tells her how worried he is, then one pleading for her to be okay. The majority of them are silent, with the person who called hanging up just as the voicemail kicks in. But the last one has me squeezing my eyes shut, hard.

Charlie sobs on the other end, insisting it isn't real, that Emmy just lost her phone, and that she will walk through the door any minute.

The call ends, and I go back to the home screen, staring at our smiling, happy faces.

“Come on, son. We gotta get back. Nothing else we can do here,” my dad says, coming up behind me and placing a hand on my shoulder.

“What the fuck do you mean there’s nothing else we can do here?” I demand, whirling around to face him.

“Look, we don't need the cops involved any more than they are right now. They are taking this as a turf war gone wrong. That Tyson and Emmy are back at the compound. I might have told them I’d have them by the station to check in, but I’ll worry about that later. Right now, we need to get back to the compound and tell five Old Ladies that their husbands are dead. Tell our men that their brothers are dead, on top of the fact that our enemy has kidnapped my son, daughter-in-law, and granddaughter. I’m hurting too, you know. But I need to keep my head on and make smart choices. Your people need you, and so do mine. So let's go.”

Charlie sobs in the corner while Evie tries to console her. Ben and Talon are huddled in the booth looking shattered and broken, all while Queenie is ranting in vivid detail about what she's going to do to Dagger when she gets her hands on him.

My ears are ringing, and my brain is going haywire. Too much. It’s all too much.

Picking up my glass of whiskey, I chuck it at the mirror behind the bar.

“Shut up!” I roar, grabbing handfuls of my hair and tugging on it. I need the noises to stop. I need the pain to go away, to feel numb. I need my girls in my arms and my brother at my side. Not to be sitting around here, doing fuck all while God knows what is happening to them.

The room is silent now. Only the sounds of Charlie’s quiet hiccupped cries can be heard.

"How the fuck can you just sit there!" I yell at Ben and Talon, then turn to Charlie. "Crying isn't going to bring her back. All it's doing is giving me a fucking headache."

Charlie's eyes go wide, before she turns and tucks her face into one of the Old Lady's shoulders, letting out another round of sobs. The Old Lady shoots me a death glare as she rubs Charlie's back, soothing her.

"Look, we get it. You're pissed, hurt, and fucking scared. We all are!" Talon shouts, getting out of the booth and walking over to me. "But that doesn't give you the right to take it out on us. What the fuck do you want us to do? Hop in a car, drive down there, and knock on the fucking door? Maybe if we ask nicely enough, they will just hand them over? No. They would put bullets in our brains before we could even open our mouths."

My chest is heaving, the pressure in my head becoming too much. Deep down, I know he's right, but I'm not myself right now.

"Oliver," my dad says, stepping in between Talon and me. "I know you're hurting, but don't take it out on your family. You need them right now more than ever, and they need you. How would Emmy feel if she knew you were taking it out on them?"

"You don't understand!" I shake my head. "I was supposed to protect her. From the moment I met her, as a five-year-old little boy, I vowed to myself that I would protect that girl with everything in me, at all costs. And what have I done? Nothing. I've failed her over and over again, so many times I've lost count. And now? Now, I fucking failed my daughter too. They're fucking better off without me."

"Don't. Don't talk like that. That girl loves you with all of her soul, Oliver. You're her best friend, first love... First, everything. She needs you just as much as she needs the others," my dad states.

"I should have been able to save her, Dad," I growl in frustration, my eyes burning with tears. "And now they have her."

"And we will get her back," he says with pure determination, as he grips my shoulders. "We will burn that place to the ground trying. They *will* come home."

"I'm so fucking scared." My voice cracks, tears breaking through.

"I know, son. I know." His voice sounds so sad. He pulls me into him, wrapping me in a tight hug.

I feel like a little boy needing the comfort of his father again. I'm slowly losing touch with reality, and the only person who's ever really anchored me isn't here this time. So I cling to him, letting everything out that I've been holding in, needing him to be my temporary rock.

"Don't worry, your pretty little head, Olly-boy," Queenie's voice comes from behind me after I get a hold of myself. I turn around to look at her. She's standing there like a fucking badass. Guns and knives strapped to her tight, black jeans, paired with a red leather corset top. Her hair is in a high ponytail, and her lips are painted blood red.

When the hell did she change into that?

"Don't ask," Neo says, appearing at my side. "Trust me, this is what she actually looks like ninety percent of the time." I startle, looking up at the very scary man.

"You should really come with a bell," I grumble.

His eyes light up, making me raise a brow. "Oh! With a collar too?" He looks over at Harlow, who's glaring at him so hard that if he wasn't her lover, he would probably be dead by now. "Right. Not the time. But like, can we talk about this later?" Harlow growls, showing her teeth a little. "Fuck," he groans, then cups his junk. "You know how hot that gets me when you go all lioness."

"Neo!" She barks, but the crazy fuck knows when to shut up. He mutters something about dying from all the blood going to his dick, before turning around and leaving.

"Dagger will die. His men will die. There's no doubt about that. But my sister, my niece, and my best friend? Nah. We'll get to them before anything happens."

"Don't make a promise you can't keep," I warn her. Normally I would never talk to her like that in fear I might lose a finger or two, but I'm not someone to be messed with right now.

"I'm not," she says matter of factly.

"Well, alright then. Let's start making a plan and get my world back."

CHAPTER 1
Emmy

"GIVE ME MY daughter, you cock sucking, mother-fucking, piece of shit!" I roar at the locked door, as I pound my fist against the wood. I've been doing this for hours. My hands are numb, and my throat is raw, but I won't stop until Melody is back in my arms. It's been over twelve hours, and she's still solely breastfeeding.

Are they taking good care of her? Have they at least tried to bottle feed her? Or are they leaving her alone in a room, hungry and crying?

The thought has the back of my eyes stinging with tears. I would have thought that I already cried out everything I had in me. I guess I was wrong.

"Please!" I shout, my voice breaking as the words slip past my lips. "I'll do whatever you want. Just, please, give my daughter back. She needs me."

Needing a minute, I turn around and lean my back against the door, sliding down until my ass hits the ground. Tucking my legs to my chest, I wrap my arms around them tight and bury my face into my knees.

Another wave of sorrow takes over my body, and the tears come back with a vengeance, as I think about the last twenty-four hours.

Happy. I was so utterly happy. Going out for my birthday, which happened to be the best one to date, then coming home for my men to rock my world.

Now here I am, alone in Hell while God knows who has my daughter. And Tyson. My gut turns, as a million horrible things flash before my eyes at what they would be doing to him, the son of their enemy. I will fucking kill them all for laying a hand on my man.

Oliver and the others must be going out of their minds with worry and fear right now.

They would have woken up thinking that I'd be gone an hour or two only to find out that I'm not coming home at all.

I don't know how long I've sat here crying, but when I hear the sounds of keys clanking, I quickly scramble to my feet.

A lock clicks, and a moment later, the door swings open, revealing a tall, blond haired man.

Damn it! If this asshole didn't take me by surprise, I would have grabbed the lamp on the side table and knocked him out.

Then what? You have no weapons, no idea about this place, and by the time you found Melody and Tyson, they would have realized what was going on. You're screwed, face it.

"Feedings. You get her for feedings only. Then I will come back to get her," the man says.

"What? You can't do this!" I seethe, clenching my hands, as I try not to punch his stupid face.

"I can. And until Dagger thinks you're broken enough, – meaning you won't try and escape– to be a good, little daughter that he wants, this is how it's going to be. You really have no choice. Now, do you want your daughter or not?" he asks in a bored monotone voice, while crossing his arms and blocking the exit, as he stares me down.

Narrowing my eyes at him in fury with my chest heaving, it takes everything in me not to tell him where to go and how to fucking get there. But I won't. I can't risk not getting to see her. "Fine," I say through gritted teeth.

He lets out a grunt, before stepping back into the hallway, closing and locking the door again.

Letting out a frustrated sigh, I start to pace the room, biting the side of my thumb as I wait for the big, meathead to come back with my daughter.

When I woke up, seeing Dagger's face was the last thing I wanted. I had the desperate need to squeeze my eyes shut and hope that it was all a dream. Well, more like a nightmare.

Dagger didn't say much, before he left me locked up in this room, but he did manage to spew some crazy bullshit about me finally being where I belong. About how there was no way in Hell he would allow his daughter to be with the enemy and how excited he was to be a grandpa.

It was all the ramblings of a crazy man. He doesn't want me. He just doesn't want his enemies to have me. I guess the idea of me dating the sons of his rival MC was enough for him to be petty enough to do all this. But what else can I expect from an unhinged psychopath?

He can think whatever he wants, because we will NOT be staying here. I will find a way to get Tyson and my daughter, before getting the fuck out of there. Then I'll send his own flesh and blood to finish the job. I know Harlow is itching to add him to the list of evil men she will rid from this world.

The sounds of a baby crying has my head snapping over to the door. The lock clicks, and in walks meathead with my screaming child in his arms.

"Here. Take the little brat. She's hurting my fucking ears," he growls, thrusting Melody towards me.

I quickly take her from his arms, hugging her to my chest. "You have thirty minutes to feed her. Then I'll be back. You will get her again two hours after that." Then he shuts and locks the door once more.

Looking down at Melody with blurry eyes, I can't help the massive smile that takes over my face, as I start to rock her from side to side to calm her cries.

"Hi, baby girl," I choke out, tears sliding down my cheeks. "Mama is so glad to have you back in her arms."

It takes me a few minutes of soothing and rocking her to get her to stop crying. My heart breaks hearing her like this. What the fuck have they been doing with her to make her so upset? Have they even fed her in the past twelve hours?

Walking over to the bed, I climb up and get comfortable, leaning back against the pillows. Adjusting her, I pull down my shirt and position her to my nipple. She immediately latches on, sucking like she's starving. My lip curls and my vision goes red. *Fucking bastards were starving her!*

There's nothing I can do about that now. What matters is that she's getting what she needs *now*. At least the room they have me locked in has an en-suite bathroom. Nothing fancy, but knowing that I can shower and have a drink of water when I want to is better than nothing.

Not wanting my milk supply to dry up and the fact that my tits were so fucking engorged they hurt like a bitch, I had to express my milk into the sink.

It was a waste when it could have been used to feed the baby they fucking kidnapped.

Once Melody's swallows begin to slow, she relaxes in my arms. I hum *Somewhere Over the Rainbow* to her while rubbing her curly, red hair.

I try to enjoy this time with her before that asshole comes and takes her from me, but thoughts of Tyson creep in. *Where is he? Are they torturing him for the fun of it? Is he locked in a room like me?* Being the enemy's son and someone who's probably killed a few Savage Hellhounds over the years, I don't think they would be pulling out the welcome mat for him.

Once Melody has drained one breast, I switch her over to the other. My poor baby girl is so hungry. I really wanna kill someone right now.

Just as Melody starts to feed again, the lock on the door clicks, and someone that I would gladly volunteer as the first person to die walks in.

"Times up," he grunts.

"She's still feeding."

He looks down, watching her eat. Scowling, I grab her baby blanket and cover her up.

"Hurry up then," he grunts.

"Oh yes, I'm gonna tell the starving baby to start chugging, so that you can take her away again," I sneer. "Has anyone even fed her since Dagger's goons kidnapped us?"

"They tried. But she wouldn't drink from the bottle."

"So you thought making her go hungry would encourage her to drink it? God, I hope none of you have kids and never do. Because all of you know shit all about caring for a baby, when she didn't drink, you should have brought her to me."

"Well, she's here now. And now I'm going to take her, and you will get her in two hours. Don't try and fight me on this, or we will be forced to use her against you."

Okay, so I'll be offering him up to Harlow too. Or maybe Tyson will want a crack at him when he finds out how this ass-wipe has been treating his baby girl.

Melody falls asleep, detaching herself from my nipple. She looks so peaceful and all milk drunk. Smiling at her little, parted mouth as she makes her cute little noises, my heart starts to shatter, knowing that I have to hand her back.

Taking a deep breath, I hold back the tears threatening to fall while telling myself to be strong.

Kissing the top of her head, I whisper, “Mama and Daddy T will get you out of here, my sweet girl. Don’t you worry. I love you more than life,” and kiss her again.

Fixing my shirt, I get off the bed and reluctantly walk over to him. “If she gets hungry before the two hours are up, please bring her back. Fuck with me however you think you need to, but don’t use her as a pawn. It will only hurt her in the end. She’s innocent, and it’s not fucking right.”

He nods and holds out his arms. I look at them, hesitating for a second, before handing my life over to him. He looks down at her, a hint of a smile. “You know, she's actually kinda cute when she's not screaming her head off like a banshee.”

“Fuck you,” I hiss, letting the words slip past my lips before I know what I’m saying.

“Nah, sweet cheeks. I’m not into that kind of thing.” He chuckles, before leaving once again.

What the fuck does he mean by that?

That fucking sound of the lock clicking into place has quickly become the sound I hate the most in the world.

Dragging my feet across the wooden floor, I head back over to the bed. I could scream, pound on the door, and call them all the names in the book again. But that’s not going to do anything. I need to be smart, clear my head, find my man, get my daughter, and get the fuck out of here.

Dagger will regret the day he fucked with the Phantom Reapers because there's gonna be a war real soon, and they sure as hell won’t be on the winning side.

Curling up onto my side, I close my eyes, hoping sleep will make the time go by faster, so that I can have Melody back in my arms.

But thoughts of my other lovers consume my dreams. My sweet, sweet loves.

I'm so sorry for any pain you might feel by our absence. It won't be forever. Not when you have Queenie on your side.

CHAPTER 2
Tyson

THE IMPACT OF his fist to my stomach is nothing but a dull sensation at this point. I don't know how long I've been hung up like a slaughtered animal, but after a few hours of their torture, my brain did its best to shut down. The pain eventually turned my body numb.

"You know, if she wasn't the boss's daughter, I would have taken that sexy, little ass for a ride. I bet she would take my cock perfectly," the bald meathead of a goon tries to goad me.

Every man who came in here spewed the same kind of filth. At first, I was fighting against my restraints, trying to get to them, so I could rip their fucking throats out, but it only spurred them on even more. Now, I've shut myself down. For the time being, I'm trying to block out their words, while filling my mind up with all the fucked up things I plan to do to them once I get free. Normally, the things Queenie does to her victims would be too much for me, but right now, it's a brand of fucked up that I would love to take part in.

"This isn't fun anymore," the little weasel looking one says, his voice annoying as fuck. He sounds like a male version of 'Janice' from *Friends*. Honestly, I'd say listening to his hyena laugh has been the worst punishment they've done to me so far, and that's saying something. Especially, seeing how they've used blades, chains, and their fists. "He's not even reacting. Maybe we fucked him up too much. Dagger said we can't kill him yet, so maybe we should stop."

"Should we stop, little Reaper?" the bald one asks, stepping closer to me. He grips my bloody face in his hand and yanks my head up. "Have you had enough? Maybe I'll give you a little break and go see what Emmy is up to." He gives me this big shit-eating grin, and I use this moment to spit the blood that's been pooling in my mouth since his last punch to my jaw. The blood coats his face, some getting on his nasty yellow teeth. "Fucking piece of shit," he roars, the smug look falling from his face, replaced with pure venom.

He spits back at me, before letting go of my face, to smash his fist into my jaw again. My head whips to the side, and I spit out a new mouthful of blood. This time it lands on the floor next to his feet.

As much as I'd love to do it again, I don't want to be eating through a straw, with my jaw wired shut until the broken bones heal. Also, how would I eat my Princess' sweet pussy that way?

Not being able to bury my face between her sweet, creamy thighs would be a much worse punishment than anything they have thrown at me yet.

"Fuck this guy. He's not worth my time anymore. Leave the fucker to hang here until Dagger tells us what to do with him next."

I watch them through my swollen eyes as they walk up the stairs, leaving me bloody and beaten.

I'm a fucking mess. The smell of piss, sweat, and blood invades my nose. I've been hanging here for hours; you really think they let me down to run to the toilet? Nah, I tried to hold it in as long as I could, but one of the fuckers thought it would be funny to punch me in the bladder and watch me piss myself. He's gonna pay for that. It wasn't my finest hour.

My arms feel like they are popped out of their sockets, even as they try to support my body weight. It feels like only minutes before the next person makes their way down the steps, feet thumping against the floor. I must have fallen asleep.

"Wakey, wakey," someone says. This voice is new. Mustering up all my strength, I lift my head enough to see who my next tormentor is. I can't see much; the light from the window is long gone, leaving only the low light of the single bulb in the middle of the room to glow over him. His hair looks to be a shade of blond, a little shaggy, but longer than Talon's. He's tall, about my height, if not taller. He has this bored look on his face like he would rather be anywhere but here. Me too, buddy, me too.

"Let's get you down and cleaned up. I don't think your little girlfriend would be too happy with you looking and smelling like a homeless man." He raises his arms up, a hunting knife in one hand. On instinct, I try to move back. He looks down at me with a raised brow. "I'm not gonna stab you. I need it to cut down the rope," he says, rolling his eyes, as he starts to cut away at the ropes, that have my wrists bound and hung up on this fucking hook.

The moment he makes the last cut, my body drops to the ground because I have no strength in me to catch myself.

I groan, rolling onto my back, as I blink up at the roof. This feels amazing, but it also hurts so fucking much as my muscles get some much needed relief.

“Need some help?” he asks.

“No, I don’t,” I grunt as I pathetically move to stand. Once on my feet, gravity fucks with me, and I almost go toppling back to the ground, before the guy grabs a hold of me, keeping me upright.

"They really did a number on you, didn't they?” he asks, examining my face.

“You think?” I sneer.

“Look,” he says, before looking over my shoulder at something. “Not here,” he says, lowering his voice.

He guides me up the stairs, every step more painful than the one before. When we step out the door, we enter into a dark hallway.

“Where are you taking me?” I rasp, my voice laced with exhaustion.

“Somewhere a little more accommodating than the basement,” he says, as we pass a few doors.

“Where are we?”

“You sure do ask a lot of questions for a prisoner. Isn't that my job?” he chuckles. *Asshole.* When I say nothing, he sighs. “We’re in one of the houses on the Hellhound compound. Lucky for you, everyone is at the clubhouse celebrating the death of a few of your men, while mourning the loss of ours.”

My body ignites at that. My men, my brothers, dead? Fucking Hellhounds are gonna pay for that. But good, I’m glad we took out a few of theirs.

“What happened to your guys?” I ask, as we stop outside a door. He shifts my weight, reaching into his pocket to grab a set of keys. Unlocking the door, he helps me into the room, flicking the light on as we enter. I flinch away from the sudden brightness, squeezing my eyes shut and regretting it, as my swollen eyes throb in response.

He kicks the door shut behind him before taking me over to a plastic chair.

"Didn't think you would want the bed smelling like piss," he says, when he sees me looking at the much more comfortable option that my body would appreciate more. But he has a point.

"And to answer your question, some of our men died while being a distraction, keeping your men behind bars, so Dagger could get you, Emmy, and the baby here."

Good. They all deserve to fucking die for what they did. "Where's Emmy?" I demand. "Where's my daughter?"

"Both are safe. Emmy is in a room much like this but in another house. The baby is with the Old Ladies."

"She should be with her mother." Melody is breastfeeding, but even if she wasn't, Emmy is the best place for her to be.

"I agree, but Dagger wouldn't be Dagger if he didn't use some sort of emotional blackmail. But the baby would not take a bottle, so he's allowed me to bring the baby to Emmy every two hours to feed."

So she gets to see her, that's good. Wait. "Why you?" I ask, brows trying to furrow in confusion.

"Because I volunteered." He shrugs, taking a seat on the bed.

"Why?" I ask again, my confusion increasing.

"Because I need access to both of you, and as much as I can get, if I'm going to get all of you out of here."

"What the hell do you mean by that?" *Is this some kind of trap? Or some fucked up joke?*

"I mean, there's a war coming, and as fucked up and blood thirsty as the Savage Hellhounds are, there's no way we're going to win. You have Queenie on your side, and fuck... I know what that woman can do. I do *not* want to be on the wrong side when she comes in here and burns this place to the ground."

"But these are your men," I say slowly. Is this man a traitor to his people? Tossing them under the bus to save his own ass?

"All you need to know is I've never belonged in this place. I don't agree with their ways and what they do. But if I tried to leave, I'd be dead. So no, these are not my men. They are Dagger's men, and I'm here as a fucked up little puppet. I don't like how this is all coming about, but this is the chance I've been waiting a really long fucking time for. To be able to cut those puppet strings."

I don't trust this man as far as I can throw him, but something is telling me that he's being honest.

And if that means having someone who doesn't want to kick my ass for the fun of it, be the one to deal with me while I'm here, I'm not going to argue.

"Anyways, you smell disgusting. Go shower. I'll bring by some food after I drop Melody off with Emmy," he says, standing up to leave.

"Is she really okay? Has anyone hurt her?" The idea of someone laying their hands on her makes my blood boil.

"No. No one but me and Dagger have been in contact with her since she was put in the room. As for Melody, she's only been with me or the Old Ladies since getting back. The old bats aren't the most lovable people, but they do know enough about babies to care for her when she's not with her mother."

He turns to leave, heading towards the door. "Thanks," I find myself saying. "I'd rather it be you dealing with them than those disgusting pigs. Some of the things they said they'd do to her..." I close my eyes and take a deep breath, my anger rising at the thought of their threats. "Just, please don't hurt her."

"I won't. I have no interest in hurting either of them. As for the others, they won't lay a finger on her. Dagger has forbidden them. Well, all but that creepy fucking teacher, but I won't let him near her."

Teacher, what fucking teacher? Before I can ask him what the hell he was talking about, he's gone, locking the door behind him with several locks clicking into place.

It feels like I am frozen in ice, and now my body is unthawing because, with each passing second, I start to feel more and more pain due to the extent of my injuries.

"Fuck," I hiss as I stand. I limp my way into the bathroom, each step feeling like I'm walking on a bed of broken glass.

Flicking the light on, I take in the small bathroom. A shower, but no tub, a sink, and a toilet. At least it's better than where I was.

Stripping off my filthy clothes, I toss them to the side and turn on the cold water. I'm too sore and raw for hot water. I bite back a scream as the water hits my skin. The water pressure is weak, but my skin is marked up and bruised, plus I'm sure I have a few broken ribs as well.

Doing the best that I can, I wash the grime away from my skin. I half ass wash my hair, unable to lift my arms very high.

I fucking hate feeling so useless, unable to care for myself. Fucking weak.

Grabbing one of the ratty towels left for me, I dry myself off the best I can, before dressing in the sweatpants and T-shirt that was left for me.

Hobbling back into the room, I sit on the edge of the bed. Running a hand down my face, I let out an exhausted sigh.

How did our lives end up like this? After everything we put into place to keep this from happening, it was all for nothing. They got to her in the end. At least they took me with them. Knowing that she's close by, that I can get to her faster if shit hits the fan, gives me the smallest amount of comfort ever known to man.

And *now* this mysterious man is helping us. I don't trust him; I'd be a fool to. But he seemed serious about helping us, and I can't turn down his help when it comes to getting my girls out of here. Back to safety.

Climbing under the blankets, my body shakes as the pain of my injuries hits me full force. Closing my eyes, I think of her smile, her big brown eyes, and that laugh that has my heart exploding every time I hear it. We will get out of here, and she will be the source of my strength.

Hold on, Princess, I'm coming for you.

CHAPTER 3
Ben

OUR WHOLE WORLD has been turned upside down. The love of our lives is gone, and our daughter is in the hands of the fucking enemy. And we can't do shit all but sit here and worry.

It's been forty-eight hours. FORTY-EIGHT miserable hours of pain and heartache. Oliver has been busying himself with MC stuff. Talon insisted we be let in on whatever they have planned, but Steel told him that we will know what we need to know, because we're not patched-in members or even prospects.

I get it... But I don't like it. And Talon has expressed his feelings towards it more than once.

"How are you doing?" I ask Talon, giving his shoulder a squeeze, as I stand behind him at his spot at the kitchen island. Placing my hands on each shoulder, I give them another gentle squeeze. He's leaning over a bit, his arms resting on the counter, as his head hangs low, staring blankly at his cup of coffee.

"Not good," he says, sounding defeated. My heart hurts for him, seeing one of my loves aching for our other. I know how he feels, because it's the same thing I'm going through too, but someone needs to be strong. If he needs to break, I'll be here to pick up the pieces and keep him from falling down.

"Wanna talk about it?" I ask, taking a seat next to him.

He looks up at me, and my heart breaks all over again as I see the dark rings around his eyes. I know he hasn't been getting any sleep, tossing, and turning all night. "And say what? That it feels like a part of my soul is missing? How I can't stop thinking about if they hurt her? If Tyson is alive? If our daughter is being taken care of? The Savage Hellhounds are sick fucks. What makes us think Dagger won't let his men loose on Emmy? Ben, if they lay a hand on her, I will fucking kill them all with my bare hands and bathe in their blood."

I know he means it. I can see it in his eyes. I've seen the darkness that lurks deep within him.

"And I'd be right there next to you. I will always be by your side," I promise.

Talon stares at me, saying nothing for the longest moment before he stands up. He steps into me, taking my face into his hands, and captures me with a bruising kiss.

I try not to moan because now is not the time, but it's so hard not to. He and Emmy have their ways of making me turn into a horny puddle of goo almost instantly.

He pulls back, his chest rising and falling as he catches his breath. "Take it away." He looks so fucking broken that tears sting my eyes. "Please. Help me take the pain away, even if it's just for a moment. It hurts so fucking much," he chokes, a clenched hand hitting his chest over his heart. "I need you."

I want to. I want to help him in any way I can. But is this the right way? Should we be using sex to cope with the hurt of them being gone?

"Ben," he says, seeing the conflict on my face. "Emmy loves us. We have our own relationship outside of her, and she's okay with that because she's our number one. She's told us so many times not to stop being who we are with each other because of her. I want her here too, so bad, but right now, you're here. She's not. Please."

He's right. He needs me, and I love him too much to watch him hurt. If I can take his mind off things, and make him feel something other than like a piece of him is missing, then I want to do that.

"Come on," I say, holding out my hand. He places his in mine, squeezing it hard. I guide him upstairs to our room. A part of me is breaking alongside him. I need this distraction just as much as he does.

Talon likes to be the one to take charge in the bedroom, and Emmy and I both love it. But, right now, he needs me to be the one to take control.

"Sit," I tell him after bringing him to the edge of the bed. He does so, looking up at me with lost eyes. I cup his face, leaning over to kiss him slowly. He moans into my mouth, grips my hips, and pulls me down onto his lap. I can feel his hard cock against my ass, and I grind against him, loving the noises of appreciation I'm getting from him. I need him so fucking much.

I slide my hands down his back as he devours my mouth with urgent need until I find the hem of his shirt. He lifts his arms for me as I pull it off.

"Lay down," I say, pushing lightly on his shoulders. When he's flat on his back, I run my fingertips over the hard ridges of his abs and all the way down his delicious V that disappears below the waist line of his jeans. His skin ripples under my touch.

Leaning over, I leave open mouth kisses over his chest, slipping my tongue out when I get to his abs, tracing every inch with my tongue.

"Fuck," he hisses as I take his nipple into my mouth. My tongue plays with it as I suck lightly before biting just hard enough to have him bucking under me.

"Does that feel good?" I ask, my voice husky. My attention is on my man as I push all other thoughts to the back of my mind for the moment.

"So fucking good," he groans, as I repeat the action to the other nipple. "But I need more."

Moving away from his nipple, I kiss down his chest, stopping just above his jeans. Climbing off him and onto the floor, I move between his legs.

I start to rid him of his pants, un-doing them and sliding them down. He lifts his ass up so I can get them fully off, leaving him in only his boxers. His cock is hard and presses against the thin material.

He moves so that he's leaning back on his arms. My eyes lock with his. His pupils are blown wide with lust, and I bite my lip. A part of me wishes this was the part where he pulls me off the floor, throws me on the bed, and whispers dirty things into my ear as he fucks my ass hard. But, maybe this time, I'd be okay with being the one to do those things. It's not something I've done with him much, but Emmy seems to love it.

Standing up, I start to strip out of my own clothes, feeling Talon's heated eyes roam all over me. I love the attention, the visible way to measure how much he craves my body.

"Tattoos are so fucking hot," he growls, sending a shiver through my body. "My lovers are like my own personal works of art. The rarest forms. Priceless."

God, I love this man.

When I'm bare, I take my cock in my hand, needing to relieve some of the pressure. Talon licks his lips as he watches me give my length a few strokes, stopping to smear the pre-cum that's gathered on the tip.

"Next time, it's mine. Don't waste it," he says, and my cock twitches in response.

I thought I was running this show? "Take your boxers off. Show me that cock I fucking love. Show me how hard you are with the need to be inside me." I say, my hand stroking my cock a little faster.

"Fuck, I love it when you talk dirty to me," he groans, quickly ridding himself of the last thing that's standing between us.

"Move to the center of the bed," I direct him.

When he's where I want him to be, I climb onto the bed myself. His hungry eyes watch my every move like he's desperate to devour me, as I crawl to him until I'm draped over his entire body.

His thighs widen for me, and I lower myself between his legs until my cock is pressed against his. He sucks in a ragged breath. "I love you, Talon." I'll tell him all day, every day, for the rest of our lives, so he knows he's never alone.

He swallows thickly, his eyes flicking between mine and my lips. "I love you, too." He reaches up, pulling my face to his. I moan into his mouth as his tongue tangles with mine. I can never get enough of the way he tastes.

"Ride me?" He asks, breaking the kiss. We're both worked up, and playtime is over. "I wanna touch you while you fuck yourself with my cock."

I groan, putting my hand to his chest. "Baby, you can't say shit like that. You're gonna have me cumming all over your chest, before you even touch me."

Grabbing the bottle of lube out of the bedside table, I straddle his thighs so that I can have access to his cock. Squirting some gel onto my hand, I grip his cock, coating it completely so that it's ready for me. He moans, jerking his hips causing his dick to thrust into my hand.

Moving, I position my ass right over the head, his tip brushing against my tight hole. "Don't look away." I tell him as I start to sink down on his thick cock. We both let out lusty groans, and Talon bites his lip hard, his hands flying to my thighs.

"So fucking tight," he rasps.

Once he's fully inside me, I take a moment, giving both of us time to adjust before I start to rock my hips. It doesn't take long until I'm riding him hard, both of us filling the room with our cries of pleasure. My body is humming with ecstasy because of him. He always makes me feel so fucking good.

Leaning over, I tuck my face into his neck, kissing, licking, and sucking. He thrusts up into me as he grips my cock, jerking me off.

His hand around my length is punishingly tight as he starts to fuck me hard. I can't think straight anymore. My mind is too far gone from the sensation of him alone.

I know I'm not gonna outlast him. "Fuck." I curse as his speed starts to quicken. "Talon, baby, I'm gonna cum." I grunt, then a second later, I roar into his neck as my hips thrust forward. Jets of hot cum shoot out and coat Talon's abs.

Before I even get a moment to think, he has me flipped onto my back, my legs over my head, as he starts to fuck me hard and fast. The look of determination on his face has me hurting for my man. He's trying so hard not to think about anything other than us at this moment. But I know he can't. It's impossible.

He keeps fucking me, unable to look me in the eye the more intense he becomes.

"Damn it," he grunts. "Fuck. Fuck. Fuuuuck," he screams, as he cums hard in my ass. His chest is heaving. His breathing is wild as he releases my legs and leans over to tuck his face into my neck.

I hold him, rubbing his back. His breathing doesn't even out, if anything, it starts to pick back up.

His body starts to shake as he breaks apart in my arms. Tears fall from my eyes, as a broken sob breaks from his lips.

"We'll get them back," I tell him, trying to hold myself together, trying not to break down right alongside him.

"I miss them, Ben. I miss them so fucking much," he croaks. "Emmy should be here, between us. Happy, safe. Melody should be in our arms where she belongs. This is all wrong. So *fucking* wrong. I need them back. If something happens to them, I don't know if I'll survive." He starts to cry. I just hold him, unable to say anything to make it better.

He is right, though. As much as I love Talon–and he's just as much a part of me as Emmy is–but if I lose her and my daughter, I don’t think there would ever be anything that could repair that kind of loss, that kind of pain. We would be broken shells of ourselves.

But it won't come to that. We won't let it. We have the Phantom Reapers and Queenie on our side. I hope the pieces of shit who have my girls are ready, because we are about to rain Hell down over them all, and I expect to come back soaked in their blood.

CHAPTER 4
Emmy

IT HAS TO have been at least a week since that asshole kidnapped us. I haven't seen Tyson since we got here, but the guy who brings me Melody, whose name turns out to be Seth, tells me he's fine and locked up in a room just like mine in another building.

I know he didn't get off unharmed. It's not the Savage Hellhounds' style to not be sick bastards, and it makes me ill knowing I can't be there for him. But he's strong. If I can survive this, so can he.

But they want you alive. They're only using Tyson until he no longer serves a purpose, whatever that might be.

I plan on us getting the fuck out of here before that happens though. How? I have no fucking clue. I'm starting to get cabin fever from being locked up twenty-four-seven. All my meals are brought to me just like Melody is when she needs her feedings. All I have in here to entertain myself are a few magazines from the late 2000's that Seth was able to sneak in for me a few days ago. I've read every single word in each of them five times by now.

Is this my new life? Just being held as a prisoner, stuck in this room? What's the fucking point of keeping me if they have no use for me? Why not just kill me? Am I just some pawn in this fucked up game they have with the Reapers? Because let's be real, there's no way Dagger woke up after all these years and said, 'Hey, I wanna be a dad and a grandpa.' Stupid fuck doesn't have a loving bone in his body.

It's all about power and control. So, now I'm forced to sit here and wait for however long. But at least I have her, my sweet baby girl. They seem to be taking good care of her. She's putting on weight and feeding well. She's all smiles and giggles that I, sadly, don't get to enjoy for very long.

I'm sitting here in bed, feeding Melody like always. I can't help but smile as I watch her drink.

Her little noises are adorable as she soothes herself by opening and closing her little fist while the other one is wrapped around her red curls.

The door opens, and I look up to tell Seth that my time isn't up, that he just dropped her off, but it's not Seth.

"Well, look at that. If it isn't my whore of a daughter." My mother sneers as she barges into the room with Seth behind her, glaring at her back like he would love to stick a dagger in it.

"Poor little thing. She's gonna grow up to be just as fucked up as her mother," she says, looking at Melody.

"What the hell are you doing here?" I growl. "And you have no room to speak. I'm already a better mother in the last four months than you've been in the eighteen years I was in your care."

"Well, what can I say? I should have gotten an abortion like your father said to. Stupid me, thought having his baby would get me him. But all I got was another mouth to feed and an ungrateful bitch."

I snort. "Yeah, mouth to feed, sure, seeing how all the money we had went to your drugs. Do you remember why I was always taken into foster care, or were you too high to notice?" I shake my head. "Doesn't matter." I look over to Seth. "Why is she here? And not just in the room, but here at your compound."

"Your father wants his family now." She gives me this smug as fuck smile that I just want to wipe off her face. "I'm his Old Lady now."

Seth chokes out a laugh, and she shoots him a glare. "No, you're not. You're just a warm place for Dagger to stick his dick. Once he gets sick of you, you will be tossed aside or dead like the others."

"Watch your tone with me, or I'll tell Dagger you were bad mouthing his woman," she juts her chin out.

In a flash, Seth has my mother against the wall, his hand wrapped around her throat as he squeezes tight, making her eyes pop with panic.

"Listen here, you stupid bitch. Talk to me like that again, and Dagger won't be the one ending your pointless life. You're a hole to fuck, that's it. Why he came back for seconds, I don't fucking know, but he sure as hell doesn't plan on making you his *Old Lady*. So learn your place before I put you in it."

Is it fucked up that I'm enjoying this? Seeing her like this, scared and vulnerable instead of cocky and cruel. Looking down at Melody, I see she's fast asleep, not even waking from all the commotion. She must be milk drunk.

Seth lets go of her, and she starts coughing. She doesn't say anything, just pats at her skin tight dress.

"Now that you're done causing a scene, wanna tell me why you're here?" I ask again. *Is it a hard question to answer or something?*

"I wanted to see my granddaughter."

My brow furrows. "Let me get this straight. You hate me, want nothing to do with me, but you care about my kid?" I look back at Seth. "What kind of drugs is she on this time?" He just grins and shrugs.

She glowers at me. "If you're going to be rude, I'm leaving."

"Good. Hope the door hits you on the way out because you're not here for her or me; you're here to gloat. You think because Dagger is fucking you that you're better than me now. That because he is in charge here, you have some say. Fuck off; you're still nothing."

"Time to go," Seth says, grabbing her by the arm and shoving her out the door, shutting it behind her. I can hear her bitching as it fades away down the hall.

"Well, that was a lovely family reunion." I give him a forced smile as I move Melody, placing her on my shoulder so that I can burp her.

"Fucking crazy bitch," he scoffs, stepping closer.

"Why are you being so nice to me?" I ask. The question has been bugging me for days.

"What do you mean?" he grumbles, crossing his tattooed arms as a piece of his blond hair falls over his eye.

"I know MC men are not all sunshine and rainbows, but this club is one of the most ruthless ones in Canada. They kill for fun and laugh while they dance on your grave. So why haven't you tried to rape me, beat me, or at least call me degrading names?"

He cocks a brow, a smile teasing his lips. "Like I said before, I'm not into that kind of shit. I'll tell you what I told your man, Tyson. A war is coming, and the other side has Queenie. That's not someone I want to make an enemy of, not for this lot.

They deserve everything coming to them, and I plan on being on the winning side."

"So…you're gonna help? You're gonna get us out of here?" I ask, hating how hopeful I sound.

"I'm trying," he says slowly. "It's not that easy. Dagger knows I'm not like the others, it's why I can get away with being the one to deal with you all, but the moment he catches wind that I'm not on his side, I'm dead."

Letting out a breath, I nod. "I get it. Do you know what his plan is with Tyson and me? Is it just to keep us locked up forever?"

"Tyson, no. He's only keeping Tyson alive to keep the Phantom Reapers from charging in here right away. He plans on killing him once he wins, or so he says."

My stomach drops. There's no fucking way I'm letting Tyson die and not at the hands of that monster.

"As for you and her… Well, he just wants you so that his enemy doesn't." I fucking knew it. "So what he plans on doing with you, he hasn't really said. The only orders he's given me are to keep you alive."

"You think he'll kill us?" Is he that fucked up and heartless that he would kill a baby?

"That…or keep you alive and get off on being in control. So, yes, the plan is for me to help get you guys out before he can change his mind."

Not knowing what else to say, I hand over Melody, knowing that because she's done eating, it's time to give her back. "I'll see you soon, my little love," I say, placing a kiss on her forehead.

"You got this," he says, giving me a half smile before leaving.

Flopping back onto the bed, I throw an arm over my face and try not to cry. I just want to go home. I want to be between the warm bodies of my lovers, safe and protected.

I miss Charlie's laugh, Ben's sweet words, Talon's stupid jokes, Oliver's hovering, and Tyson's banter.

I'm going to be strong and not give up. I've survived so much already; I won't be taken down so easily.

CHAPTER 5
Charlie

I DON'T WANT to get out of bed. What's the point? The moment I open my eyes, I know she won't be here next to me. At least if I stay asleep, I can see her in my dreams. I can hear her laugh and see her smile. I can touch her, kiss her, love her.

"Wake up, sleepy head." A voice snaps me out of my Emmy induced dream.

"Go away," I groan.

"Sorry. But Harlow said it's time to get up. You're no help to Emmy if you stay in bed and smell like a three day old hamburger," Evie says. I can hear her walking across the room.

"I'm no help to Emmy anyways. What can I do? I'm just in everyone's way," I argue with her. She throws open the curtains. The summer sun blinds me, and I screech like a vampire getting burnt, as I shove my face into the pillow, pulling the blanket up over my head.

"Dramatic much?" Evie laughs. The bed dips next to me. Evie grips the covers and starts to pull them off.

"It's been a week. It's time to get dressed. Come to the clubhouse and let the Old Ladies make you something to eat.

"Just leave me alone."

"No can do. I wouldn't be a good friend if I let you waste away. Time to be strong for Emmy."

I fling the covers back. "Be strong? That's all I ever fucking am. I'm always the one with the smile on her face, seeing the bright side of everything. Whenever something happens to one of us, I'm always there telling everyone else it's going to be okay, that everything will work out. But you know what? I can't do it anymore because it doesn't feel like everything is going to be alright. It feels like my world is crashing down around me, and there's nothing but darkness, because my light isn't here to keep the darkness from swallowing me whole. I can only be so strong before I break!" I snap at her, as tears fall from my eyes.

"I know how hard it is to try and be strong when someone has taken the love of your life away. But you're not helping Emmy by staying in bed," she states sadly.

I know about Harlow and her fucked up life, but I thought they were always together throughout the whole thing.

"How do you know what it feels like?" I ask, but there is no anger behind my words.

She pulls her feet up and crosses her legs facing me. "Because not too long before Harlow found out about Emmy, a monster from our past who we thought was dead and gone, came back to take away the love of my life. It's not my story to tell, but the whole week she was gone, it was pure Hell. I felt fear unlike anything before. At least you know where Emmy is. We're just waiting for the perfect time to strike. When Harlow was gone, we didn't know who took her or if we would ever see her alive again. You deserve time to feel, to break, but a war is coming soon, and you need to be ready."

She's right. I might not be able to help much with what the others are planning, but I can't let my heartache consume me. I had my pity party, and now it's time I let reality sink back in and fight.

"Fine," I sigh. "Let me shower, and then we can go to the club house."

"Perfect, because there's a few people Harlow wants you to meet," she says with a smile of amusement.

"Charlie!" Harlow shouts when she sees me. She waves me over from the other side of the bar.

"Hi," I say, still feeling like crap, but at least I don't smell like death anymore.

"I want you to meet a few people," she says, turning to some guys I haven't met yet. "This is Dean," she says, introducing me to a tall man with nicely styled brown hair and beard who's in, what looks to be, a very expensive suit.

"Hey." He nods.

"And this is Axel." She turns to a very angry looking man, and my eyes widen slightly. She sees my reaction and giggles.

"Ah, don't let this broody fucker's face scare you. Deep down under all that muscle and ink, he's a big old teddy bear."

Axel turns to Harlow and cocks a brow, but I can see how much he adores her from the look in his eyes alone. "Teddy bear? You're just asking for a spanking now, aren't you?" he growls.

Harlow's smile turns playful. "Oh, I'd like to see you try, Mountain Man. I'd have you on your knees, where you belong, in seconds."

"Guys! As hot as it is to watch you two banter back and forth as foreplay, now is not the time," Dean says.

"Later," Axel growls. Harlow presses herself into him and leans up like she's about to kiss him.

"Can't wait to see you on your knees, big boy," she purrs, before reaching up and pinching Axel's nipple.

"Fuck's sake, Queenie," Axel growls. "What the hell is it with you and pinching the fucking nipples?"

"It's fun." She states, grinning while taking a step back and moving over next to me. "Come, let's get you fed, and I'll tell you what we have planned so far."

Harlow and I sit and talk while we eat lunch. The clubhouse is busy with people coming and going, but it doesn't have the same vibes as it used to have. No one is drinking, playing pool, and just hanging out. They're all waiting, waiting for Steel and Queenie to tell them what to do.

She explained to me that with all the threatening text messages they've been getting about Tyson, they don't think now is a good time to storm the place. The Savage Hellhounds are on standby, waiting for us to make a move so they can put a bullet in Tyson's head. So, much to Harlow's disgust, we have to wait.

After a while, Harlow leaves, and I sit here alone, just watching people go about their day until Neo sits down where Harlow was.

"I'd ask you how you're doing, but your Queen is gone, so I know it's not good," he says, taking a swig of his beer.

"Thanks. And yeah, you're right, I'm not doing good. But I'm no help to anyone laying in bed."

"We're going to get them back. If it wasn't for those pieces of shit on standby, ready to have Tyson killed, we would have already burned them all."

"How's Harlow taking it?" I ask, knowing that Harlow switched into Queenie mode after the shoot out the day Emmy was taken. The way she's been acting today is the most sane she's been since then.

"She doesn't take kindly to having assholes hurt her people. She might look fine right now, but that's only because Axel and Dean are here. Once their welcome has worn off, she will be back in 'deadly mode'. I'm just glad to be here. I've already had to tie her to the bed to keep her from sneaking out at night," he chuckles.

My brows shoot up. "And you're still alive?"

"Oh, I got my punishment." He wiggles his eyebrows. "If it was anyone else besides me, Evie, or the other guys, then they would've been gutted like a fish."

"So, how are you going to keep her distracted until it's time?"

"Sex," he says with a mischievous grin.

"Sorry I asked." I smile, and it feels so strange.

"How are your people doing?"

I let out an exhausted sigh. "Talon is doing just about as good as me, but he has Ben to help. Oliver has buried himself deep into club stuff, so I haven't seen much of him."

"That Ben kid, are you sure he's okay? Saw him not too long ago out back. He looks destroyed."

My brows furrow. Ben's been the strongest one of us all. I haven't seen him break yet. "I'm going to go find him."

Saying bye to Neo, I head out back to the patio. Ben's sitting on a bench, facing the back fence.

"Hey," I say, taking the seat next to him. He startles at my voice, his head jerking up to look at me. My heart sinks when I see the tear tracks staining his face.

"Hey," he sniffs, wiping at his eyes. "Nice to see you up."

"Ben." My voice is soft as I shift closer. "It's okay not to be okay."

"I know." He lets out a harsh laugh. "But I need to be strong for Talon. We're his only family. His parents are dead, not that there is anything to miss, but we are all he has while his friend, girlfriend, and daughter are gone. He needs me."

"How about we take care of each other? I need you all just as much. I might still have my parents, but they're not my family. I don't have my lover next to me, but I could use a best friend?"

He gives me a sad smile and a nod. "I'd like that." He lifts his arm, and I snuggle into his side, putting my head on his shoulder. We sit, talking about Emmy and all the times she made us laugh, or how she made us feel loved until we're crying again.

It's a lot to handle. Each passing day we miss watching our daughter grow, hearing her babbling, and seeing her smiles.

I envy Ben. He doesn't have to fall asleep alone. He has someone to hold him at night.

We head home once it starts getting dark. I follow Ben up the stairs, saying goodbye as we break off and go to our own rooms. Slipping into bed, I snuggle with the Marie stuffie I got Emmy, and the tears start to fall again. I can be strong, I know I can, but at night when the silence becomes deafening, and all the bad thoughts take over my mind, I don't wanna have to pretend.

I don't know how long I've been crying for when I feel the bed move. Looking up, I see two figures in the moonlight as they each take a side of my bed.

"What are you doing?" I ask as they move in close.

"We don't want you to be alone," Ben says. "Emmy would want us to take care of you too. You can't always be the mother hen of the family."

I smile into Marie, trying not to cry harder at how much this means to me.

It doesn't take long before I hear soft snores coming from Ben's side.

"Thank you," Talon whispers.

"For what?" I whisper back.

"For being there for him when I was too broken to be."

It's the first time in a week that I don't feel so alone.

CHAPTER 6
Tyson

IT'S BEEN A week. A whole fucking week of Hell. A hundred and sixty-eight hours of thinking about my girls and about how I can't be with them. Even when I'm sleeping, they're the only thing that my mind focuses on. It's always the same dream. I'm walking through a forest at night, with only the moon's glow to see by for light. I hear a baby crying, so I follow the sounds. When I reach it, I see Emmy standing there with Melody in her arms. The moment she looks at me, she turns and runs away from me. I chase after them while calling Emmy's name, begging and pleading for her to stop, but she never does. She runs, always just out of reach. Melody's pained cries break my heart. Then I wake up in a cold sweat, heart racing, and the reminder that even though they're both close by–somewhere on the same property–they are still just out of reach.

The cold sweats on the first few nights were mostly due to how much pain I've been in. Thankfully, Seth has been bringing me pain meds when he brings me my food. He can't do anything else to help, that would be too obvious just in case Dagger sees and finds out he's helping me.

The bruises on my face are an ugly yellow now, but I got my sight back, and my lips aren't swollen anymore. As for the broken ribs, they didn't puncture anything from what I can tell, and other than hurting like a bitch when I bend over, the meds help with the pain.

I keep telling Seth that whatever his plan is for helping us, it needs to happen soon. I know they won't keep me around forever, and I'd really like to get the fuck out of here before it's too late. He keeps telling me *'he'll do it soon'*, but he won't tell me what his plan is. Hell, I think at this point he's probably just winging it.

I'm just lying here, staring up at the roof, even though the room is pitch dark. I'm unable to go back to sleep when I hear the lock on the door click.

I'm immediately on guard because Seth only comes here for meals, so I don't know what he would be doing here in the middle of the night. To be safe, I sit up in bed, ready for whoever comes through the door. I don't grab anything to defend myself because that's only asking for trouble. If I need to fight my way out of something, I'll deal with it then.

"Get up," Seth says in a harsh whisper.

"I am up," I answer back, my voice low. He clicks on a flashlight, shining it in my face. My arm comes up, shielding my eyes from the blinding glow. "Dude, do you mind?"

"Come on, we don't have much time."

My brows furrow. "Much time for what? Are we getting out of here?" *God, I hope so.*

"Ah, no. Sorry man, still working on that. But the whole MC is drunk out of their minds or passed out. So, if we leave now, I can sneak you over to Emmy for a little bit before I have to bring Melody in for her next feeding."

I'm up and out of the bed in seconds, ignoring the sharp pain in my ribs from the sudden movements. Grabbing the sweatpants and shirt from the edge of the bed, I get dressed, before slipping on the pair of sneakers Seth gave me.

As I get to the door, I pause next to him. "Thank you for this. You have no idea how out of my mind I've been, being away from her." I wish I could see Melody too, but as long as Emmy confirms our baby is fine, I'll live. I've been aching to have my baby girl back in my arms again, my little princess. Fuck, I miss them both so much. My soul feels empty.

"Of course. Emmy is being strong for the both of you, but I think she could use this just as much as you. Just stick close behind me, and stay quiet."

We exit the room, Seth locking it behind him. He leads me down the dark hallway, the flashlight the only thing lighting up our walkway and out of the building that I've been staying in. When we get outside, he clicks the flashlight off. "We need to keep this off so we don't draw any attention."

We make our way behind the building, down a path that leads to another structure much like the one we just left. He unlocks a side door and holds it open for me before locking it again behind him.

"Emmy is the only one in here, but people can still hear you from outside, so try not to be too loud," Seth says, stopping next to a door. He unlocks it before pushing it open enough for him to get inside.

"Is everything okay with Melody?" Emmy's worried voice meets my ears, and I almost sob in relief. As the days went on, I held onto the memory of her beautiful voice like it was a life raft, afraid it was getting harder and harder to remember. But hearing her now it's music to my ears.

"Everything is fine with the baby," Seth answers. I stand behind the partially opened door.

"Then why are you here?" She questions sassily.

"I thought you could use some company," he sighs, as if he's tired of having to defend himself.

"Umm, thanks? You seem like a nice guy, and it sure beats sitting here talking to the walls when Melody is gone, but not to sound rude, I'd much rather be sleeping at two am."

I can't help but grin as she politely tells him to fuck off. My girl loves her sleep. But I think she would be more than happy to lose a few hours if it meant seeing me.

"Thanks, kid," Seth laughs. "But no, not me." I take that as my cue to enter the room. There's a bedside lamp on, casting its light over Emmy as she sits up in bed.

Her eyes go wide in surprise, and the tears are immediate. "Tyson." My name comes out a broken sob, as she throws back the blankets. She rushes from the bed and across the room in seconds, throwing herself at me. I catch her with a grunt, ignoring the jolts of pain in my ribs from the contact, as I clutch her to my body. I'd suffer through all the pain in the world if it meant being able to hold her in my arms like this again.

"I thought I'd never see you again." She cries into my chest. I bury my face into her hair as I rub her back.

"You can't get rid of me that easily, Princess. You're stuck with me, in life or death."

She pulls back to look at me. Her eyes are filled with so much pain but an overwhelming amount of relief too. She reaches up and touches the bruises on my face, anger filling her eyes while she promises to make whoever hurt me pay. Seeing her so protective over me is such a turn on.

Pulling my face to hers, she presses her lips to mine in a bruising kiss. I groan, loving the feeling of her lips against mine again, especially after so long. She tastes like happiness, love, and light.

She whimpers as I dive my tongue into her mouth, pulling her lower half against mine, showing her just how much I missed her. My heart yearned for her, my mind craved her, and this might not be the best moment, but my cock aches for her. To be inside her, to own her. To be where it fucking belongs.

"One hour, and I'll be back with Melody. I can't risk any longer than that," Seth lets us know. I don't break away from my girl to acknowledge him. I hear the lock click, indicating we're now alone. Good, because what I need to do to my girl, I don't want an audience for.

"I love you so fucking much, Emmy," I growl against her lips, before gripping her face and fucking her mouth with my tongue. I'll never have enough of her. Her fingers fall from my head to my shirt, gripping the fabric in her tiny hands and whimpering as I start to back her towards the bed.

"I love you too, Ty. So much it hurts to be away from you, even for a day," she says breathily, as the backs of her legs hit the bed.

"Soon, baby girl. Soon we will be out of this Hell, and I'll never have to be away from you again. But right now... I. Need. You."

My chest is heaving, my cock is throbbing, and my mind is screaming for me to claim her. This past week showed me that you never know when it could be your last moment with the person you love, so make *every* moment count. And if I only get an hour with her until God knows when again, then I'm gonna spend it with my dick deep in her tight cunt.

She bites her lip, her eyes glazing over with lust as she drops to her knees. Fuck, I missed my dirty girl.

Looking up at me with her big brown eyes, she pulls my sweatpants down to my ankles, making my heavy cock fall forward, pointing exactly where it wants to be. She licks her lips, casting a glance at the pre-cum dripping from the tip before her soft hands touch my thighs.

"You know I'll always take care of your needs, Tyson." Her voice is full of need as she runs her hands up my legs, making my cock twitch. "I've missed your touch, your kisses." Her tongue pokes out, licking the pre-cum, and making me hiss. "Your cum." Her hand wraps around my cock, giving it a hard squeeze, and I curse as she takes me into her mouth. I make sure to watch everything she does to me. She starts to bob her head, her eyes locked with mine. Taking me all the way to the back of her throat, she gags a little, before pulling back, then repeating the motion.

My hand tangles in her hair, gripping a handful so that I can take control. She loves how much pleasure she brings us, loves when she drives us so fucking mad we lose control.

"That's it, Princess. Take my cock like a good girl. So fucking beautiful," I groan, as I start to thrust my hips.

Loosening her jaw so that I can fuck her throat, she grabs a hold of my thighs for support. Ignoring the pain in my ribs, I get lost in the ecstasy of her. I fuck her mouth until her eyes are wet, and she is breathing as hard as I am, but for a completely different reason. Her moans are intoxicating, and I can't take it anymore. Pulling her off, she sucks in a breath. "So fucking perfect." I groan, as I wipe the spit from the corner of her lip. She smirks up at me with this cock-sure grin, loving what she does to me. It makes me want to slap her bratty ass. "I need your lips wrapped around my cock, Princess."

She cocks a brow, looking at my throbbing dick then back to me. "Wasn't that what I was just doing?"

Sassy, she is. "Not those lips, pretty girl." I give her a sexy smile. Her eyes brighten, and she's on her feet, stealing another kiss.

"Fuck me, Tyson. Make me forget about where we are, the hell we've been through. I only want it to be me and you, nothing else."

I can see the hurt in her eyes. She misses her other lovers just as much. But they aren't able to be with her right now, and I am. So if she needs to feel me, to escape for a bit, then that's what I'll do. I'd do anything for her. She never needs to ask.

"Clothes off. I wanna see your gorgeous body."

She gives me a seductive smile as she shimmies out of her pyjama pants, her baggy shirt just covering her panties, leaving her legs on display.

I lean over slightly, brushing my fingertips against the tattoo I fixed for her, loving the tiny gasp she lets out and the shivers she gives me.

"You're so fucking perfect, you know that?" I ask her, my hands skimming up under her shirt and over her sides, feeling the stretch marks on her belly. I know she's still insecure about them sometimes, but we all make sure to let her know how fucking stunning her body is, no matter the shape or form. "My sexy tigress," I growl, dipping my head to kiss and suck her neck. She moans, her body melting into me.

I pull back and remove her shirt, groaning at the sight of her plump breasts spilling out of her bra. "Like what you see?" she says with a smirk.

"Hell yes."

She puts her hands behind her back, undoing her bra and letting it fall to the ground. "How about now?" My cock throbs with the urge to push her onto the bed and thrust my dick between her tits. Her nipples are hard, just asking to be sucked into my mouth. "Fucking perfect." I groan, leaning over and flicking my tongue over the perked point.

"Tyson," she breathes. "As much as I love it when you drive me crazy, we don't have a lot of time, and I need your dick inside me like yesterday."

Chuckling, I nip at her breast, causing her to let out a surprised squeal.

"Quiet now, Princess. You don't want to have this cut short." I grin.

She cocks a brow then rolls her eyes, a smile forming on her lips. She grips the edge of my shirt to pull it off, but she's too short. I lean over so she can get it over my head, cursing when I feel a sharp pain in my ribs.

"Are you okay?" she asks, concern lacing her words. She lets out a gasp when I straighten up, showing her my body. "Tyson," she breathes, her face morphing into anger. "I'm going to fucking kill them." She seethes, as her fingers brush over the bruises.

"I thought your face was bad, but fuck, Ty, are you okay? How are you even walking?"

"I'm fine, sweet girl. It looks worse than it really is. And no, you won't kill them." Her eyes snap up to mine, and she glares at me. "Don't give me a look like that, love. You won't live with blood on your hands if we can help it, no matter whose it is. That's what me, Oliver, and your sister are for. Now, lay back for me, I'm going to fuck that pretty, pink pussy of yours until you scream my name."

"About damn time," she mutters.

"What was that?"

"Nothing." She smirks, laying down on the bed. Her hair fans out around her head, making a brown halo. She brings her legs up, placing her feet on the bed before letting her thighs fall open, revealing her soaked center.

"Look at you." My voice is heavy with lust. "So fucking wet for me." She watches me as I dip my fingers into her juices, lightly grazing her clit, and making her moan before bringing them up to my mouth. I suck them clean, closing my eyes as I savor her taste. "Fuck, you taste like Heaven, Princess. I can't wait until I can bury my face between these thighs and eat you for hours."

"Tyson," she whines, needy and desperate. I don't waste any more time, knowing we don't have much longer.

"I got you, baby girl." I step closer to the bed, thanking the gods that it's level with my dick because I really don't think I can bend much right now. "Legs up," I tell her, and she lifts her knees up. Grabbing each leg, I straighten them out and put them over my shoulders. Then I grab her by the hips, dragging her pussy closer to me. "I need you to be quiet as I fuck you raw. Can you do that?" I ask, grasping my cock, giving it a few pumps before lining it up with her sweet cunt.

"Have you met me?" She sasses back, lifting a brow. "Quiet and sex don't go together in the same sentence when it comes to me."

"Well, time to learn, baby girl." I grin before entering her in one hard thrust. Her eyes widen at the sudden intrusion, biting her lip to hold in her scream. There's no more time for teasing, no time to warm her up. I start to fuck her like a crazed man. The feeling of her tight pussy wrapped around my dick is indescribable. *Best feeling in the fucking world.*

Her breasts bounce with each thrust as her eyes roll back into her head. Her hand covers her mouth as she does her best to smother her cries of pleasure, but it doesn't do much.

"Fuck, Tyson." She lets out a strangled moan. "God, you feel so fucking good. I've missed your cock."

"Yeah?" I grunt, picking up my pace. I wish this could last all night, but I haven't had any sort of release in over a week, and her pussy is just too fucking magical. "You like it when I fuck you hard and deep?"

"Yes, Sir!" she cries, her hand covering her mouth again. I love it when she calls me that.

"Grab your shirt and bite it," I tell her, nodding to her t-shirt laying next to her on the bed. She grabs it, shoving a piece in her mouth. "Good girl," I praise, and she whimpers. I swear my cock twitches at that sound. "Now, give your clit the attention it deserves, Princess. Work yourself up on my cock and cum for me."

Her hand slides over her belly, and she moans, her eyes rolling in the back of her head again as she starts to rub her clit. Watching her like this feels like a dream I never want to wake up from.

Slipping my hands under her ass, I raise it up a bit to get a new angle. And by the way her eyes fly open while she screams around the shirt and her fingers moving faster, I know I hit her sweet spot. Gripping her ass, I fuck her harder until I work myself into a frenzy.

Emmy is sobbing in pleasure against her gag, her free hand tangled in the sheets. Her core grips me, and I know she's seconds away from cumming. She circles herself a few more times before her back arches off the bed, her hips thrusting out and pushing her body further onto me, while tossing her head back. Her muffled screams are still pretty loud, and she cums hard, squirting all over my cock.

I wrap my arms around her legs, holding her as close to me as I can as I rut into her for another minute, before lightly biting her leg to muffle my own release. I groan a desperate sound of relief as I bury my cock deep, emptying every last drop of my cum inside her.

Neither of us moves for a moment, only the sounds of her heavy breathing filling the room.

"I so fucking needed that." She huffs, taking the shirt out of her mouth. "After two years of mind blowing sex from all of you, my fingers just don't do it."

Resting my head against her leg, I close my eyes and grin, letting out a chuckle. "You won't have to ever use your fingers again if you don't want to, Princess. We are more than happy to take care of any needs you have."

"Tyson." Her voice is shaky, all joking gone. My eyes snap open, and I get a sick feeling as I see her eyes start to tear up.

"What's wrong, baby?" I ask, my brows pinching. I know what's wrong. *Everything* is fucking wrong.

"Hold me?" she asks in a small voice.

"Always." I kiss her leg, pulling out and helping her put her legs back down. "I'll be right back." She nods her head, and I take off into the bathroom she has, finding a washcloth on the counter. I wet it before going back to her and cleaning her up. When I'm done, I toss it back into the bathroom. I get dressed, helping her do the same, then climb into bed with her.

Opening my arm, she snuggles into me, resting her head on my chest. My arm pulls her as close to me as I can get her. We say nothing, just enjoying being in each other's embrace because what else can we say?

We have no plan, no way out right now. We're away from our home and family. All we have is right here, right now.

We lay there for a while before she tips her head up to look at me. Tears fall from her eyes, and I wipe them away with my thumb. "Don't cry, pretty girl. We'll be home soon."

Emmy moves so that she can kiss me. I cradle her head as I move my lips against hers slowly, memorizing every touch and caress, as I dip my tongue in and over hers. We stay like this, kissing and tasting each other until the lock to the door clicks.

"Sorry to be a party pooper, but time's up," Seth says, as he walks into the room, a little cry coming from his arms.

"Little Princess?" I breathe. Emmy moves off me, letting me get up and go over to take my daughter. Seth hands her over, seeing the need to hold her on my face. "Hi, my sweet baby girl." I choke, tears stinging the back of my eyes. For just a moment, everything feels right in the world. "I missed you so much." I kiss her little forehead, inhaling her baby scent.

"Daddy Ty loves you so much. I never want you to forget that. We will be home soon, where we belong." I hold her close to my chest. She feels like she's grown so much in only a week.

Emmy sniffs as she wipes her eyes, a watery smile on her lips. "We really gotta go," Seth says, standing there looking uncomfortable.

"Right." I nod. Moving Melody so that I can see her little face. I kiss each cheek before handing her over to Emmy. "You're going to be okay, little one," I say, rubbing Melody's red curls. "Both of you will be." I pull Emmy into one last kiss, my heart breaking as the kiss does.

"I love you." Her voice cracks.

"I love you too, Princess. To the fucking moon and back."

Seth clears his throat in warning, and it takes everything in me not to punch him in his stupid face for taking me away from my girls. But I know he's already risking a lot for this time, and I don't want to risk Emmy getting in trouble or not getting to have Melody like she does now.

With all the strength within me, I turn and head out of the room, leaving my heart and soul behind.

"You better have a plan to leave, and it better be soon," I tell Seth as we enter the room I've been locked in. "Because it's already been long enough."

"One week," he says. "In one week, we have a big shipment coming in. All the men will be helping unload it. People will be distracted. I'll get you out then."

"One week," I say it back to him as a warning.

He nods and leaves, locking me back in.

Seven days, Princess. Seven days and I'll have you back where you belong.

CHAPTER 7
Emmy

"HELLO, DAUGHTER." A booming voice makes me jump to my feet from my spot on the window sill where I was watching the lightning storm rage outside.

"What do you want?" I sneer.

He cocks a brow, a smirk hitching on his lips. "Now, is that any way to talk to your daddy?"

"You're not my dad. You're just the crazy bastard who kidnapped me, my child, and her father."

"You sure that's his baby?" he chuckles. "That bright red hair makes me think she might be from that nerdy, tattooed one you're fucking."

I scoff. "She might not be his by blood, but she's still his daughter. Unlike you, he's a real man who cares for his child, matching DNA or not. What's your plan with us anyways? Why go through all the trouble of taking people you don't want in the first place?"

He lets out a laugh that's dripping with venom. "Because I *can,* little girl. I can do whatever the fuck I want. And what I want is for my flesh and blood to be far, *far* away from my enemies. You know how bad it looks for me to have my daughter fucking our rival's sons? Hell, you're probably fucking their old man too. Four dicks not good enough for you?"

"Fuck off!" I spit.

"Not today, spitfire. You're coming with me," he says, taking a step forward. "Now be a good girl, and let's go." He pulls out his gun, aiming it at my head.

"And what if I don't? You're just gonna kill me?" I counter, trying to sound braver than I feel. This man is fucking crazy. I have no doubt that if I push him hard enough, he would, in fact, kill me.

"Nah, but I'd shoot you."

Knowing he would do it, I start walking towards the door.

We leave the room and start heading down the hall where he is directing me to go. I look over and see Seth standing there like a good little soldier, but the look in his eyes tells me he wishes he could help me.

We're supposed to be leaving tomorrow.

The shipment is meant to come in during the night, so with them being distracted, Tyson, the baby, and I should all be able to get away and be far gone before they notice us missing.

We head down a set of stairs that leads into an open foyer. I knew I was in a house because the room I'm staying in is a few stories up, but I didn't think it was this *nice*. Well, it would be nice if all the furniture didn't have white sheets covering it. Looks like my room is the only room being lived in.

Voices from one of the rooms has my body tensing, completely on edge.

"Look who I brought by for some social time," Dagger says, pushing me into the room with the barrel of the gun. "Thought it was about time we all hung out."

My eyes take in the room, and I immediately want to turn and run, but the muffled grunting from the corner of the room has my feet planted in place. Tyson is bound to a chair, a gag shoved in his mouth, and he looks at me with fury in his eyes. Not at me, but at Dagger.

"Tyson!" I cry, taking a step towards him.

"Ah, ah, ah. Not so fast," Dagger says, grabbing a hold of my arm and tossing me into an empty chair. "He's here to watch and listen. Pretend he's not here."

I glare at my sperm donor as he takes a seat on the couch in front of me, putting his arms up along the back of the couch and crossing his legs like he thought he was some kind of king.

Looking around, my eyes land on the people that had me wanting to run just moments before. My mother sits on a chair to the side of Dagger, grinning at me like she is the queen of the fucking world. But she's not the one who has my skin crawling. Standing next to the couch Dagger is sitting on is Mr. Park. The fucking sleazebag teacher from Emerald Lake Prep. The person who kidnapped me and delivered me to the devil's door.

"We're just waiting on one more guest, and we can get started with this little family meeting," Dagger says, and a moment later, the door we came through opens.

A lady with grey hair in a sloppy ponytail, leather pants, and a black halter top walks in with my fucking daughter in her arms. I move, getting up to take her, but the bitch hands her over to Dagger.

"Give her to me, please," I plead, not wanting to push my luck by sassing back.

"You can have her when she's hungry. But now it's her papa's turn to hold her." He moves her so that she's laying down on his lap, her feet in the air as she grabs them, making her adorable cooing sounds. "Well, aren't you just the cutest?" He smiles down at her. It looks so wrong to see an innocent child in his clutches. He looks up at me. "You know, when you were born, I was young and in my prime. I wasn't ready for kids."

A snort of laughter slips out, and I bite my lips, forcing myself to shut up. He glares at me before continuing, my eyes going back to Melody as he talks, not trusting him for a moment.

"But now, looking down at my granddaughter, I can't help but wonder what I missed. So here's what's gonna happen. She is *mine* now. I'll allow you to keep feeding her until we can get her on a bottle, and I'll let you live on the property. You can be her aunt."

My heart starts to pound in my chest as pure fear and panic fills my veins.

"Are you fucking crazy?" I breathe. "You can't have my fucking baby!" I shout.

"Why not?" He cocks his head to the side, giving me a smirk like he's saying all this to get me riled up. "I think I'd make a wonderful dad."

"Please tell me you're joking," I reply, my voice shaking from nerves.

He stares at me a moment before bursting out laughing. "Of course, I'm just fucking with you. You should have seen your face."

I let out a sigh of relief, sinking back into the chair as I will my pounding heart to calm down. I really want to bash his stupid fucking face in.

"But, you two will be living here from now on.

Unfortunately, I don't have time to make sure you behave or keep you in your place. So as of this weekend, once we deal with the Reaper scum, you will be staying with Jimmy."

Like fuck he's going to be doing anything to Tyson. We'll be out of here before he gets the chance. "Who's Jimmy?" I ask, my brows pinching in confusion.

"That would be my real name, love. Jimmy Rogers," Mr. Park, who apparently isn't actually Mr. Park, says as he steps over to me. He bends down, getting in my face, and I rear back. "I'm a Hellhound, and your father so kindly offered up his beautiful daughter if I got a job at that stupid excuse of a school to get close to you. I would have taken you that night if he..." He looks behind me to Tyson and sneers. Tyson starts to sound like a feral animal, his chair knocking against the wall as he struggles. "But no worries. I stayed in town, waiting for my chance. Now that I have you, I will never let you go." He reaches out to caress my face. Not wanting that pervert to touch me, I bite his hand hard before he can make contact with my face.

"You little bitch!" he roars. A second later, he cracks me across the face. My head whips to the side, causing me to cry out at the sudden impact. He roughly grabs a handful of my hair so painfully that I feel some strands being ripped from my scalp, as he yanks my head up so that I'm looking at him. "You're mine now," he hisses.

"Mine to fuck. Mine to punish. Mine to control. Whether you like it or not. You're going to be the mother of my kids and be the perfect Old Lady, or you'll pay the price for disobeying me."

"Now, now, Jimmy. Save the foreplay for the bedroom." Dagger chuckles darkly.

The pervert lets go of my hair and uses the same hand to wrap his fingers around my neck. He pulls me into a pained kiss, and I try not to puke at the feeling of his vile lips on me. "Until later." He grins before taking his place at Dagger's side again.

"You know, baby, if you want to be a daddy again, we can always try for another." My mom purrs from her seat, pushing her saggy tits up in her skin tight dress.

Dagger laughs a cruel sound. "Oh sugar, why on Earth would I want another child with you? I didn't even want the first one."

"It's different now. We're starting fresh, turning over a new leaf."

Dagger cocks a brow. "We're not starting anything. You're a wet hole to put my cock in. An easy blast from the past, but there's nothing special about you. All you offer is a fucking headache."

Her face grows red with fury, and she stands up, ready to cuss him out. "You can't talk to me like-" She doesn't get to finish her sentence because Dagger pulls out a gun, shooting her right between the eyes, making me jump back in horror.

She falls back onto her chair but slumps down to the floor with her face pointed to the ceiling as her dead eyes stare blankly. Dagger looks at me while my mouth hangs open in shock.

"Oh please, we all know you hated the cunt. And she was starting to get on my nerves. Don't know whatever possessed me to allow her back in my life. She was so fucking annoying. Never shutting up, even when I was fucking that used up pussy of hers."

I say nothing, no words able to form. He was right, though. It might make me a horrible person, but I feel no loss from watching my mother die. She meant nothing to me for a very long time. All she ever did was bring me pain and suffering. But the image of a hole in her head will stick with me longer than I'd like it to.

"Anyways, I have work to do," Dagger says, handing Melody over. Taking her in my arms, I snap out of the shock and hold her close to my chest. Dagger looks at Jimmy before instructing, "Take them back to her room." He then looks to Seth. "Lock that one back up," he nods at Tyson. "I don't have time for any more fun and games today," he says, giving Tyson a grin made of nightmares. "But soon, pretty boy. Soon, I'm gonna have me some real fun. I'm gonna make you scream. Make you beg for your death, all while I live stream it for your dear old daddy to watch."

No, no, this can't be happening. I won't let him hurt Tyson. I turn to Seth with pleading eyes. He shakes his head, telling me not to say or do anything. He better get us the fuck out of here soon.

"Let's go," Jimmy says, grabbing me by the arm and hauling me out of my chair. He pushes me towards the door while I hold Melody tight with my other arm. I don't protest as he drags me out of the room, fearing he might do something to me that could end up with Melody getting hurt.

Risking a look back towards the room as we get to the stairs, I see Seth pushing Tyson out into the foyer. His eyes lock with mine, and I see them filled with a burning love and determination that gives me hope that we will be okay. Thank God we have Seth, or we would be screwed.

I mouth 'I love you' before the asshole who has my arm in a death grip pulls me in front of him. "Move," he barks, and I do as I'm told, not wanting to trip up the stairs.

He brings me back to my room, unlocking the door and pushing me inside. The knowledge that he has a key to my door sends fear into my heart.

"Be a good little girl, and maybe I'll reward you when I come back," he says, licking his lips as he looks me up and down like I'm something he wants to eat. I'm unable to hide the shiver of repulsion, and this fucker's eyes light up. Not sure if he thinks I'm reacting like I enjoyed his words or because he loves a fight. Either option wouldn't surprise me.

He leaves, locking the door behind him, and I let out a breath I didn't know I was holding in.

"We're going to be okay, baby girl," I tell Melody as I sit back in the bed to feed her. "Mama or Daddy T won't let these monsters hurt you. We'll be home soon. I promise."

CHAPTER 8
Emmy

I DIDN'T SLEEP at all last night after that pervert dropped me off. Too much nervous energy.

When Seth came back to get Melody after dropping Tyson off wherever they were holding him, he told me that we were leaving the next night no matter what. That it's now or never. If we didn't leave now, then I would truly be stuck in Hell until Harlow and the others came storming through the gates. It's not worth the risk.

Now, I'm pacing the room while biting my lip as I wait for Seth. My stomach is in knots, and fear prickles my skin. There are so many things that could go wrong. And with Melody on the line, it's even more risky. She comes first. We have to get out of here without a scratch on her head. But that means listening to Seth, keeping alert, and being ready for anything.

The lock clicks open. I stop pacing, my gaze swinging to the door. Just as I'm about to let out a little breath of relief, knowing that it's time to go, Jimmy walks into the room.

My heart stops, air getting caught in my lungs.

"I've missed you," he says, slamming the door behind him. "You have no idea how fucking ecstatic I am that your Pa gave me the green light on making you mine. Do you have any idea how hard it was staying away from you? Having you so close by for two weeks and not being able to touch you, to taste you?" He starts towards me, making me take a few steps back. My wild eyes flick from him to the door, praying Seth walks through any second now.

"Now, I get you all to myself," he purrs. I have nowhere left to go, the wall hitting my back as he crowds into my space, caging me against the wall.

"You will *never* have me," I sneer, holding my head high. Like fuck I was letting this nasty pig touch me. "I would rather die."

"Now, now, why such harsh words?" He growls, his hand grabbing me by the throat. I yelp in surprise, making him chuckle in enjoyment.

"Be a good girl, and I promise I'll make you feel real good." My eyes squeeze shut as his nose grazes my cheek, his rotten breath invading my nose and making me want to gag. I start to struggle to get away from him, but he tightens his grip making my eyes bug out as I struggle to breathe. "You're only going to make this harder on yourself. You need to get it through your head that this is your new life now."

I look around for something, *anything,* as he dips down and licks the side of my fucking face, groaning against my cheek. Looking down, I see the lamp on the bedside table next to me, and I see my only chance. "You taste so fucking good."

His hand paws my breast, and that's it, my brain kickstarts into fight mode. My knee comes up, kneeing him as hard as I can in the dick. "Fuck!" he roars. His hand releases my throat, moving to cup his junk, and I use that opening to grab the lamp. Pulling the plug out of the wall, I swing it like a bat so that the brass part of the base bashes him in the head. He lets out a grunt, before dropping to the floor with a thud.

"Holy shit." I breathe, my heart beating like I'm running a marathon.

"What the fuck?" Tyson's furious voice hisses as he walks into the room with Melody in his arms and Seth behind him.

"Thank fuck," I breathe, feeling the weight of the world fall from my shoulders. I jump over the asshole's body and into Tyson's arms after he hands the baby over to Seth. "I was so worried you guys weren't coming. Then he showed up, and well...let's just say I'm very fond of that lamp now."

"I will always come for you, Princess. Nothing will stop me from getting to you." He hugs me hard before taking my face into his hands to place a passionate kiss on my lips.

"Sorry to break up this love fest, but we have to go," Seth says.

"What about him?" I ask, looking down at Jimmy.

Tyson moves away from me, bending over to grab the lamp. He wraps his hand around the cord, yanking hard and pulling it apart. He tosses it on the bed, taking the cord to tie Jimmy's hands tightly.

"Here," Seth says, handing Tyson his belt. Tyson ties up Jimmy's feet before dragging him over to the closet.

"Hopefully, no one notices he's gone before Queenie can get her hands on him," Tyson grumbles, pulling me back into his arms again.

"I'd say a day or two. The sack of shit is known to lock himself in the house, spending his days drinking and watching porn. Fucking disgusting." Seth's lip curls. "And I'm normally the only one who comes around here."

"Well, I shoved one of the old socks that was at the bottom of the closet in his mouth so that he can't scream for help when he wakes up."

Seth grins. "Nice." He hands a backpack over to me. "This has food, water, a GPS, flashlight, and first aid kit. Plus, I shoved a few diapers and a pack of wipes in there too. It's going to take you all night to reach your compound this way, but it's the best option we have for you guys not to get caught."

Seth tells us what direction we need to go, telling us to keep to the trails he marked off on the map. He says he's been out there in the past, making escape routes in case it was ever needed in the future. He explains that we should follow the orange markers that should reflect in the light of our flashlight to help guide our way.

"You ready, Princess?" Tyson asks me, cupping my face. His thumb caresses my cheek, and I close my eyes. Leaning into his touch, I take in a deep breath to claim my racing heart.

"Yeah. Let's do this. Let's go home." I smile up at him. He places a kiss on my lips before handing Melody over to me. I smile down at her sleeping face. I hope this trip isn't too hard on her.

Seth leads us out of the house, stopping by the door to make sure that no one else is around. When he's satisfied, he motions us to follow. Leading us behind a few buildings, we stop once again. "You see that warehouse?" he asks, pointing to a big gray structure about thirty yards away. "Behind it, I cut a hole in the fence a while back. Thankfully, one of my jobs is to make sure the gate and fences are secure. It helps that Dagger is pretty cocky and thinks no one has the balls to fuck with him, so he has nothing to fear. His stupidity worked in our favor. It's gonna be a tight fit. This is where we part ways. Good luck."

"Thanks...for everything. I'll make sure to tell Queenie not to kill you when she comes to burn this place to the ground," I say, smiling kindly at him.

"Thanks," he chuckles.

Tyson says goodbye too. Checking to make sure we're clear before we race towards the building. I hold Melody to my chest as we jog, making sure she doesn't bounce around too much and praying that she stays asleep.

"You go first," Tyson says as we get to the fence. "I'll be right behind you."

Giving him a quick kiss, I turn so that my back is to the fence, keeping Melody's body protected. Shouting starts in the distance as I shimmy my way through the fence, and just like that, Tyson and I are separated. Tyson's eyes snap to mine, fear and panic shining bright and only visible because of the moon's light.

"Come on!" I hiss, my heart starting to pound faster and harder with each passing minute. "Let's go before they get here!"

"Hey, you! Stop!" The voices sound closer.

"Go," he urges me, his voice hard, but I can hear the pain laced in it.

"What!" My eyes go wide. "No, not without you."

"They saw me, not you. You have time to get away. Go, Emmy, *please!*" He whisper yells, grabbing the chain links that stand between us. I twine my fingers with his through the fence.

"I can't leave you behind," I sob, my voice cracking as tears start to fall. This can't be happening. We're so close to freedom.

"Melody needs you to be strong. Get her out of here. Get the both of you to safety. I'll be okay. Bring your sister back here, and let's bring them to their knees, okay?" His eyes glisten with his own tears. "I love you so fucking much, Amelia Knox. You are the love of my life, the light of my world, and the reason my heart beats. You own me in every way. I am yours, forever."

Why does this feel like a final goodbye? I'm about to argue with him when he squeezes my fingers, before he takes off. Without his help, I wouldn't be able to get back through the fence to go after him.

I'm frozen in place, my heart conflicted on what to do. Part of me wants to find a way back to him because if we can't leave together, then I don't want to leave at all. But a soft cry has me making one of the hardest decisions of my life. Melody comes first, always. I have to go, even if that means leaving a piece of myself behind.

I don't even want to think about what they are going to do to him for trying to escape or what they will do to Seth for letting it happen. The thought has another sob ripping from my throat.

Kissing the top of Melody's head, I rush behind the tree line. Quickly moving flashlights create a strobe effect while they look for where Tyson just was.

I step through a couple of trees, stumbling after a few steps. Looking back, I see big floodlights turn on, lighting up the compound. What I see further down the fence line has me holding my breath.

"Tyson," I breathe, seeing him on the ground, his arms behind his back as men above him argue, holding a gun to his head. "Fuck, fuck fuck!" I whisper shout. It feels like my heart is being ripped from my chest and crushed before my eyes.

As if Tyson can feel my eyes on him, he looks over. I can see his face in the light. He mouths "go" just as the Dagger demands he give up my location.

I need to go. I know Tyson won't give me up, but they will most likely go back to that room to confirm that I'm not there and then come back to the fence line, looking for me. I intended to be as far away as I can get before that happens.

Shifting Melody to my side, I shake the backpack off and place it on the ground. Digging around to look for the flashlight, my hand makes contact with something cold and smooth. Pulling it out, I see that it's a pistol. Well, that could be handy. Making sure the safety is on, I slip it back into the bag and pull out the flashlight.

Choking back a sob, I put the bag back on, light up the flashlight, and start walking. Moving it around to see the surrounding trees, I find an orange tag flashing back at me. Taking one last look back, I start running down the trail with only the light in my hand and of the moon to guide me.

God, please get us home safe, and please keep Tyson alive until we get him back to where he belongs.

CHAPTER 9
Emmy

I'VE BEEN WALKING for hours. My feet are numb, my arms are sore, and I can barely keep my eyes open. I've stopped a few times after I felt like we were far enough away for it to be safe enough to rest. Melody was pretty good for a while, the motion of being carried keeping her asleep in my arms. But after an hour of walking, she got hungry, so I stopped to feed her, and am now sitting on the cold forest ground.

Placing the bag on the ground, I sit down next to it, leaning back against a tree to feed Melody. When she's done, I lay her blanket down and change her before scooping her back into my arms, shaking out her blanket, and wrapping her back up. "We're almost home, sweet girl," I tell her as I rock her back to sleep. Honestly, I don't know how far we have to go to get to the compound.

The map was good for a while, but at some point, I got off the trail and was no longer able to find the orange markers. Not wanting to get lost, I noticed a river on the map that wasn't too far from our trail, so when I heard the rushing water in the distance, I found the source and have been following the river upstream ever since. I know that where this river ends has to be right by the Phantom Reapers compound. There's a big lake not too far from home with a dam that is, most likely, the source of this river. I just need to keep following the river upstream, and we'll be okay.

Now, the sun is starting to rise. My head is spinning, and as much as I know I have to keep going, I can't. My eyes keep closing, and if I don't take a break to get a little bit of sleep, I'm gonna be a danger to Melody and myself.

"It's okay, baby girl," I soothe as Melody starts to stir in my arms, my voice cracking from all the crying I've done on and off through the night. Any time my mind drifted to thoughts of anything but keeping to the right trails or getting us to safety, it went right to Tyson.

His broken eyes staring back at me as I left him there in the enemy's hands. It was hard not to wonder if he was okay, if they beat him like before, or was it worse this time? Did they finally decide to kill him?

My heart squeezes as my eyes start to burn. Unable to hold it in, I let the tears flow. I know I had to go, to take Melody and run. But something broke in my heart, leaving him behind like that. And I know for a fact that if I didn't have Melody with me, I would be right by his side, right now. I know he wants us to be safe, and he would give up his life for us in a second, but I don't want him to. Never. Because he has an army of people by his side. I hope he knows that I don't plan on leaving him there for long. The moment we get back to the compound, I'm getting everyone, and we will finish this war that the Savage Hellhounds started, once and for all. No one but Seth and any innocent people in that compound will survive. I know Harlow will enjoy every moment of burning that place to the ground.

My eyes start to droop with my head nodding forwards. I can't fall asleep, not yet. We are almost home. Taking out my hoodie that I ended up stuffing in my backpack after the summer air made it too hot to wear anymore, I lay it on the ground and place Melody on it, needing to splash cold water on my face from the river.

Once I know she won't roll, I quickly move over to the water, cupping handfuls of the ice-cold liquid and enjoying the feeling of it against my warm skin. I rub some on my arms to cool myself down before taking off my sneakers and stepping into the water. I groan at the soothing feeling against my aching feet. Once my toes start to feel numb, I put my socks and shoes back on, not caring about getting them wet, and make my way back over to Melody. My muscles are aching, and those ten-minute stops aren't helping at all. I need a little bit longer of a break this time, or I'll keep having to stop again, making this take much longer than it needs to.

Taking the book bag, I put it next to Melody and lie down on the ground, using it as a pillow.

I smile at her sleeping face as she sucks on her thumb before looking up at the sky, watching the clouds drift by. Just a half-hour this time, and I'll be good to go again.

Crying has me jolting awake. I must have fallen asleep. Fuck, Melody!

I look over to where I laid her down, but she's not there. My stomach turns, my heart starts pounding as I scramble to my feet, ready to tear apart this forest until I find her.

"Hello, sleeping beauty." A voice a few feet away has my eyes widening in panic, when they land on a strange man...with Melody in his arms. "You know, it's not very responsible to take a nap out in the middle of the woods with your child and no shelter. A wild animal could have made her their dinner," he tisks. "It's a good thing I came along, isn't it? I'll make sure you two get back where you belong nice and safe." He gives me a sinister grin, his yellow teeth on display. He's wearing a Savage Hellhound cut. Fuck! They found me. I knew stopping was a bad idea. I should have just kept going. I came so fucking far, and we won't be going with him. It's not happening.

"Give her to me, please." My words are shaky as I try to put on a brave face, holding out my arms as I take a cautious step towards him.

His eyes flick from me to the baby and back. "Nah. I think I'll keep a hold of her. Grab your stuff; we have a long hike back to Hades." He turns around and starts walking, not bothering to check to see if I'm following, knowing I would never let him take off with my daughter. But there's something he doesn't know I have.

Bending down, I grab my bag, but I don't put it on and start walking. No, I stick my hand inside, making contact with the handle of the gun. Pulling it out, I flick the safety off and level it with his head.

"Stop!" I shout, my hands shaking.

He turns around, his body tensing when he sees the gun. "Don't be such a foolish kid. I have your baby. You're not *really* going to shoot me and risk her; now, are you?"

"Put her down on the ground and step away," I growl. It can't be healthy for my heart to be beating this fast. I feel like I'm going to pass out, but the need to get my baby girl back in my arms takes over.

"Put the gun away, and no one gets hurt."

"I said, put her down, and step the fuck away," I say through gritted teeth.

Melody starts to cry, and I so desperately want to turn my attention to her, but I can't give him the one up on me. "You don't think I won't shoot you? Have you met the man who shares my DNA? My sister, Queenie? I come from a bloodline of fucking crazy, and you are between me and the most important thing in my life. I will not hesitate to put a bullet between your eyes."

He says nothing, studying my face for any hint of a lie. But there is none. I might not be the one who gets off on killing people, but I would take a life if it meant protecting the ones who mean the most to me. Just like they would for me.

My finger twitches on the trigger, and I see his eyes flash with panic. "Alright. You can hold her while we walk," he says, slowly putting my screaming baby on the ground. I hate hearing her cry like that, and these past few weeks have already been so confusing and hard for her. I feel like a horrible mother for not being able to keep her safe and away from all this, but I will do better. Be better. Starting with getting us home.

"Back up," I say, moving forward to get my daughter. When he's far enough, I bend down, placing the gun on the ground so that I can gather Melody in my arms, never taking my eye off him.

As I shift her to get a better hold of her with both hands, the man's eyes look from the gun to me. He uses that opening to dive for the gun, but he's not fast enough. My hand shoots out, grabbing a hold of the gun, and just as his hand is about to make contact with me. I shoot blindly, popping off a few shots and hoping one of them hits him.

Melody's cries become shrieks as the sounds of the gunshots echo through the forest, sending birds flying out of the trees.

Dropping the gun, I hold Melody to my chest, bouncing her back and forth. "Shhh. It's okay, baby girl. Mama is so sorry," I sob.

My eyes are on the man on the ground. He's not moving, not groaning in pain. Needing to know if he's dead or not, I move around him with shaky legs.

I suck in a gasp, my stomach lurching as I take in the massive hole in his forehead and the matching one exiting the back of his skull.

He's dead. Deader than dead. And *I* killed him. I killed a man, something Tyson wanted to keep me from having to experience. But I can't think of that right now. I need to get out of here.

Grabbing the gun again, I make sure the safety is back on before tucking it in the waistband of my dirty jeans. I grab the backpack and hoodie, before getting the hell out of there before any more of Dagger's men can find me. If they are out here, they would have heard the gunshots and would be trying to find out where it came from. I don't plan on being here when they do.

Leaving his body there on the riverbank, Melody and I start walking upstream again. My brain is numb; my body is on auto-pilot as my only thought is keeping Melody comfortable and my feet moving.

We stopped a few times for me to change Melody, get her latched to feed while I walked, or to grab a bit to eat and drink. I'm not risking a moment longer.

After what feels like hours, I finally see the dam. It's big, and we were at the bottom of it. If something happened and it broke, we would drown. The thought had me looking around to find a trail to get to higher ground. Once we get out of the valley, the compound isn't far away.

My eyes start to water at the thought of being home, in my lover's arms again, *safe*. But then I cry for a whole other reason. Tyson isn't going to be there with us. He's back in that hellhole, and my heart hurts to think about what we might find when we get him back.

The walls of the valley are all rock, and there's no way for me to get up and into the woods. Looking back, I see that I should have started up towards the trees further back, but instead, I walked deeper into the valley.

My eyes skim over the dam, scoping out a set of stairs. It must be what the civil engineers use when they need to do any maintenance or repairs.

Thank God.

Once I get to the bottom of the stairs, I look up and groan. It didn't look that high when I was further back.

"Alright, little one. We're almost there, sweet girl."

The climb up the stairs had me realizing just how traumatized my body was from this whole trip home. My feet are bleeding, my clothes are dirty, and my hair is a matted mess.

Sweat soaked through my T-shirt, so I take off the blanket Melody has wrapped around her, seeing some of her hair sticking to her face. Thankfully, the sun was at our back for most of the trip, so she was shielded by my body. But my back, however... I know there's going to be a wicked sunburn left behind.

When we get to the top, I can see the service road that leads out to the main road that's next to the compound gates.

It feels like we're so close, yet so far away. Every step down the gravel road is like five steps back, the feeling that it's never-ending.

Then I see it, the main road. Getting a burst of adrenaline, I hold Melody tight and start running with every last ounce of energy I have in me.

The compound walls come into view, and I let out a sob of relief. The men guarding the gate start shouting at me to stop, but I don't. They raise their guns, shouting some more, but when I get close enough, they seem to know who I am, because they lower their weapons, shouting at each other before a few race over to me.

"Take her," I croak. One of the men grabs ahold of Melody from my outstretched arms, and then everything goes black as my body gives out on me, giving in to the exhaustion the moment it knows we're safe.

CHAPTER 10
Talon

"IT'S BEEN TWO fucking weeks. If you tell me one more time that we will get them back *soon,* I'll punch you, man. I'll hit you so damn hard in the nuts that you won't be the next one to give Emmy a baby," I growl at Oliver from across the booth.

He drops his hamburger, glaring at me. "Look, you might not understand how much of a risk going in blind would be, but I do. We already lost men, and that was just in a fucking diversion. They won't hesitate to take us all out at whatever cost. They have my fucking brother, just waiting to take him out. I might be willing to sacrifice the whole fucking world for my family, but I can't live with the way Emmy would look at me if I gave our men up for slaughter just to save her and my brother."

"It's not just them," I spit. "It's our fucking daughter!"

"You don't think I know that?" Oliver roars, his fists slamming down on the table, making the cups rattle as he leans over, baring his teeth. "You don't think I sit up awake *every* fucking night wondering if she's being cared for properly? Emmy and Tyson can handle a hell of a lot. But she's just a fucking baby. I'm just praying they're not monsters enough to hurt a fucking baby."

"If we don't go get her back by tomorrow fucking night, I'll go do it myself," I warn him in a deadly tone.

"And get yourself killed?" he scoffs. "Leaving Ben and Emmy heartbroken for life? I know you don't think much about your self worth, no matter how many times we tell you how valuable you are to us, but you need to remember: you are a part of those two's souls. By hurting yourself, you're hurting them."

Shouting outside has me looking out the window to my right. Men run past, barking orders to each other.

"What the fuck?" Oliver says, his brows creasing as he moves to stand up.

Steel flies out of the back room like a bat out of Hell in the direction of the clubhouse exit.

"Dad!" Oliver shouts. Steel's head snaps over to his son. "What the fuck is going on?"

Steel's face splits into a massive grin. "They're here. They're at the front gate. Oliver, your girls are home."

I don't hear anything else he says, because I'm out of my seat, pushing past both of them as I run towards the front gate. My legs pump as fast as they can, my heart pounding against my rib cage, as I hold back tears that burn my eyes. Footsteps tell me Oliver isn't far behind me.

My brain is all over the place. I want to feel happy, excited, relieved, but I won't until the moment I lay eyes on her, hold her in my arms, and know she's safe.

As we get closer to the gate, my eyes are met with the loud pitched scream of a baby's cry, and as much as I hate to hear my baby girl in any distress, that sound is the best sound in the world right now. A sob rips from my chest as I push myself harder in time to see one of the men walk through the gate with a baby, her bright red hair shining in the sunlight. Behind them, another member is carrying a limp body in his arms.

"Emmy," I croak out, my voice filled with so much pain at the state she's in, but pure and utter bliss to see her behind these doors again.

I stop before them, not knowing what to do. Do I hold my daughter or my girlfriend?

"Give her to me," Oliver barks, taking Melody from the man. When I see she's safe in Oliver's arms, I give Melody's little, wet, red cheek a kiss. "I love you so much, sweet girl."

Turning to the man with Emmy, I gather her in my arms. She's passed out, covered in dirt and scratches.

"Fuck," I sob, holding her tighter. My knees give out, everything hitting me at once. Every thought that's been plaguing my mind for weeks, wondering if I'll ever see her alive again, comes flooding out.

Clutching her to my chest, I sob into the crook of her neck.

"Talon!" Ben's broken voice sounds distant and faint. A hand grabs my shoulder. "Talon, baby, we need to get her inside." Moving my face away from Emmy, I look up to see Ben's distraught face. I look down, making sure this is real. She's really in my arms where she belongs.

"Give her to me, man. We need to get her looked at," Oliver says, bending down to take her.

I hold tighter, not ready to let her go.

"Let him take her. She's home; she's safe. It's okay," Ben encourages.

As much as I don't want to let her go, I know she needs to be taken care of. I don't know what happened, but the idea of her hurting and seeing her like this has me ready to murder anyone who looks at me the wrong way.

I let Oliver take her from my arms, already missing the feel of her.

"Come on, baby." Ben holds out his hand. "Charlie has Melody. Let's go take care of our little girl."

The MC medic has been in there with Emmy for far too fucking long, and I'm fucking pissed off that Oliver gets to be in there with her. The room they use as an infirmary isn't very big, and I don't want to be in anyone's way, but the need to touch her, to show myself that this is real, has my hands twitching.

I want to hold Melody too, but my body is vibrating, and I don't want her feeding off my stress.

Looking over, I hear her giggles, and just like that, any anxiety I had melts away. She's sitting on Charlie's knee as she bounces her while Ben makes her favorite bunny, the one that got left behind when those monsters kidnapped them, talk. It's causing Melody to let out full belly laughs.

Charlie's eyes are gleaming with happy tears, but I know that she and Ben are just as worried about Emmy as I am.

I was too far gone in my own head to know how the others reacted when seeing our girls come through the gate. When we got inside, Charlie was a mess as she held Melody, trying to get her to stop crying as Harlow looked her over. Ben was barely holding on as he tried to stay strong for me.

Once my brain had a moment to settle down, I felt the pressure that's been on my chest lessen. When Oliver came out to update us, saying that Emmy only had heat stroke and exhaustion,

I felt like I could finally breathe. She was here, safe, and didn't have any broken bones.

I tried not to think about the things we would have to ask her when she woke up. If someone forced themself on her, I would find them and kill them myself. I will show no mercy.

Steel is sitting at the bar, waiting for her to wake up so he can ask where his son is and why he's not with Emmy and the baby. Is he dead? Did he leave with them, and she lost him on her way? Or did he even make it out of their gates?

"We leave tonight, this ends now," Harlow's voice echoes through the room, causing everyone to turn their attention to her. She's talking to her guys as they try to reason with her. But who are they kidding? She's Queenie. Telling her to hold back from murdering is like telling the wind not to blow or the sun not to shine.

"But what about Tyson?" Dean asks. "What if-"

"No! I know my best friend. If he didn't come back with my sister, it's because he couldn't. There's no way he would have just let her go. We need to get him back because with her being gone, there's no reason to keep him alive!" Harlow roars. "He could be fucking dead by now. No, we leave tonight and pray to fucking God that they decide to torture him before ending his life, so we might have enough time to get him out."

"She's right," Steel says, getting up from his stool and walking to the middle of the room. "Listen up, Reapers! Tonight, we start and end this war with the Savage Hellhounds. Tonight, we spill the blood of our enemies, get revenge for our lost ones and what they did to our people. Redemption will be found!" Steel roars and the whole room erupts into bloodthirsty cheers.

"Alright, Prez, let's get to planning," Harlow says, following Steel into his office.

"Shouldn't they already have a plan by now?" Charlie asks, walking over to me with Melody in her arms. "They had two weeks to decide on a course of action."

"Steel and Queenie butted heads a lot, never agreeing on what to do. Things are different now. Queenie is right; with Emmy and Melody gone, they have no leverage or reason to keep Tyson alive. That changes everything," Neo says, before smiling down at Melody, who looks up at him and lets out an adorably excited squeal.

"You're lucky. If I didn't know how much you needed time with your daughter, I would take that little butterball of cuteness," he mutters, placing a kiss on Melody's head, before walking over to his cousins.

"Guys, is this real?" Charlie says, as Melody grabs a handful of her pink hair and starts to chew on it.

"I keep asking myself that." I smile down at my daughter, gently taking the hair from her. "This might look like bubblegum, Melly Belly, but it's yucky." Her lip starts to wobble, and my heart breaks. "You know what, here," I say, giving it back, and she starts to suck on it again, making her cute little babbles. "You can have it. You can have anything you want."

"Thanks," Charlie says, as Melody yanks on her hair.

"What? Do you want to break her heart? Did you see that look she gave me? Nah, she can have anything her little heart desires."

"She has us so whipped," Charlie laughs.

"And I don't think we would have it any other way," Ben says, looking down at Melody with such love in his eyes it has me swooning.

"Thank you," I say, wrapping my arms around his waist, pulling his body to mine, and giving him a kiss.

"What for?" He asks, his voice low and husky as he nips at my bottom lip. So not the right time for this, but my cock seems to know everything will be okay and is alive and alert.

"For being amazing, for keeping me from destroying myself until our hearts came home."

"I will always be there for you both. We are your family, Talon. We have your back no matter what."

"I know," I smile.

"Guys, she's waking up," Oliver calls out from the doorway of the room Emmy is in.

We all head towards him, eager to see her.

When we get into the room, she's fighting with Oliver as he tries to get her to lay down.

"Firefly. You need to calm down," Oliver urges.

She stops struggling, looking up at him with wide blinking eyes. "Olly?" she asks, her voice breaking with disbelief.

"I'm here, Firefly. You're home; you're safe." He pulls her into his arms, holding her like she might leave again. She starts to cry, her shoulders shaking roughly.

"I'm home," she says between sobs.

Biting the inside of my cheek, I hold myself back from going over there and interrupting.

"Melody?" She pulls back, her eyes looking around frantically. When she sees Melody in Charlie's arms, she lets out a big sigh. Then she realizes we're all standing here, and she breaks all over again. This time we all rush over, each of us taking different spots on the bed and reaching out, so she has skin to skin contact with everyone.

We lay there, comforting her, enjoying her touch while she enjoys ours. She tells us about everything that's happened since she was taken. What her father had planned, what he was gonna allow that fucking perverted teacher to do to her. And when Oliver asked what happened to Tyson, she broke down all over again, telling us that they got him before he could get out. That he told her to leave, and as much as she didn't want to, she needed to keep Melody safe.

"We'll get him back," Oliver says with so much confidence that I hope he's right. "We're ending this once and for all...tonight."

"I want to come," she demands, and Oliver snorts out a laugh, but shuts up fast when he sees the look she is giving him. "You can't be serious, Emmy," he growls. "We just got you back! There's no way you're going back there. No. You need to rest."

"I can take care of myself," she insists.

"We have no doubt that you can, Firefly, but do you think it's safe for all of Melody's parents to be fighting in this war?" Oliver asks.

"Because I know I'm going tonight. There's no way in hell I'm not," I growl.

"Stay here with me and Melody, Emmy. Please," Charlie begs, looking like she's going to start crying. "We need you."

"I'll be here too," Ben tells Emmy, taking her hand in his and lifting it up to place a kiss on it.

"On one condition," Emmy says after a moment of silence. "You bring that sick fuck who thought I'd ever be his woman back...alive. I want to see how my sister works."

"Why is that such a turn on?" I groan.

“Don’t be turning into Neo now,” Charlie laughs.

“Sorry, but the idea of my sexy, strong, badass woman wanting to see the ones who did her wrong pay? Yeah, it’s fucking hot.”

Oliver snorts, shaking his head. “What about Dagger?” he asks her.

“If you can get him alive too, sure, but I’m not gonna be picky. I just want them to pay. I want this to end so that we can move on with our lives and not have to worry if there's someone out there who wants to hurt us.”

“We will, baby.” Oliver kisses her forehead.

“Olly,” she says, her voice cracking. “He can't be dead.”

“He’s not,” Oliver says, cupping her face. “He would never leave you, baby girl. He loves you and our little girl way too fucking much to ever be without you.”

She nods her head and looks at all of us. “There’s one more thing.” She bites her lip. “Melody and I took a break this morning after walking all night; I just needed to lie down and rest. But I was so fucking stupid, because I fell asleep without meaning to, and when I woke up, one of Dagger’s men had caught up to me. He had Melody and was demanding I follow him back. There was no way that was happening, so I did what I had to do to protect us.”

“What happened?” Charlie asks.

“I did something Tyson never wanted me to have to live with. I killed him. I pulled a gun and told him to put Melody down. When I put the gun down to pick her up and get a proper grip, he dove for it. But I was faster. I pulled the trigger without even thinking and shot him in the head.”

“Good,” Oliver growls. “I never wanted you to have any blood on your hands. But Firefly, you did the right thing. You protected our daughter and brought her home.”

“I know,” she nods. “And as fucked up as it might be, I’d do it again. I would kill anyone who threatened me, Melody, or any of you.”

“And we would and will do the same,” I say.

“I love you,” she says, tears starting to well in her eyes again. “So fucking much. Being away from you all hurt more than any physical pain I’ve had to endure in my life. I don’t want to be without you guys ever again.”

"You won't be," Ben assures her.
"Can we go home now?" she asks, looking at each of us.
"Yeah, baby, we can go home now."

CHAPTER 11
Emmy

"THIS IS KILLING me, you know," Oliver rasps, his forehead pressed to mine as we say goodbye. "I just got you back; the last thing I want to do is leave you again. But knowing you're safe behind these walls makes me feel a hell of a lot better about it."

"I know," I whisper, trying not to cry. I will, but not in front of him, not now. The last thing he needs to see before leaving is me breaking down all over again. "But, you have to go. Your brother needs you. Bring him home to me, Oliver. And you and Talon better be with him, in one piece. I can't lose you guys. Losing you is losing a piece of myself; I'll never be the same."

"We'll be okay. We're gonna get him back, burn the place to the motherfucking ground, and end this bullshit once and for all. We'll finally be safe to live our lives," he promises, pulling me into his arms. He holds me tight to this chest like if he lets go, I'll drift away.

"I love you so much, Olly. Always have since the moment I met you," I murmur into his chest, clutching the back of his jacket, never wanting to let him go.

"You owned me the moment I looked into your pretty, brown eyes, Amelia Knox. There's no one else in this world I'd rather give myself wholly to. Always you, Firefly."

He cups my face, pulling me into a bruising kiss as tears spill down my cheeks. "One more taste before I go." He groans, before dipping his tongue past my lips and over mine. I whimper as I melt into his body, wishing we could turn around, go home, and do so much more. But I won't be whole until Tyson is back here with us where he belongs.

"Go." My voice breaks. "Go before I demand to come with you."

"I love you."

"I love you too; come back to me."

"Always," he vows.

He hesitates a moment, giving me one last kiss, before turning around and racing over to his father's bike. He puts his helmet on and swings his leg over the seat before holding on to his dad. The bike engine revs and they take off through the open gates, hooting and hollering as they go.

"We'll be okay," Talon says, slipping his arms around my waist from behind, pulling me to his chest.

"I hate that the three of you will be gone. You could all die, and I'd be broken," I sniff, trying my hardest not to break.

"Don't think like that. We have Queenie and the Phantom Reapers. We have a plan. Find Tyson, get him to safety, and then let Hell rain down." He kisses my neck, my eyes closing as I lean back into his body.

"Ready to go kill some dirty dogs?" Harlow asks, coming over from the car she was standing by, her guys splitting up, taking two cars.

"Bring them home to me, please," I beg my sister.

"Baby sis, this is me we're talking about. Nothing is going to happen to them, and if anyone looks at them funny, I'll bring you their heads." She winks at me. "We'll get your boy back and bring all three home safe and sound. You'll get your gang bang soon."

Even though my heart is bleeding right now, I can't help but choke on a laugh. *Man, she really does not have a filter.*

"Well, come on, my Queen, let's go bathe in some blood. Then you can have a gang bang of your very own." Neo purrs, mimicking mine and Talon's pose. Harlow's eyes light up, and she giggles. *Eww.*

She says goodbye, allowing Neo to drag her over to one of the cars. "I better go; they're my ride. Unfortunately." Talon chuckles against my neck.

"Please come back," I beg him, turning around in his arms so I can see his handsome face. Brushing some blond strands out of his eyes, I let my fingertips trail over his cheek, needing to touch him.

"I will, My Lady. My whole heart is waiting for me here." He leans in, and I cup his face, kissing him softly but with so much passion. "Let our man take care of you. Let your girl hold you. You're not alone, Emmy, remember that. You are never alone."

With one last goodbye and kiss, he jogs over to the car, getting into the back seat. Both vehicles take off. The only people left are a few prospects and men ordered to stay here and guard this compound with their life. The moment the gates close, a sob rips from my throat, and my knees give out from under me, as if I've been crushed by an invisible thousand pound weight. But before I hit the ground, arms catch me, holding me tight and keeping me from falling.

"I got you, baby," Charlie says, voice thick with emotion. "Lean on me. Let me be your strength."

"Where's Ben?" I ask, as we walk through the front door to our house.

"With Melody. I was with her while Talon and Ben said goodbye. From the red rimmed eyes he had when he came to get the baby, he's pretty broken right now too."

"I'll go check on him."

We head up the stairs, heading towards Talon and Ben's room. Quietly, I push the door open, and a piece of my broken heart mends itself as I take in the sight before me. Ben is laying on the bed asleep with Melody, who's passed out next to him in her portable bassinet crib. His hand is draped over her tummy while her little hand holds on to Ben's finger. Some pillows are piled up to build a protective wall on the other side.

"Okay, that's pretty fucking adorable," Charlie says over my shoulder. The smile on my face is so wide my cheeks hurt. My eyes glaze over with tears once again, but this time it's due to how happy I am to be out of that hell and home safe.

Then reality hits me again, making me remember where Tyson is and where my other lovers are going.

"Come on," Charlie says, closing the door. "Let them sleep. Spend some time with me. Let's take our own nap."

She laces her fingers with mine and guides me to my room.

"I don't think I can shut my brain off long enough to sleep." I sigh, scrubbing my face with my hands, willing the headache, heartache, and exhaustion to go away.

"You need to rest, babe. You're still recovering from heatstroke. How are you feeling?"

"Oliver made me take some pain meds to help before he left. Talon insisted on lathering up my back in Aloe Vera gel." I laugh. "He enjoyed that, and I know if he didn't have to go, it would have led to something more." My heart clenches at the thought of them.

"Shhh. No talking about them. Let me take your mind off of things. Lay back, only focus on me." She moves to stand between my legs, and I have to tip my head to see her gorgeous face. "I've missed you so much, Emmy." Her voice is filled with so much emotion it has my eyes stinging with tears. There's nothing I can do right now, and worrying myself sick doesn't help anyone. I'm home, I'm safe, and in the arms of the woman I love. I've thought about this for weeks, being back where I belong. I need to stop focusing on the negative and drown myself in her smell, her touch, and her love. In *her*.

"Charlie," I rasp, my voice breaking.

"I know, baby." She brushes the hair out of my face, threading her fingers through it and cradling the back of my head. "Let me show you how much I missed you. How much I ached for you. To know you're safe and alive. These past two weeks, baby, I thought I would break, unable to put the pieces back together. I need to know you're truly here."

"I'm real," I whisper, and she leans over, capturing my lips with hers. We moan, starting out slowly at first, engraving every stroke of our tongues, every brush of her lips, the way she tastes into my memory.

Needing more, we crawl back into the middle of the bed, never breaking apart.

Opening my legs, I pull her down to me, needing the pressure of her body on top of mine, to feel her close. I want to mold myself to her, to become one, and never be without her again.

Her hands slip under my shirt and over my naked breast. I didn't bother putting on a bra after my shower. It was too hot and uncomfortable for that many layers of clothing.

Her fingers find my perked nipples, rolling them between her forefinger and thumb. I gasp into her mouth, arching into her touch. My body responds to her as always, desperate for her love.

Gripping her ass, I grind her against my throbbing clit, moaning at the shock of pleasure that whips through me. She thrusts her hips, bruising my lips when she kisses me harder and sucks on my tongue. I will never get enough of her.

She kneads at my breasts, taking turns torturing each of my nipples, switching off, and doing the same to the other one. Breaking the contact, she starts to kiss down my jaw, then my neck. Lifting up my shirt, my nipples stiffen harder from the cool air from the AC.

"Fuck." I hiss when her hot wet mouth makes contact with the aching nipple. Gripping the sheets, I close my eyes, focusing on the sensation of her touch.

Her tongue swirls as she sucks, flicks, and nips at my sensitive peaks. My brain is buzzing while my pussy demands she move her attention down there.

As if she can read my thoughts, when she's done pleasuring my other breast, she kisses her way down my body. She starts by licking between my breasts and leaving a trail of teasing kisses as she goes. Her lips brush against my skin, making me suck in a sharp breath. My skin prickles, my tummy sucking in at the sensitivity of her touch.

When she gets to my mound, she places a soft kiss before speaking. "I've missed the taste of you." She breathes, pulling my shorts down and off me completely. Her hands glide up my legs, her fingers kneading the flesh of my thighs, before grabbing my knees and opening me up wide for her.

"I could say all the perfect words of how my soul was drowning and my heart dying with you being gone, and while all that is true, right now, I want you to know how much I craved your perfect body. Your wet, pink pussy on my tongue as you fucked my face. The sting as you pull my hair in desperate need of release."

Looking at her through lidded eyes, I bite my lip. A whimper escapes me as my chest heaves in anticipation of when she will touch me next.

"I need you," I beg. "Please." Because as much as I love her pretty words that warm my heart, I need to cum all over her pretty face.

She gives me a heated smile before grabbing the hem of her top and yanking it off, taking her sports bra with it. Her perfect tits bounce into place, her nipples sharp, rosey peaks.

"You're so beautiful," I say, reaching for her. She leans over, taking my hand and sucking my fingers to her mouth. *God, I love this side of my girl.*

Letting go of my fingers with a pop, she positions herself between my legs, gripping my ass and moving it towards her. "I can feel you, and my mind knows you're real and here in my arms. But I think my taste buds need a refresher." She licks me from bottom to top, her eyes rolling back as she groans. "Fuck, you taste every bit as delicious as I remembered. But the real thing is so much fucking better."

"Charlie!" I cry with my back arching off the bed and my eyes squeezing shut. She starts to eat me out like she hasn't had her favorite meal in a long time. I guess, in a way, she hasn't. *Full of myself much?* Maybe, but she sure as fuck is one of mine, and she loves to remind me I'm hers.

My breath starts coming out choppy, and sweat coats my body as my legs start to shake. I'm so sensitive and needy as I grind my core against her mouth. She moans, the vibration adding to the sensation of her touch.

Charlie sucks my clit as she slides two fingers into me. "So fucking wet for me, baby," she mumbles against my pussy. "Soak me, Emmy. It's been a while since you squirted for me."

They all love to brag when they get me to squirt. I might always be wet for them, and even though I can, squirting isn't something that happens every time we have sex. It's usually only when I'm too worked up and over stimulated. And that's *exactly* how I feel right now. After weeks without her touch, my body is humming for it.

"Cum for me, baby," she purrs. "I can feel your legs shaking, you're so close. You can do it." She hooks her finger over the sweet spot, making the heat in my belly start to burn into an inferno. "That's it," she praises. "So close." To give me some help, she starts eating me out again.

"Oh god, please, Charlie, don't stop," I beg with pleading eyes, my orgasm right there, just out of reach. The look she gives me tells me she won't.

The pleasure is too much. My eyes roll into the back of my head as euphoria takes over me. Arching into her, my fingers grip the sheets, and my nails dig into my palms with how hard I'm grasping it as I scream out my release. My thighs lock around Charlie's head out of reflex as I use her mouth to ride out the waves of my pleasure.

"Such a good girl," she says, kissing my inner thigh as she comes up for air.

"Fuck." I breathe out a laugh. "That was..." I look up at her. "Everything I didn't know I needed."

She gives me a smug grin as she crawls back up my body, her face coated in my juices. "Your body loves to obey, doesn't it?"

"Since when have you become a dirty talker?" I cock a brow with a grin of my own.

"Since I thought I lost the chance to try new things with you." Her face slips a little, but I can tell she's trying to hold back from dampening the mood.

"Well, now it's time to show you just how much I've missed this sexy, little body," I say, grabbing hold of her and flipping us. She lets out a squeal of laughter that quickly ends in a moan as I do exactly what I promised. Making her scream my name twice before we fall asleep, naked in each other's arms, and spent from everything that's happened in the past twenty-four hours.

CHAPTER 12
Tyson

PAIN. SO MUCH fucking pain. My body is heavy, my limbs unable to move. Thankfully, all they did was beat me to a bloody pulp. I don't think anything is broken, but Dagger was too busy to come down here and deal with me himself. He's dealing with the shipment from last night, so his goons have been having their fun, taking turns making me bleed.

I'm in the same room I was when I first woke up here, only this time I'm not alone.

A pained groan sounds next to me, and I struggle to open my swollen eyes. I hate feeling so weak and useless, but I can't play the hero right now. I need to stay alive, just a little bit longer, until Queenie gets here. I know she's coming. She would never let me die.

"I've been in my fair share of fights over the years, but I've always won those," Seth groans. "Never been this beaten and bruised before." He groans again, his chain clanking as he moves and hissing in pain as he does.

"Don't think telling them 'their dicks are as small as a troll's and that 'they have a face, not even a mother could love' helped your case," I rasp, my throat raw from when one of the guys would choke me until I passed out and did it again the moment I woke up.

He lets out a pained chuckle. "Not like I was lying. They act like they are king shit, but they're just shit. Ugly fuckers who have nothing to offer this world."

"Well, I'm keeping my mouth shut because I'd like to stay alive to see my girlfriend and daughter again," I mutter, shifting my body so that I'm laying on the cold cement floor. It feels good against my bruised face. Never have I felt so weak and useless.

We were so fucking close to freedom. Watching Emmy and Melody leave broke my heart, but I'm so proud of her for listening to me. When I get out of here, I'm gonna reward her so fucking hard that she will be a sobbing, stunning mess in my bed by the end of it.

"You think they're okay?" I ask Seth, needing someone else to tell me 'yes' so that my brain stops thinking up all the bad things it can conjure up.

"I might not know your girl well, but from what I saw–and how she dealt with everything while being here–I think she will be okay. She seems like a strong woman."

"She is." I smile, closing my eyes as I will my mind to show me her beautiful face. "She survived so much bullshit. More than any one person should have to ever endure."

"Like what?"

"Her first year at Emerald Lake Prep, some crazy bitch who was fucked in the head and obsessed with my brother tried to drown her. She didn't know how to swim. Oliver got to her and brought her back. She pretty much died for a minute. Then there was someone from our MC who hated the fact that one of their men was dating the 'enemy's' daughter. He knew that Emmy never had anything to do with Dagger, never even met the man once in her lifetime, and despite who she shared DNA with, she wasn't on his side. But he couldn't see past it and became fixated on getting rid of the problem himself. So he kidnapped her, and his, just as nutty, daughter who was also obsessed with Oliver–because, apparently, he attracts the crazies–tried to kill her. We got to her in time, thankfully."

"Wow, all that in one year?" he says, blowing out a breath.

"Yeah, then the crazy bitch from school got out of whatever looney bin she was locked up in and came for Emmy, believing she was the reason why Oliver would never be with her. She shot up the school, and Emmy was forced to give birth to Melody in a library with Ben, Talon, and Charlie, while Oliver and I looked for Brittany, the crazy bitch."

He lets out a whistle. "Damn, what is it with you guys and being handed shitty ends of the stick."

"No fucking idea. But thanks to Dagger, it hasn't gotten any better. Sending in that fucking pervert...he really is an unhinged bastard."

"Try living under his thumb," Seth mutters.

"My life was so chill a few years ago. But it was going nowhere. I was sleeping around, getting drunk, and not caring if I lived or died on the next run. It was no way to live.

Emmy brought me back to life. She's the light battling any evil in my world. She's worth it."

"Knowing who her sister is, I have no doubt how strong she can be. I just feel bad for anyone who has to share blood with Dagger."

"Well, how unfortunate for you, isn't it?" Dagger's voice booms through the basement. I didn't even hear him open the door. "Seeing as how you're one of my bastard children, just like the rest of them."

That has my eyes snapping open in surprise. Seth looks at me with a grin. *What the fuck?* No way, there's no way he's Dagger's son.

"Oh, now you acknowledge me as your blood? Only took you my entire life. You know, for the longest time, I thought the whispers when you weren't around were all lies, but it seems to be your thing to knock up women and leave them."

"Women? Nah, boy, they're all whores. Useless, wastes of space that are only good for opening their legs. I didn't want Emmy, I didn't want you, and I had no idea Queenie was mine. Although I must say, she's my favorite. Blood thirsty little thing, isn't she? She gets it from her Pa."

I snort, and Dagger turns his head to glare at me. "Something funny to you, boy?" he asks, taking a few steps closer. I keep my mouth shut, not wanting to give him any reason to kill me sooner.

"Just that Queenie doesn't want to be your favorite, but she does wanna kill you. And I hope she lets me watch," Seth says, a taunting grin slipping over his lips.

"You think some bitch can beat me?" Dagger growls, redirecting his footsteps over to Seth.

"Oh, I know so. She's gonna kill you all. And I'm gonna stand there and laugh."

"Fucking ungrateful, no good traitor," Dagger spits. "I should have killed you alongside your mother."

"Probably should have. Would have saved me years of living in this dump, never being good enough for any of you. But you know what I've come to realize, the older I got? I didn't want to be one of you because I knew I was better than all of you. You're all fucking monsters with no regard for anyone's life.

You don't even have a purpose other than to cause havoc. No one respects you; they fear you. And sometimes, respect is better than fear. Because then you end up in a war like the one coming, and no one's gonna miss you."

"Why you little-" Dagger sneers, his words getting cut off by the sounds of distant gunshots. "What the fuck?" Dagger growls, looking towards the stairs that lead to the exit.

"Looks like we're about to have a family reunion," Seth says, cackling like a mad man. Maybe he really is Queenie's brother. "Run along, Pops, don't want to miss out on watching your men fall. I hope she saves you for last."

Dagger lets out a roar of anger before taking off up the stairs.

"So... I guess we just sit here and wait, eh?" Seth says.

Despite the pain it's causing me, my face slips into an excited grin. "Dude, you have no idea what's about to happen. You're lucky you helped me and Emmy because, trust me, you do *not* want to be on the receiving end of Queenie's wrath. She's like Harley Quinn on crack."

"She sounds like a peach," Seth grins.

I snort. "Yeah, a real peach. But she's the best friend you can ask for and to have on your side. Although, she is also the one person in the world you do not want to fuck with or fuck over. I feel like dating her sister might also earn me some extra safety points."

"What would being her brother get me?"

"Nothing." His face goes pale. "If you're a shitty person, you're as good as dead. But like I said, you have me and Emmy to vouch for you. You will be fine." *I hope.*

I can hear men shouting and gunshots coming from outside. Not to sound ungrateful, but it's about fucking time.

"Let's hope they search the buildings for us before they set the place on fire," Seth says, lifting up his chained foot. "Because we're not going anywhere on our own, and I'd really rather not end up as an overdone steak."

"As much as Queenie loves a good bonfire, she knows I'm here. She won't do any real damage to the place until she knows I'm safe."

"Fingers crossed."

Emmy, baby, I'm coming home.

CHAPTER 13
Harlow\Queenie

"So, we stick to the plan?" Oliver asks, leaning against the car as he talks to us through the window.

"Yes and no," I shrug.

His brows furrow. "What does that mean?"

"It means, if I find something more fun to do, I'm gonna do it. This is my first real battle, and I have so many things I wanna do," I say, my eyes lighting up at all the possibilities waiting for me beyond those walls.

"She normally kills in a controlled environment. This is like telling a kid they can have whatever they want, then setting them loose in a candy store," Dean explains.

"I want them all, Daddy Dean," I purr. I grin at the heat reflecting back at me in his eyes. He says he hates it when I call him that, but we both know it gets his cock harder than steel.

"As long as we get Tyson out safely, then have at it. Although, Emmy did request that we bring Jimmy back alive."

"I know, she told me. Is it weird I'm both excited and nervous? She wants to see me at work. What if she sees me differently?"

Neo chuckles. "My Queen, the worst that could happen is she pukes and never wants to watch you at work again. She loves you. How can she not? You're fucking amazing."

"Also, did Emmy tell you about the guy who helped her and Tyson out while she was there? The one who was in charge of them and the baby?"

"Yeah," I mutter. "She doesn't want me to kill him."

"You look disappointed," Oliver laughs.

"I am!" I say, throwing my arms out. "I don't want to leave any of them alive, none. This should be a free for all."

"Even the Old Ladies and the Sweetbutts?" Oliver asks, cocking a brow.

I let out an exasperated sigh. "No. I don't like killing women if I don't have to. Something tells me none of them really chose to be there, and it's not like they can just walk away from a life like this, not if the men don't want them to." I turn in my seat to face the rest of my guys. "But, if anyone interferes, if they get in our way or try to help the Hellhounds, don't hesitate because that tells you where their loyalties lie. You would have to be an evil person to want to defend these monsters."

Everyone agrees, and we start getting out of the car.

"Wanna see my toys?" I grin over at Oliver as I open up the trunk.

He gives me a skeptical look. "What kind of toys?"

"Fun ones." I roll my eyes. "The kind that go boom."

"Oh," he says, walking over to me.

"What kind of toys did you think I meant?" I laugh. "Sex toys?"

"Well, maybe. I mean, it is you after all," he chuckles.

"He has a point," Neo says, coming around from the other side. "I could totally see you killing someone with a dildo." He grins, his eyes growing lidded like the idea turns him on.

"Enough!" I warn. "Don't look at me like that. We have a war to finish. We can play later."

"Yes, please," he groans. "But I'm serious. Remember that time you slapped Axel with his own dick? Left a nice red mark. Just think of all the damage it could do if you meant to use it as a weapon."

"Wait. What?" Oliver asks, cocking a brow as he looks over at my mountain man.

"Nothing," Axel growls at Oliver, then glares at Neo. "Fuck off with that."

"Sorry dude, no can do. That memory lives rent free in my head," Neo cackles, dodging Axel as he tries to slap Neo upside the head.

"It's okay, baby," I purr, wrapping my arms around Axel's waist, grabbing a hold of his firm ass cheeks, and giving them a squeeze. "I prefer the real thing anyways."

"You're a little brat, you know that?" His voice is low and husky, sending a shiver of pleasure down my spine. "Getting me hard as a rock, before I have to go put a bunch of dogs down."

"And you're just gonna have to suck it up." I grin, biting his lower lip before stepping back. He growls and slaps my ass before going back to the car he came in.

"Anyways. Lookie!" I tell Oliver, my body humming with excitement. I rarely get a chance to have big event kills, but when I do, I love to change it up.

"Is that a rocket launcher?" Oliver asks, his eyes going wide as he peers into the trunk. "And a fucking flame thrower?"

"Oh, that's mine," Neo says, taking it out. "Thank you." The look on Neo's face is like when a kid gets the toy he's been dying for on Christmas morning.

"Don't forget the grenades," I say, holding one up. Oliver takes a step back.

"I'm kind of disappointed that I won't be having as much fun as all of you," Talon says, walking over from where he was talking to Steel.

"Well, you still have a pretty important job. You're finding Tyson and that Seth dude and getting them out safely while we have some fun." I grin mischievously.

"Oh, oh, can we use the fireworks too?" Neo asks, holding one up.

I take a moment to think. "Actually, that's not a bad idea. Set a few off by the gate. Get as many men as we can to come running to check things out, then let the games begin."

"Yes!" Neo says, gathering a bunch up in his arm.

Shaking my head with a smile, I walk over to Dean and Steel. The smile Dean gives me has my cold, bloody heart skipping a beat like a schoolgirl with a crush. *I fucking love that man.*

We go over the plan, but really, they're only here as back up. I'm being nice enough to even let them be here because sure, the Savage Hellhounds have been the Phantom Reapers' rivals for years, and they owe them their blood or whatever, but the moment that sperm donor started messing with my sister, I made it my mission to end his life. Should have done it a lot sooner, but my pride won't let me admit out loud how stupid I feel for not slitting his throat in his sleep before now. But my days traveling to seek out my victims are rare, now that I've gone and made myself a mom and got a bunch of men. Lucky for the guys, I love their stupid faces.

The Reapers park their bikes under the coverage of the forest, and my guys move the cars onto the service road nearby so they're out of sight. They are to wait there until I take care of the dumb fucks manning the gates. That is if they're even smart enough to have anyone on the lookout. From the research Evie did, they seem to think so fucking highly of themselves, that every time I sent a drone to check out the perimeter, there was almost always no one manning the gate. Or if there was, the lazy fuckers were passed out with a beer in their hands. *A bunch of jokes is what they are.*

With my dagger strapped to one leg and my gun strapped to another, I make my way to the guard station. I felt like dressing up for the occasion and to shake things up a bit. I'm dressed head to toe in black and red camo. I mean, it does shit all for its purpose, but I don't do puke green colors, thank you very much.

Neo, of course, wanted to add his own touch, so the crazy bastard cut the tips of his fingers and used two on each hand to smear blood on my face like war paint. He was nice enough to let me lick them clean, though.

For an MC that is known for being loud and obnoxious, I don't hear much going on from outside the walls, as I walk toward the entrance.

When I get to the guard station, I peer into the windows and find myself both annoyed and excited because there are two guys hunched over a computer watching a video. Porn, to be exact. Two women fucking each other. I roll my eyes because they are *so* faking it for a man's enjoyment. Trust me, it's much hotter when it's with people who are actually into each other or in love like Evie and me. The raw lust and pure chemistry is electric. These two are just doing it for the paycheck. Can't fault them for that, though. Nothing wrong with working in the adult film industry. Your body, your choice.

Needing to get the show on the road, I knock on the window, before quickly stepping to the side, away from the door and completely out of sight. I could just shoot them through the window, but that would draw some unwanted attention if there's anyone nearby. Right now, I want to be a sneaky bitch and have a little fun before we take this place guns blazing.

"What the fuck was that?" one of them asks.

"I don't fucking know!" There's some shuffling before he speaks again. "I don't see anyone outside."

"Maybe it was a damn bird again. Three of them tiny bastards have crashed into the window just this week alone," the first one says.

"Well, go check."

"You go check," the first voice demands.

"Fuck," the second one grunts, then opens the door, stepping out. He looks left, then he looks right, making eye contact with me. His eyes go wide, and he moves to call out while he reaches for his gun, but I'm faster. Before he can get a word out, I race forward, dagger in hand, and bring it up just under his chin. I angle it into his throat, getting him right above the esophagus.

He starts to gurgle on his own blood as I pull the dagger out. I quickly ram it into his temple, ending his life and making him drop to the ground. It would have been nice to have a little bit more fun with these guys, but I'll have plenty of entertainment.

"Bob?" dude number one says.

Bob. I laugh to myself. *My Bob is much cuter than this Bob. I miss my little goat friend.*

Focus Queenie, we have people to kill.

The man steps out to check on his friend. "What the fuck is going-" he stops mid-sentence when he sees me. "You," he breathes.

"Me," I cheer, raising my arms in the air like I'm the best surprise ever. Because, well, I am. He reaches for his gun, but I pull mine before he gets the chance to.

"You might wanna rethink that," I tell him, aiming it at his head. "You shoot at me, and you'll piss not only myself off, but my men will eat you for dinner, buddy. Let's be real. You knew this was coming, and your boss was too fucking stupid or cocky to think he would be on the winning side of this war. We're about to storm this place and burn it to the ground. So, I'm gonna give you a choice, which is more than most get. You can take this gun and shoot yourself, or I can tie you up and save you for later. And I'm sure you know what I like to do when I have more than enough time with my new friends."

I can see it in his eyes, he believes everything I just said. He knows he's fucked, and he's gonna die now. So, now all he has to do is decide if he wants it to be quick or painful. He reaches for the gun I'm offering him, his hand trembling in fear as he does so. "I don't wanna die," he starts to sob, but still takes the gun from me.

"And I don't want to live in a world where people think they can rape and abuse other people, but we don't always get what we want. So, chop-chop, buddy. I got places to go and a crap ton of people to kill."

He raises the gun to his head, snot running from his nose as tears spill from his eyes. I almost feel bad.

"Tell me, before you off yourself, have you ever raped anyone?" I ask, tilting my head to the side. The look in his eyes tells me all I need to know. He's just as much of a monster as the rest of his brotherhood. I already knew he raped someone before. I've done my research on these men; they all have some sort of past that would have them ending up in one of my D-Days. It's a pity I gotta waste them all in one go. I could have found something fun to do with this lot. Oh well, there's no shortage of evil in this world, sadly. So I'll always have someone to play with.

"Well?" I huff. "What are you waiting for?"

"I can't!" he wails, the gun shaking against this temple.

"God!" I huff, grabbing the gun from him and leveling it to his head. "Do I gotta do everything myself?" Then I fire the shot, ending his blubbering. Good thing I put a silencer on this thing. I don't want my fun to be ruined before it even starts.

You might be wondering, *well Harlow, what about the cameras*? Well, believe it or not, when I had Evie hack into them, there was nothing to hack into. The cameras are broken, and they are too fucking cheap to replace them.

Now that we can waltz right on into this joint, it's time to get my troublemakers over here so we can let the fun begin.

"Ready to rumble?" I ask into the walkie-talkie.

"Does my dick threaten to rip out of my pants every time I lay eyes on you?" Neo responds back.

I giggle at his response, biting my lip. A second later, I start seeing everyone emerge from the tree line.

"So, remember. We cause a distraction. Then you two and a few of your men search for Tyson and Seth. Check warehouses, basements, anywhere you think of where they might be keeping them. I doubt they would have brought Tyson back to the room he was staying in before, because they would not have been keeping them longer than tonight."

"You think they're still alive?" Oliver asks, uncertainty written all over his face as he looks towards the entrance.

"Shut your mouth. He's not dead until I see his lifeless body, got it?" I warn him. "Don't be going into this with that mindset. It will only bring you down."

"Yeah," he nods. "Ready?" he asks, turning to his dad.

"Ready," Steel says, then signals to his men to be ready.

"After you, my Queen," Neo says, handing me the grenade launcher.

"You're so kind," I say with a southern twang.

Walking toward the entrance, my guys follow behind. Dean and Axel carry the fireworks in their arms.

Using the guard station to enter the compound, I raise my gun, ready for anything. But when I look around, I see no one. Not a soul is around. But the sounds of music blaring in the distance has me fixed on a building on the far side of the compound. *That* must be their clubhouse.

"Be alert, but they all seem to be down there," I say, nodding my head in the direction of the sound.

Dean and Axel jog over to the tree line to my left and start setting up fireworks.

"This is gonna be so much fun," Neo says, the excitement clear in his voice. Looking up, I fall in love all over again with my crazy man, that has a look of pure joy on his face. "Thank you for this," he says, holding up the flame thrower. "I love my new toy."

"Good boys get rewarded." I wink. I'll never admit it to them, but I know I've been a handful since Emmy was taken, and he's been so good at keeping me from risking their lives by coming here and trying shit too soon. Normally I'm never reckless when it comes to something like this, or anything really, but they took not one but three people who mean the world to me, and that just doesn't fly with me.

"Best reward ever."

"Really?" I cock a brow.

He gives me a devilish grin. "Next to anything you do to me, and with me, of course."

"Thought so." I wink.

Looking behind me to check on Axel and Dean, I see them running over to us, the fuse of the fireworks lit, and only seconds away from going off.

Cupping my hands, I shout. "Yo, Daddy O. Come out, come out, wherever you are! We wanna party too!"

"Fuck yes!" Neo hoots, and then all at once, the fireworks start shooting off into the sky, the booming sounds echo through the compound.

Neo takes off, laughing like the unhinged man he is as he lights up the flame thrower, setting the dead trees a flame and making them go up in blaze of golden yellow. We have men waiting outside the compound in case the fire gets out of control and gets past the walls. *See, I think of everything.*

The moment I see everyone rushing from the clubhouse, I raise the grenade launcher and aim it at some cars halfway between them and me. They explode, and I turn to Talon and Oliver, yelling at them to go. They take off, disappearing into the trees, using them as cover as they make their way to the first building in search of our treasure.

With the fighting going on over here, hopefully, it will give them time to find them without getting spotted.

The rest of the Reapers make their way through the guard station, hooting and hollering, excited to finally get their pound of flesh.

Let the games begin.

CHAPTER 14
Oliver

Talon and I run through the patch of woods on the Hellhound compound, jumping over fallen trees and dodging low hanging branches. We have one thing on our minds; finding my brother and the man who helped care for my girls while they were held as prisoners, and we will kill anyone who gets in our way.

I won't hesitate. If it's not someone on our side, I'll shoot first and *never* ask questions.

"Let's start here," Talon says, pointing to the warehouse just ahead of us. When we get to the clearing, we look around, but everyone is flipping out, heading closer to the front gate. Good, less people around here.

"Go!" I tell Talon, and we run over to the building. Finding an unlocked door on the side, we go inside.

Making sure no one is in here, we take a look around, but there's only wooden pallets with crates on top of them, no basement, and all the rooms are empty.

One by one, Talon and I search each building we think they might be held in as the war rages on. Shouting and gunshots fill the air, and I have no doubt blood has already been shed.

Just as we are about to go inside one of the houses, the door swings open, and I bump into the chest of a Hellhound.

"What the fuck?" he growls, then looks down, seeing who I am. His eyes widen slightly as he reaches for the gun, but I'm faster. Before he can pull his on me, I fire two shots. One in his head, the other in his chest.

"Nice," Talon says, looking down at the dead body.

"Come on," I tell him. We search the house but find nothing, not even some indication that someone was in the basement. "Where the fuck are they keeping them?" I growl, looking around for any places we might have missed.

"There!" Talon says, pointing to two steel doors that are peeking up out of the overgrown grass. "Looks like a storm shelter." We run over to it, working together to get the heavy steel door open.

"Hello?" I call down into the darkness. "Anyone down there?"

"Oliver?" A familiar voice calls back, and my heart jumps with relief.

"Tyson, I'm here!"

"Oh, thank fuck," another voice says, and I'm guessing that it's Seth.

Looking to the side, I see a light switch against the wall. Flicking it on, we rush down the stairs.

My gut turns when I see the state my brother is in. "Fuck," I hiss, rushing over to him.

"Long time no see, brother. How you been?" Even beaten to a bloody pulp, he's still a cocky fucker.

"Better than you." I try to lighten the mood.

"Never." He chuckles, then groans like the movement hurts. "Emmy thinks I'm the best looking out of all you dickheads."

"Sure, dude, keep telling yourself that," Talon joins in.

"Well, this seems like a lovely family reunion and whatnot, but if you're here, I'm guessing those gunshots are the start of this war. So we should probably get the fuck out of here before they come down here and kill us all."

"Not sure that's gonna be so easy," I say, holding up the chains.

"Right," Seth says, looking down at his own chains.

"Who has the keys?" Talon asks. "Can't we just shoot at the chains or something?"

"Sounds super safe," Seth deadpans.

"Well, what the fuck do you want us to do? Go out there and start asking around if anyone has the keys?" Talon growls.

Looking up, I see the chains attached to a hook in the wall. It looks like it's in bad shape, and Talon's idea just might work. These guys are in no shape to be able to rip it out of the wall, so the chains are the only thing keeping them here. But if they were at full strength, they could easily detach them from the wall. Unfortunately, we don't have time to stand here and fuck around with it.

"Talon might have the right idea. I think with a few shots, we can at least get them off the wall. We can worry about getting them off your body later once we are safe and have more time."

Thankfully, they are only tethered to the wall by one chain each. Tyson's is around his wrist while Seth's is around his ankle.

"So, you're just gonna start popping off shots? What if it ricochet's off the wall and hits one of us?"

Stepping to the side of Seth, I examine the hook. "If I shoot it at this angle, you should be okay. But just to be safe, maybe everyone should stay low to the ground."

"What about you?" Tyson asks.

"It's a risk I'm willing to take. So, everyone down, and cover your ears."

Lining up the shot, I hope and pray that this works. With a deep breath, I fire three shots around the bolts, sending chunks of cement flying.

"Fuck!" Seth grunts. "A piece almost took my eye out."

"My bad," I say, checking out the hook. Grabbing a hold of it, I wiggle it and see that it's come loose. With some force, I move it back and forth before yanking and pulling it from the wall completely.

"Hell yeah!" Talon cheers.

"Here," I tell Seth, holding the end of his chain out for him to hold. "Drape it over your shoulder for now, so it's not in the way when we get the fuck out of here."

He takes it from me, and I look him over. "Are you able to walk?"

"I should be." He groans as he starts to stand. "Tyson's got the worst of it, unfortunately. Mine was more to teach me a lesson; his was from pure hatred."

"I can't wait to see the life leave Dagger's eyes," I seethe. That man has caused nothing but hell and pain for my family. This whole world is better off without him.

"How's Emmy?" Tyson asks, shifting his weight as he rolls onto his back.

"She's fine, man. The baby too, thanks to you," I say, crouching down and gripping his hand. He looks so weak and fragile. I've never seen my brother like this before.

He's always been strong, solid, and put together. I know this must be killing him. Not being in control and left entirely vulnerable.

"It killed me knowing she and the baby would be out there alone. I worried something bad would happen. Fuck man, she walked alone in the woods for hours. I should have been there with her."

"But you distracted the enemy long enough for her to get away. She got home. They are with Ben and Charlie now, locked behind our walls. Our men are ordered to protect them along with all the other women and children with their lives. And I know Ben won't hesitate to shoot anyone. It might not be something he would like to do, but he does know how to shoot a gun. Just like us, he would kill to protect our family."

"Good. I'm glad they are okay and safe. How was she when she got there?"

My heart clenches as I think of the state Emmy was in when one of our men brought her through the gate.

Not wanting to tell him and cause him to freak out, I ignore the question walking over to the hook with his chains.

"Fuck." I hiss. "It's not going to be as easy for you."

Tyson holds up his hand, using his other one to pull at it. "It will be if I break my hand and you guys pull it off."

"What the fuck?" Talon mutters, his eyes wide with shock.

"What's the harm in a little more pain? Not like I don't already have broken ribs, a bruised body, and I'm pretty sure my knee cap is busted. That's all on my left side. I need something on my right side, so it's not too uneven."

"Don't even joke like that, man," I growl.

"Look, we don't have time to sit around here and bicker like a group of Karens, okay? One more broken thing on my body sounds a hell of a lot better than having our bodies riddled with bullets and being dead."

"Fuck," I curse, kneeling down. "How the hell do we do it?"

"Well, I'll hold my hand like this..." He positions his hand like he's going to pick something up. "Then one of you step on it hard enough to break the bones, then pull it off. Sure some skin might come with it, but Emmy thinks scars are sexy, so I see no loss."

"I fucking hate you sometimes." I let out a harsh breath.

"But you also love me. Let's get this over with so we can get out of here and home to our girl."

"Fine." My jaw is tight. The thought of hurting my brother like this makes me sick.

He lays his hand down on the ground, angling it the way he needs to.

"Just one big stomp with your steel toe boot should do it," he says, looking up at me with nervous eyes.

"Shut up," I mutter, moving to raise my foot. My body prickles with sweat, my heart beating so fast it's out of rhythm. Taking a deep breath, I will my foot to move. "Damn it!" I shout. "I can't do it." I let out a harsh sigh as I put my foot back down.

"Well, you have to so suck it the fuck up an-" Tyson is cut off, as a loud crunch fills the room as Seth does what I couldn't do.

"Fuckkkkk!" Tyson roars in agony.

"Sorry, man. But we gotta get out of here." Seth responds with no remorse.

"No," Tyson rasps, his voice hoarse from his scream. "Thanks."

Seth bends down and grabs Tyson's broken hand by the wrist before warning him, "This is gonna hurt too."

Tyson moves his head and bites into his upper arm, looking at Seth, then nods. Seth starts to wiggle the cuff back and forth as he pulls it over Tyson's hand. Tyson screams into his arms, squeezing his eyes shut as some of his skin starts to rip apart. Thankfully, Seth is able to get it off, throwing it to the ground with a clatter that echoes throughout the room alongside Tyson's panting.

"Come on," I say to Talon, leaning over to pick up my brother. "You grab his other side. We need to leave. Now!"

Talon and I struggle to get Tyson up the stairs and out of the bunker. It's not easy with Tyson's broken knee and his other injuries, but we manage while Seth takes the lead with my gun, ready to shoot.

"Wait!" Someone shouts, and I look over my shoulder to see Seth aiming a gun at one of our men.

"He's with us," I tell Seth, and he lowers the gun.

"You found him, thank God," Ricky says.

"Find Joe and Bill, and get back to the others. Join in on the fight. We have him," I tell Ricky, sending him on his way.

Gunshots, explosions, and screams fill the air as we make our way back over to the tree line, using the buildings as coverage.

"What the fuck?" Tyson says, as we stop before what used to be a big patch of trees that is now completely on fire.

"Neo really went to town, didn't he?" Talon mumbles, his eyes wide as he takes in the blazing trees.

"Neo? How the fuck did he do all this?" Tyson questions.

"Queenie gave him a flame thrower," I sigh.

"Of course, she did," Tyson chuckles. "That man needs to be supervised like a child."

"Well, I'm trading in one fucked up family for another, I see," Seth comments.

With furrowed brows, I look down at Tyson, wondering what the fuck that means. He shakes his head. "Long story. We'll talk about it later."

We better.

"Well, how the fuck do we get to the front gate now? It's not a safe idea to be out in the open."

"Waaaah-hoooooo!" Someone shouts, and we all look over to see Neo driving over to us like a mad man on an ATV. "Anyone in need of a lift?" Neo asks, stopping next to us with this look of pure bloodlust, and happiness. His face is splattered in blood as well as his clothes.

"Having fun?" Talon asks.

"Dude, this is almost as amazing as sex with my Queen. But like, not, because that pussy is fucking gold," Neo groans.

"I'm sure it is. Now can you please take him to the front gate and get him to the other side so some of my men can get him to the hospital?"

"Why, of course. It would be my pleasure. Hop on, big boy, we're going for a ride." We get Tyson on the ATV. "Hold on, Ty man," Neo says before taking off with a lurch. Neo starts hooting and hollering as they speed towards the front gate. He has one hand on the handlebars to steer, but the other is holding onto a machine gun that is wedged under his armpit so he can shoot any incoming enemies. Or at random like he is now. *He better not hit any of my fucking men.*

"Come on. We gotta go. With Tyson not slowing us down, we should be able to get out of here easier," Seth says.

"You two go, get out of here. Now that my brother is safe, I need to go find my dad and help him."

"Oliver," Talon protests.

"Go. I have more training in this than you do. Plus, this way, there is one less lover of Emmy's at risk, meaning more people to go home back to her."

"You better come back to us alive, man, or I'll find you and kill you all over again!"

"Nothing will keep me from Emmy. I won't fail her again."

"You never failed her in the first place, Oliver."

"Yeah, yeah. Enough lovey-dovey shit, get out of here," I tell him, pulling him in for a hug, then looking over at Seth. "Help keep him alive. Or I'll kill you."

"He's Emmy's, so I got his back."

I don't know why he feels the need to protect Emmy, but I'm grateful for it, nonetheless. *And* I can tell it's not in a romantic way. Thank God for that because then I'd have to beat his ass.

With one last look, I take off towards the clubhouse, where I see Queenie chasing after some people. As I run with my gun in hand, I look around, seeing that the war has died down. Literally. There's bodies littering the ground, and I have to jump over a few to avoid tripping. From what I can see, they all seem to have Hellhound jackets on. Some bodies are unrecognizable because they are burnt to a fucking crisp. Better be some dirty dogs and not my men.

I don't allow myself to be relieved because it would be foolish to think we are getting out of this without any casualties of our own. Is it selfish to hope we don't end up losing my dad? I know he would die for his men, but I don't want him to. He's my dad, and I'd be wrecked if he was gone.

He might be a badass biker who can make people piss themselves with one look, but he also has the kindest heart. He's loyal, loving, and honest. He thinks the world of my girls and would lay down his life for them too. He's the kind of dad I'm aiming to be with Melody and any future kids I may have.

Just as I'm about to follow Harlow into the clubhouse, I'm hit from the side.

My body goes flying before crashing into the ground. A fist meets my face, and pain throbs throughout my left cheek. Quickly realizing I'm being attacked, I start fighting whoever is on top of me. He goes to punch me again, and I bring up my knee, getting him in the balls. He grunts in pain, bringing his fist down, but I dodge it, making him punch the ground instead. I manage to push him off of me and roll to the side, but just as I'm about to get up so I can shoot the fucker, I feel the barrel of the gun at the back of my head.

"Not so fast, little boy," someone coos. "You think you can come in here and fuck with us? I don't think so. I'm gonna put you down like I did all the others."

"You sure you managed to get any of my guys? From the look of it out there, there's more roasted hounds littering the ground than anything else." Okay, so taunting him might not be the best idea, but I'm not gonna let him think he's winning in any way.

The guy who I was just fighting with gets up off the ground, heading over to me with this pissed off, constipated look. He pulls his gun out and aims it at me too. Guess he didn't like being kneed in the balls.

"You're gonna pay for-" he starts, but his head explodes like an overripe watermelon before he gets the chance to finish.

"What the-?" Same thing happens to the guy behind me. I'm now covered in human remains.

Wiping my hands down my face, I try to get as much off as I can. When I blink my eyes open and look at pieces of brain and hair, I can't help it. Leaning over, I heave everything I have inside my stomach right at my feet. This will haunt my dreams for the rest of my life. Something new to talk to my therapist about if I ever manage to get the chance to go. Life's been a little crazy lately.

"First time seeing someone get their brains blown out?" Someone new asks me, and I turn to see Dean lower his gun.

"Don't worry, after you're around it enough, it gets easier. It's an everyday thing for us. We're practically immune to it by now," Axel adds, lowering his own.

"What kind of life do you live?" I ask them in disbelief, still a bit in shock.

"A very exciting, eventful one. You do know who our woman is, right? I'd honestly be a little concerned if we *didn't* see some brains at least once a week."

"I have mad respect for Queenie, and don't take this the wrong way, but I really hope Emmy doesn't have the urge to be like her big sister the way most girls do."

"It takes a special kind of person to love a serial killer," Dean nods.

"Or someone who's just as fucked up in the head," Axel shrugs.

"Both." Dean grins, and they both chuckle. And here I thought Neo was the only crazy man Queenie had in her pocket. Sure, they might not be on his level, but these guys are not far behind him.

"Now, did you see our Queen around here anywhere? She mentioned something about finding Dagger, but we were in the middle of offing a bunch of dogs, so we didn't see which way she went," Dean asks.

"Yeah," I say, lifting up my shirt to wipe my face. That will help get it cleaner than just using my hands. "I saw her go inside. Not sure if she was following anyone, though."

"Did you find Tyson?" Axel adds.

"Yeah, took a while, but we found him and Seth in an underground bunker," I growl. "I really wish I got to fuck up a few of these guys for what they did to my brother."

"I mean, we do have a few tied up as a gift to Queenie. Maybe she will let you get a few shots in before she has her fun," Axel says. "She doesn't really like to share her toys, but I feel like this could count as a special occasion."

"So, where are they?" Dean asks.

"Neo found us. He took Tyson to the guys waiting out front. Hopefully, he's halfway to the hospital by now. Seth and Talon took off in the same direction right after."

"Oliver!" Someone shouts. Turning around, I see my dad running over to me. My face splits into a grin. He's covered in blood, but I can tell by the look on his face he's okay. I run over, meeting him in the middle, and we collide in a bone crushing hug.

"I'm so fucking glad you're okay," I tell him, pulling back.

"Gonna take a lot more than some stupid mutts to put me down." He chuckles, then his face drops. "Did you find your brother?"

"Yeah, we did. The fuckers had him chained up. Had to break his hand to get him out, but he should be on his way to the hospital. Talon and Seth, hopefully, made it out too."

"Why didn't you go with them?" He asks, his brows furrowing.

"You didn't think I'd just leave you here to fight this war all on your own, now did you?"

"Dude, not to burst your bubble, but you did fuck all in this war," Neo says, walking towards us. *Where the fuck did he come from?*

"Where's the ATV?" I ask.

"Crashed it. Found a few stragglers, so I plowed through them. One of them got caught in the wheels and ended up flipping it. The asshole." Neo rolls his eyes like it was a big fucking inconvenience that a mangled body fucked with his joy ride. "I did this awesome tuck and roll just in time to see it go ka-boom."

"So, is it over?" I ask.

"I think so." My dad grins. "I have some men searching around, but between the pyro over here and that badass of a best friend, they were taking out groups of people. If it wasn't for them, our body count would be a lot higher."

"There were casualties then?" I ask, hating the idea of losing any of our men.

"So far, only two. Bullet and Roco." Dad nods. "Some damn good men, but they went out doing what they loved. I think living to be fifty-five in this life is pretty damn good."

"Don't say that. You're forty-five, and I refuse to think we only have ten years left with you."

"Well, maybe I'll make it to sixty-five now that these fuckers are gone," he laughs.

"Come on, fuckers! The Queen is waiting," Neo says, as he walks past us and into the Savage Hellhounds' clubhouse. Dad, Axel, and Dean follow him, but I stay back for a moment to look at the state of this place. The trees are burnt, but thankfully the fire hasn't spread past the wall. There are burning cars, bodies littering the ground, and the smell is horrible. I hate that so much death had to come from today, but it had to be done. Dagger would never have stopped going after my girl, and it's not like these men even deserve to be breathing fresh air anyways.

They were all evil men who did unspeakable things. Knowing these guys and what they do, I'm so fucking grateful that they didn't lay a hand on Emmy.

With one last look, I follow them. Dagger and Jimmy better be alive because they do not get a fast death. No, we want them to feel every excruciatingly painful thing Queenie does to them. And I wanna watch right alongside my girl.

CHAPTER 15
Neo

I FUCKING LOVE vacations. This is by far the best one I've had in my life. Sex, blood, and murder, what more could I ask for? Sure, most of it was spent worrying that Emmy was kidnapped, but everything worked out in the end. Plus, I got some wonderful memories out of it.

And, we are not even done.

"My Queen!" I shout into the empty bar.

"Back here, Pet!" She calls back from somewhere further inside the building. We follow the direction of her voice down the hall.

"Marco," I call again.

I can hear her giggle. "Polo," she calls. I grin, heading into the room where she's at. "About time! Now the whole gang is here."

She looks like a fucking wet dream, all covered in blood, and I almost want to pout because her camo outfit hides the rest way too well. She always looks her best in red.

Queenie sits at a big wooden desk. Her feet are propped up and crossed as she leans back in the chair. Taking a puff of the cigar in her hand, she tips her head back and blows the smoke upwards, which leaves a cloud above her head.

"Look who I found," Queenie says, pointing to the two fuckers gagged and tied to a pair of chairs.

"My Queen, did you get them tied up all on your own?" I tease, walking over to her.

"Of course I did." She rolls her eyes, but I see a smirk creeping onto her sexy red lips. "Knocked this fucker out after I shot him in the foot. Wanna know something funny? He was in his safe over there getting money and fake IDs. Big, bad, daddy Dagger was gonna abandon his men for us to slaughter while he skipped town." She looks at the man who is screaming against his gag while also thrashing in his seat. "If I wasn't already ashamed to have his blood running through my veins, I sure as hell am now. Like really?

I thought you were this big, bad, biker who had no heart. You look like a pansy-ass little bitch to me," she snorts.

"And this one!" She laughs, pointing to some man next to Dagger who has snot running down his face.

"Mr. Park," Oliver growls behind me. "That's the teacher who tried to rape Emmy."

"Yeah, fucking pathetic excuse of a human, found him hiding in a closet. Fucker even pissed himself when I took out my dagger. So fucking gross, and I had to haul his snotty, piss covered self out. Not so tough now, eh?" Queenie's feet fall from the desk, and she moves to stand, leaning over it on her hands. "You thought you could try and rape my little sister? Nah, now I get to shove fun things in *your* holes by force." She gives him this smile that has my cock throbbing, but I'm sure to anyone else it would strike fear in their heart with how excited she looks about torturing him right now. "I think I'll leave you gag-less. That way, I can hear you cry and plead for me to stop like I'm sure many other women have while you ignored them. It'll give me a good laugh, one that will have my sides hurting."

"I can help too, right?" I ask, licking my lips as my eyes fall to her sexy blood red ones, wanting to suck the specks of actual blood off her upper lip.

"You know you can play whenever you want to, Pet." She winks. "And maybe Beast will want to play with good ol' Pops over here." She nods at Dagger, making him scream in anger against his gag as he thrashes in his chair some more. His hands pull against the tape as his nostrils flare like an angry bull.

"I think he has something to say. Should we see what it is?" I grin.

"Why not?" Queenie says with a laugh, sitting back in the chair again.

Walking over to Dagger, I get a whiff of piddle pants. Looking down at him, I give him a sneer. "Fucking nasty. I think we might need to hose you down with a pressure washer before taking you back home with us."

He whimpers, a bubble of snot popping from his nose as he tries to lean away from me.

Shaking my head, I reach over and grab the gag from Dagger's mouth. "Woah there." I chuckle as he tries to fucking bite me. "Bad dog," I scold him, wagging my finger at him. "No biting."

"Fuck you!" he spits.

"Nah, but I'll fuck your daughter." I give him a pearly white smile.

"Pet, don't," Queenie scoffs. "Sick fucker would probably get off on watching." I look over to see her shiver in disgust.

Shrugging, I hop up on the desk, swinging my legs like a little kid as I wait for my Queen to do her thing.

"So, I bet this isn't how you thought it would end," Queenie says, with a fake pout. "Poor, big, bad, biker gang is all dead and gone with their leader about to meet the same fate, but in a much slower and more painful way."

"I'm gonna kill you!" he snarls.

"Oh my God, Neo!" she coos. "He's so cute!" I snort a laugh at her taunting. "I'd really, truly love to see you try."

"You think you're so tough. You're just a stupid, useless woman!" he shouts, while curling his lip in disgust.

"And you're just a silly, little man with a small dick. If I didn't hate you so much, I'd pity you." She looks over at Axel, asking, "Do you think that's why he's so angry? He's so pissed off that he can't make it more than an inch into a pussy?"

"Oh yeah," Axel chuckles. "That's gotta be the reason."

"Knew it." She snaps her fingers.

"Shut up!" Dagger barks. "You think you're so funny, you stupid bitch. You're a joke."

"Blah, blah, blah." Queenie rolls her eyes, before getting in his face with a dagger tight against his neck. "More like joke's on you." Her voice went from playful to deadly. Dagger's eyes flash with fear, realizing she can slit his throat and end him with a flick of her wrist. "What was the point of all this? Why come after a kid you never wanted in the first place? She was never a bother to you."

"She became best friends with him." He sneers at Oliver. "Doesn't matter if I wanted her or not. I wasn't gonna let my blood hang out with Reaper scum."

"That's why you blackmailed me into selling drugs for you and then turned me in to the cops?" Oliver growls. "Thought getting me sent away would fix that problem of yours?

Nah, it just brought us closer. Now, she has my daughter, my love, and the love of my brother. She's a Phantom Reaper, so is your granddaughter. In the end, you're left with nothing. Your club is wiped from the face of this earth, and it all could have been avoided if you didn't let your stupid pride win. Oh well, the world is down some trash now."

Steel makes his way over to Dagger, silent and deadly. He stops in front of him, crossing his arms, all while loving the fact that he gets to look down on his enemy. "You were never the better man, Dagger. Real men don't rape. They don't kidnap. They are everything you and your men were not. And now, the better men stand in front of you while you're destined to die." He smirks down at Dagger. "*Checkmate.*" Is the last thing he says, before bashing Dagger upside the head, knocking him out cold. "Man, it felt good to do that."

"Pity you don't live closer, I'd let you play too," Queenie says, lifting Dagger by the hair and using a black sharpie to draw a dick and a mustache on his face. She takes a step back and nods in satisfaction at her work. I chuckle when she smiles over at me. *I fucking love this woman.*

"Maybe I'll make the trip for something like this," Steel says. "I'd love to give him everything he deserves for fucking with my family."

"I mean, you *are* due for a vacation. Cali is the perfect place to go," Queenie grins.

"So, who's gonna carry pissy pants out of here?" Oliver asks, looking down at the fucker who passed out from fear alone.

"Not it!" Me, Queenie, Steel, and Dean all shout at once.

"For fuck's sake!" Axel curses.

"Sorry, man, I got my girl to get to and a brother to check on," Oliver says, before looking at Queenie. "Thank you for everything."

"You never have to thank me when it comes to my own family. I would burn the world down for those girls and Tyson."

"She's lucky to have a sister like you," Oliver says.

"I'm the lucky one."

"I'll grab the in-law." I say, cutting the tape off, getting him free before throwing him over my shoulder. "I wanna see how his legs bend when I stuff him in the trunk."

CHAPTER 16
Emmy

"BUTTERFLY, CAN YOU please stop pacing? You're going to wear a hole in the floor," Ben asks me from his spot on the couch. He has Melody in his arms, giving her a bottle. She's been pretty fussy, and I think she is feeding off the energy in the room. We're all nervous, and the suspense of waiting to see if everyone is alive and well is exhausting.

I'm surprised I was even able to nap with Charlie earlier. After we woke up, we all went to the clubhouse. The Old Ladies made us some lunch, and we hung out there with them. Staying in the house was driving me crazy, but we needed to come back to feed Melody and put her down for her second nap of the day. Only she didn't want to nurse from me, and she's overly tired.

"I'm sorry." I let out a harsh breath. "But it's been hours. How long does a war last? Could this be an all night thing? I don't think I could wait that long to hear any news." Was Tyson alive by the time they found him? Have they even found him? Did they get shot fighting? Are we winning, or does Dagger have everyone I love locked up somewhere?

"I see your mind is in overdrive, babe," Charlie says, stepping in front of me, stopping me from making my next round of pacing. She grabs my shoulders, holding me still. "We will win this. It's your sister we're talking about. There is no way they can beat her."

"Yeah, I kind of wish someone could have videotaped it for me," Ben chuckles. "I bet she's having the time of her life right now."

The sounds of people cheering outside makes its way through the open window, and I rush over to see what's going on. People are running from their houses in the direction of the gate, and from the smiles on their faces, I know they're back.

Spinning on my heel, I race for the door. I pull it open and take off down the steps, completely ignoring Charlie and Ben shouting behind me.

Cars and bikes start entering the compound. Excitement and dread takes over me as I push my legs to move faster. The heat exhaustion from earlier reminds me of what my body went through just this morning and causes my head to spin. But I don't care, I need to see everyone with my own eyes.

The sun is setting, casting an orangey-pink glow over everyone at the gate, almost like the heavens shining a spotlight on the soldiers coming home. And I know we won this war, because from the looks of it, pretty much everyone who left this evening has come back.

A sob slips past my lips when I see Talon get out of a car, followed by Harlow and Neo.

"Talon!" I shout, his head snapping over in my direction. He starts running for me, and we meet in the middle, our bodies crashing together in a soul crushing hug. Talon holds on to me like I'm his saving grace, and I let the tears flow as I clutch onto his shirt. He soothes me, petting my head and back, telling me everything's okay. Another body wraps around my back so that I'm sandwiched between Ben and Talon.

"Thank God you're okay." I hear Ben's voice breaking, as he clutches onto Talon, crushing me, but I don't give a single fuck.

"We won," Talon tells Ben. "We lost a few people, but other than that, every single one of the Savage Hellhounds are dead and gone." We break apart. Talon looks down at me with a smile filled with pure joy. "It's all over, baby. We can be happy for once in our fucking lives. No fucked up parents out to get us. No stalkers, creepy teachers, or crazy bitches. We get to live our lives the way we want, no one else getting in our way."

"So Oliver and Tyson are okay?" I ask, sniffing and wiping the tears from my eyes.

"Yeah, they're okay. Tyson is a little beat up, a few broken bones, but he's going to be fine. Oliver is at the hospital with him, Seth, and Steel right now."

"I want to go see them," I insist.

"You sure? You had one Hell of a night. I don't want you overworking yourself."

"Do you really think you can keep her from two of her men while one is held up at the hospital?" My sister laughs from behind me.

I whirl around to see her covered in blood. It's the first time I've seen it with my own eyes, but I'm not surprised in the least.

"I'm glad you're okay," I smile.

"Oh, baby sis, that was just child's play compared to what I do." She gives me a wicked grin.

"I don't doubt that," I laugh. "So, what's the deal with Dagger and Jimmy?"

"Axel and Dean are bringing them back to LA on our jet right now. They're gonna keep them locked up until I'm ready to bring them out and play." She wiggles her eyebrows.

"I guess that means you're going home?" I ask, a sadness washing over me. I enjoyed having Harlow around, having my sister there for me when shit hit the fan.

"Well, about that," Evie says, walking over to Harlow. She pulls her into a sweet kiss; not a bit of worry shows on Evie's face, but I know she was. How can you not when the love of your life is in a life or death situation?

"Did it go through?" Harlow's eyes light up. Evie just smiles and nods.

"What's going on?" I ask, my brows furrowing in confusion.

"How would you guys feel about moving to LA?" Harlow grins.

My eyes widen. "What?"

"The people who were living in the house next to ours just moved out. We bought it. I just wanted it, so we didn't have any neighbors, but if it was you guys living next door, I sure as hell would rather have that."

Biting my lip, I process what she's saying.

"We should talk to Oliver and Tyson about it," Charlie says, stepping up to my side with Melody fast asleep in her arms. "But, I think it would be a good idea. A place where we can start over fresh and new. You would have your family, a home for Melody to grow up in. So many options."

"I don't know," I say, looking around at all the MC members hugging their families, celebrating their win. "Tyson and Oliver love the MC life. I can't ask them to leave that behind."

"Actually, I have a solution to that problem too," Harlow chirps and then giggles at my shocked expression.

"Of course you do." I roll my eyes, waiting to hear what it is.

"The Phantom Reaper chapter in LA made some piss poor choices, and they are out of a President and Vice President. None of the other fuckers are qualified to run the MC, so I think Oliver and Tyson would be perfect to take it on."

"Can you even decide that?" I ask.

Neo barks out a laugh. "She's cute." I narrow my eyes, making him grin wider.

"Sis, I own LA. I have my fingers in every gang, club, and business. That gives me some sort of control in it all. If I tell them they are getting Tyson and Oliver, then they have no choice. Although, I don't think they would care too much. Their chapter has been trying to get Steel to move down there with them for a while now. Tyson as well."

"I mean, I do love the idea of living in LA. I fucking hate Canadian winters," I groan.

"Well, it's always warm and sunny in LA, even during their winters. Our winter is your sweater weather at best."

"I'll talk to the guys," I say with a smile. With each passing second, I'm loving the idea of starting over somewhere new and with family. "What about Seth? Now that he has no MC, no home, what do we do with him?" The idea of him having nothing after everything he's done for us doesn't sit well with me.

"I'll meet with him, get to know him, see if he's worthy. If anything, we can set him up in the Savage Hellhound chapter down there too."

"You really can do anything, can't you," I laugh.

"Everything you can think of and so much more."

Tyson

"For the thousandth time, I'm fine," Oliver growls at the nurse. It's the same one from when he was shot. Funny thing is, this is a different hospital. Apparently, she was transferred to this one. *Just our luck*. "I'm not even the one hurt!"

She turns to look at me. “No,” I say, no longer finding it funny. “Go now, please. As much as I’d love to see our girl eat you alive for not taking the hint, I think you should go before she gets here.”

“Too late.” A sexy growl comes from the doorway, and my cock perks up. I love when she gets all possessive. She glares at the nurse. “I think it's time for you to go. And not come back.” The nurse huffs, gathering her things, and leaves.

“Good thing she left, not sure if I’d bother trying to hold Emmy back,” Talon laughs.

“Are you okay?” Emmy asks, making her way to my bedside. She looks me over, her face falling. “Of course, you're not. Look at you.” Her eyes start to glass over.

“Hey now, Princess. Don’t cry. Everything will heal. I’ve got a broken knee and a few rips on my hand. That's it. It could be so much worse. I could have lost a limb or be dead.”

“Don’t talk like that!” she cries.

I hate seeing my Princess upset. Holding out my good arm, I invite her onto the bed with me. I just want her close, to feel her body next to mine. I missed her so fucking much and watching her leave broke me. I need her to put me back together like she always does.

She doesn't hesitate, carefully getting into bed and curling up next to me. I wrap my arm around her, relaxing at her touch. She’s safe, the war is over, and I’m alive.

“Oliver,” Emmy says, poking her head up from my chest. “Get your ass over on this side now,” she demands. Oliver grins, finding her fiery attitude just as hot as I do.

“Anything you want, darling.” Oliver chuckles, bringing the chair over to the other side of the bed so that he can drape his arm over Emmy’s waist, lacing his fingers into hers.

“Better.” She sighs, snuggling into me.

“Where's Seth?” Talon asks, as he and Ben take the other empty seats in the corner of the room.

“Getting checked over. But I don’t think anything is actually wrong. Steel’s with him, talking things over,” Oliver answers.

I still can't believe he’s Emmy and Harlow’s brother. I need to be there when they find out. I’m not sure if they will be happy or if Harlow will make him a new playmate.

"It's really over now, isn't it?" Her voice sounds so at peace, and it makes me so fucking happy. "We can finally just be a family." She cries, but I know they're happy tears.

"We're going to give you and Melody the best life we can, Firefly," Oliver promises her, and I grunt in agreement.

"About that," she says, moving carefully to sit up.

She tells us about the house Harlow offered us and the new jobs at the MC. I can hear the excitement in her voice at all the possibilities this new life could bring. Oliver and I look at each other, but we don't interrupt her. He doesn't look put off by the idea. Could we run an MC together? Sure, I've been helping dad, but this would be a big change for the both of us. I know dad would be all for it. He just wants us to be happy, and if moving away does that, he would never make us feel bad about it.

"What does Charlie think about it?" I ask. Charlie chose to stay back at home with Melody. They agreed it would be best not to be dragging Melody around after everything she's been through.

"She loves the idea," Emmy replies.

"What about you two?" I ask Ben and Talon.

"I don't care where we live as long as I'm with you guys," Talon says.

"I mean, it's gonna suck to be away from my parents and sister, but at the same time, I know they would want us to be happy," Ben says.

"We can come back and visit any time, and they can come down to see us. I just happen to know a billionaire with her own private jet." Emmy smiles, making Ben laugh.

"You're right. Everything will be okay," I say, coming to a conclusion.

"So, are we moving to LA?" she asks, looking over at Oliver. He simply nods.

"Eeeeekkk!" Emmy squeals with joy. *See, that right there?* Being able to make her feel that, it's what I live for. I will give her the world just to see that smile.

CHAPTER 17
Emmy

TALON, BEN, AND Oliver went home after spending a few hours with us all stuffed in a small hospital room. We were all torn between staying together and wanting to be at home with Melody. It sucks being away from her for any amount of time, but I know she's in good hands with them, and I have enough frozen breast milk for her to get her through the night.

The nurses tried to ask me to leave too, but finally gave up when I told them they would have to physically remove me. It also helped that Steel said something. After that, they were quick to let go of the subject.

Tyson passed out pretty soon after the guys left, his pain meds taking effect. I'm glad he needs the rest. But now, just a few hours later, while the world has gone to sleep and everything has quieted down, I lie wide awake in the hospital bed, cuddling up with Tyson. My head rests on his chest as I listen to his steady breathing and strong heartbeat. I know I need some sleep too, but every time I close my eyes, all I can hear is the gunshot going off, as I shot that man in the head. The wide eyed look he had before his life was taken from him. I know it's what had to be done, that it was him or Melody, but it doesn't change the fact that I took a life.

Even if that wasn't stopping me from sleeping, the idea of losing Tyson–him going to sleep and never waking up–has me laying here, listening for myself that everything is working properly. The only sounds are his breathing and the annoying as hell machines in the room.

I could have lost him. I left him there with monsters who knew he was trying to escape. I was the only thing keeping him alive, and without me, he was useless as leverage.

Tears slip down my cheeks, causing my shoulders to shake with a silent cry.

"Princess," Tyson's sleepy voice rasps, his arm tightening around me. "Please, don't cry."

"I'm sorry," I sniffle. "I just can't help but think, what if I had lost you? Tyson, I would be destroyed if I had to be without you, without any of you."

"Shhh, sweet girl. It's over now. I'm fine, alive and well. And so are the others," he tries to soothe me.

"I wouldn't say you're *well*. You have a shattered hand and metal knee," I chastise.

"I thought you loved my scars," he jokes, letting out a deep, sexy chuckle that makes me want to remind him how much I'm glad he's *alive and well*.

"You know I do. You could look like the Hunchback of Notre Dame, and I'd still wanna ride you like a pony." I smile against his chest, as he threads his good hand through my hair.

"I can be your broken man. You can take care of my crippled ass," Tyson says, tugging at my hair to tilt my head back to look at him.

"Always and forever, Sir," I say, biting my lower lip. Tyson's pupils darken, a growl vibrating in his chest.

"Such a brat." He kisses me, pulling my lip into his mouth, biting down hard enough for me to feel a slight sting before he soothes the pain away with his tongue. Moving to get a better angle, I deepen the kiss, coaxing a groan from deep within his throat.

"I might be a brat..." I breathe against his lips, as I cup his stone hard cock, making him moan. "But, I'm your brat."

"Emmy." He hisses, using my name as a warning, but his throbbing dick in my hand tells me another story. "Brats get punished."

"Well, you're gonna have to wait for that. But I promise when you're healed and back to your *old* self, I'll take my punishment like a good, little girl." I smirk, before sliding down his bed until my face is level with this erection.

"Princess, you just went through Hell and back. Have you had any sleep at all since leaving that hellhole?" he asks, his voice straining. I know he wants to take care of me, but I'm being a tease, and I know he is all too happy to enjoy what I'm about to do.

"I got a few hours' nap," I say, pulling back the blanket to reveal his length, tenting in his boxers, the hospital gown doing nothing to hide his massive cock.

"I can't sleep right now anyways. Maybe this will help me relax." I move his gown up, my fingers playing with the edge of his boxers.

"Sucking my dick is supposed to help you sleep?" He lets out a strangled laugh, his breathing growing heavy. It turns into a curse as I let his cock spring free before sliding my palm along his silken skin.

"It helps me do a lot of things," I grin. My fingers tighten around him as my hand glides up and down his steel rod. Pre cum wells up on the top of his swollen shaft and teases me with how good I know it tastes. My tongue slips out to moisten my dry lips before I bend forwards, licking the tip and enjoying how he spasms in my grasp.

"Fuck me, baby girl." He sucks in a breath, his fingers tangling in my hair and gripping a handful as he forgets all about his half assed attempt of talking me out of it.

"I think you mean suck me, baby girl." And so I do. I wrap my lips around his head and swirl my tongue before taking him all the way to the back of my throat and swallowing him whole.

He tosses his head back against the pillow as he groans, his eyes squeezing shut and his hand pulling at my hair. His hips try to thrust his cock deeper, but I hold him down. I slide off him as the evidence of what we're doing makes its way down my chin.

"No moving, or I'll stop," I tell him, giving him a death glare. "You're gonna hurt yourself."

His eyes open, and he gives me a glare of his own, before giving my hair another little tug. "Put my dick back in and shut that bossy little mouth of yours," he growls, as he guides my head back down to his cock. I grin as he enters, my slick lips gliding down his length again. I love messing with him. He gets super sexy when he takes control.

"Fuck yes, Princess! That's it," he praises as I bob up and down, hollowing out my cheeks. "You look so fucking perfect with my dick between those pretty, pink lips." He starts to control my movements by using the grip he has on my hair, pulling me off before forcing me back down.

I'm soaked and desperately want to slip my hand between my legs to get rid of the ache. I squirm in the bed, trying to find some friction.

"Is my girl wet for me?" Tyson asks, his voice thick with lust. I hum around him in answer, making him curse. "Touch yourself, Princess. Make yourself cum while I use your mouth to fuck my cock."

Whimpering at his dirty words, I'm quick to do as I'm told. He takes complete control of the blow job, and with my jaw staying slack, it's easier for him to move me. While he takes his pleasure, I take mine. I push past my pants and underwear until I'm able to slip my finger between my folds. I glide it to the bottom of my pussy and back up to my clit a few times, matching the movements of his cock in my mouth. I'm already so turned on that all I care to do is dip my fingers into my wet heat while wishing it was his cock deep inside me.

"So fucking good," he pants, his pace increasing. I pull my fingers out, sliding them against my throbbing clit, continuing to match the movements of my head. "I can hear how drenched you are as you fuck yourself, Princess. Does it feel good?" I moan around his cock, and a spike of pleasure shoots up my spine. I alternate between thrusting my fingers inside myself and playing with my clit, finding what works best. When I find the right rhythm, I try my hardest to concentrate on the orgasm that's just out of reach. But it's hard when I'm gagging on Tyson's thick cock.

His moans and erratic breathing have my pussy throbbing. I love it when my guys voice their enjoyment. It makes me feel powerful that I can make them feel so good.

"Cum with me, baby girl. Cum around your fingers as I make you swallow down every last drop of my seed."

He doesn't have to ask me twice because I'm seconds away from climaxing.

"Fuck, fuck, fuckkkk." He chants, before cumming hard down my throat and letting out a sexy snarl. I swallow each jet of cum, before taking him out of my mouth and putting my forehead against his abs. With one more circle over my sensitive nub, I follow him into ecstasy. My thighs have a death grip on my hand as I thrust against it, the waves of my orgasm taking over me. I bite Tyson's arm to muffle my scream, making him groan in pleasure.

"Such a good girl," Tyson praises as he smoothes out my hair.

"You took my cock so good, baby. I can't wait until I can fuck that tight cunt again." His husky promises have tingles racing throughout my entire body.

"I can use *you* for my own pleasure next time, if you want," I mutter against his skin, my breathing still all over the place as I slowly come down from my high.

"And watch your gorgeous breasts bounce as you ride me? Fucking sold."

I laugh lightly, exhaustion finally taking over me. Removing my hand from my panties, I move to go wash up, but Tyson stops me.

"What?" I ask, my brows furrowed.

He just takes my hand, bringing it to his lips and sucking my fingers into his mouth, licking them clean.

"No need for it to go to waste," he purrs. *Fuck,* why does he have to go and say shit like that? It has me dripping for him all over again!

"You're bad," I groan.

"So fucking bad. Now, come here." He pulls me up to his chest, wrapping me back up in his hold. "Sleep," he commands.

"You just gonna leave your dick out for everyone to see?" I laugh, pulling up his boxers and fixing everything until he's fully covered again.

"I would be doing them a favor," he says, and I can almost hear the smile in his voice.

I snuggle in close, relaxing in his hold. I feel safe, loved, warm, and wanted. It's perfect.

The sleep that my body has been fighting for the past forty-eight hours finally takes over, putting me in a deep, and this time peaceful slumber.

CHAPTER 18
Emmy

"STOP WHINING, YOU big baby." I laugh, as Oliver helps Tyson get into the car.

"I'm not whining," he mutters. "I just said it wasn't fair, that's all."

It's been a few days since everything happened. Tyson is being released today, but his casts have to stay on for the remainder of the summer. He did *not* like that news.

You know how they say, 'men tend to act way more dramatic when they have a cold than women do'? Well, try having a biker who loves his job, taking control, and being active. He absolutely hates the idea of anyone taking care of him, saying he doesn't need to be babied, but he sure is acting like one.

"I know it's not, but you need to heal. It's only a few weeks, and by doing what the doctor says, you should be back to your old self in no time," I say, climbing into the back seat and scooting over to the middle so I can talk to my guys in the front. "Plus, I get to give you all the sponge baths your little, biker heart desires." My playful tone earns me a heated look which makes me bite my lip.

Oliver starts up the car before taking off out of the parking lot. "Don't worry, brother. We'll make sure to take care of any sexual needs you're unable to meet." A cocky as fuck grin takes over his face, but he doesn't look away from the road.

"I can still have sex, you idiot," Tyson grumbles.

"Yeah, you just can't tie her to the bed and fuck her until she passes out like you two love to do," Oliver chuckles. He does have a point. Tyson and I can still have sex, but I'll be doing all the work. Not that I mind. I love riding him, watching the desire burning bright in his blue eyes, as I use his dick for my own pleasure. But I also love when Tyson takes control too. I love handing over all my trust to him.

"Keep reminding me what I get to miss out on, fucker. I'll use this damn cast as a weapon if you don't shut the fuck up."

"Now, now, boys, no fighting," I laugh.

"Yes, ma'am." Tyson rolls his eyes.

"Have something to say, Sir?" I grin, loving how his bad mood slips into a hungry one. I need to stop teasing him so much.

"Do you need your ass spanked? I have one good arm that works just as well," Tyson growls.

"Okay," I breathe, getting a rumble from his chest.

"Do you know how hard it is to drive with a raging hard on? Please refrain from crawling over into the front seat and fucking him, or we're all gonna crash and die." Oliver groans, reaching down to readjust his dick.

The car is silent for a moment before I burst into a fit of giggles as Tyson chuckles.

We talk about all the new, exciting changes that are coming up soon on our drive back to the compound. We decided to wait until the summer is over and Tyson gets his casts off before moving. That gives everyone some more time. Tyson and Oliver can spend some time with their dad, Ben's family can come over to visit, along with Rick and Amy, so we can soak up as much family time as we can before we leave. It's going to be hard being away from all the amazing loved ones who have been with us through so much, but I'm excited to see what the future brings for us. Now that there's nothing in the way, there are so many possibilities.

Harlow, Neo, and Evie leave tonight after the party that the club is putting on in celebration of our win. I asked Harlow what she plans to do with Dagger and Jimmy since I won't be there to watch her deal with them until the end of the summer, but she just told me she will keep them locked up like the animals they are. Then she said something about '*loving the idea of having prisoners in her dungeon*'. When I asked her if she actually had one, she gave me a playful look and said, "Not that kind." Yeah, I didn't bother asking what she meant by that. I have a feeling I already know, but I don't need her clarifying that because I already know way more about my sister's sex life than I should.

When we pull through the gates, the whole MC is there waiting. I grin as I see everyone cheering. See this?

This right here is a real biker family. Always having each other's backs. I know Tyson is going to miss this. It's been the only life he's known, but I have a feeling he will take that broken MC and make it into a family too. Tyson and Oliver are meant to be leaders.

I think one of the biggest changes for him will be not living on a compound. Do presidents even do that? Live away from the rest of the MC? I mean, we could if we had to, but I like the idea of living next to my sister more. That sounds a thousand times better than being around a bunch of strangers that I don't trust.

"Look at you, Ty-Ty!" Harlow greets, pulling him into a hug.

"Hey, Har. Sorry I missed out on all the fun, you know, on account of me being kept prisoner and all," he chuckles. "I heard I missed out on a fun time."

"Fuck yeah, you did." Neo grins but pulls Harlow from Tyson's arms. Harlow rolls her eyes but snuggles into her crazy boyfriend. "That place is burnt to the ground now. Wonder what will happen to the land."

"It's ours now," Steel says, joining us. "The walls are still intact, so I'm thinking of cleaning it out and building some low income townhomes. Give some families in need a place to live that won't break the bank. Make something light out of what was once dark."

"Look at you, dad, being all poetic and shit," Oliver laughs.

"Emmy!" a voice behind the crowd calls for me. Stepping away from the group, I look past everyone to see Ethan standing close to Charlie. She's holding Melody and flanked by my other guys. Next to him is Leah holding their newborn, Mason.

A massive grin takes over my face, and I wave like a crazy person. "I'm gonna go say hi," I tell Oliver and Tyson. They look over to see what I'm talking about.

"Love you, Princess," Tyson says.

"I love you too." I give him a kiss.

"I'll come with you," Oliver says, but I don't wait for him. I take off, running over to my best friend. He steps away from the others, holding his arms out. Leaping into them, he wraps me up in a tight hug.

"Fuck, I missed you," he mutters into my hair.

"I missed you too."

"When I found out what happened, it took everything in me not to come over here and demand they get you back. Leah convinced me that was probably not the smartest idea. She said they most likely knew how to handle everything better than I would, so all I could do was sit and wait for you to be okay."

"Do you know how much of a mess he was?" Leah laughs softly. "I could not get him to keep still. He was up most nights, unable to sleep."

"I didn't see you complaining about getting a full night's sleep while I stayed up with Mason," Ethan counters with a laugh.

"Well, you were up already, so..." she shrugs with a grin, then looks at me. "I'm glad you're okay. I was worried too."

"So, is it true?" Ethan's smiling face suddenly falls. "Are you really moving away at the end of the summer?"

I give him a sad smile. "Yeah. My sister offered me an opportunity that I couldn't refuse. It's a good place to start fresh."

"He could come too, you know," Harlow teases as she breaks away from people greeting Tyson.

"What do you mean?" Ethan hopefully asks.

"You can move too. I mean, there's no other houses around where we live, but I have an open two bedroom apartment above my club. Or, we can get you a place to stay close by. I'd help out, of course, until you got on your own two feet."

"You would do that for us?" Ethan asks, his eyes wide.

"Why not? You were there for my sister, a true friend. She doesn't have many of those outside of her lovers. Plus, do you even have anything you really need to stay here for?" Harlow asks, cocking a brow.

Ethan looks to Leah, her eyes wide with her own surprise. "No." Leah answers. "Our parents kind of disowned us for not being what they wanted us to be. So, we don't have anything keeping us here. As long as we're all together, that's all that matters to me."

"Then it's settled. You're moving too," Harlow says, before turning around and heading back over to Neo, who looks seconds away from stabbing one of the MC members.

"Did that really just happen?" Ethan asks me.

"Yeah, I think it did," I laugh. "There's really no denying her when she's like this. It's not worth the fight. But, if you really don't want to go, I can let her know."

"Are you kidding me?! California is my dream place to live," Leah says, her face full of excitement. She looks at Ethan. "Thank you for making amazing friends."

Ethan rolls his eyes and smiles at the mother of his child. "Seeing as you're one of them, I'll take that praise."

After everyone gets the chance to welcome Tyson home and I greet all my loved ones, we put the babies down for a nap. The crowd disperses, all going their separate ways to get ready for the big 'Welcome Home' party they've planned. I go in search of Tyson to check on him when I stumble upon him, Harlow, and Seth standing outside. As I walk over to them, I hear Tyson introduce Seth to Harlow.

"So. What do we do with you?" Harlow asks, as she circles around Seth, looking him up and down. Then looks at me, "Are you sure we can trust him?"

"I think we can. He could have ignored me, did as he was told, and went on with his life, but he risked his own ass to help us. On top of that, he treated us with respect and kindness."

"Why?" Harlow asks, turning her attention back to Seth. "Why did you care so much to be nice to a girl you'd never met, to a man who was supposed to be the enemy? Why betray your own MC to get them out? And what is the excuse behind you switching sides?" she interrogates, firing one question after another.

I can tell she wants to stab him. He hasn't done or said anything that would warrant that, but Queenie is Queenie. She doesn't always need a reason to kill.

"Because I'm not like them. The earliest memories I have is of how much I despised them. I knew the things they did were fucked up and wrong. I had to watch how I acted, all while trying not to end up like them. I did as I was told but I never interacted with them unless it was necessary, I just wanted to live my life but couldn't get out. I didn't kill anyone who didn't deserve it. I never slept with a woman who wasn't willing. I tried to blend in as best as I could to avoid trouble without becoming one of *them*."

"Why not leave? How were you tied to that MC?" Harlow glares at him.

I can tell she's pissed that there's things that Seth isn't very forthcoming about. She doesn't like not knowing everything about him. She told me when Evie did a search on him, there was almost no record of his existence. No medical records or birth certificate.

"My father was in the MC. My mother died after I was born. I had no other choice. Once I got old enough to leave, it was too late. He would have tracked me down and killed me for trying to get out." He says it all in a very matter-of-fact way, almost like he is emotionless.

"What happened to your mother?" Harlow asks the second he finishes his sentence.

Seth looks over to Tyson, a slightly worried look taking over his face. Tyson gives him an encouraging nod. *What the fuck is going on?*

Seth watches Harlow for a moment before running his hand down his face and letting out a defeated sigh. "From what I was told by some of the women who were still in the MC, she was a sweet butt. But somehow, she was claimed by one man. He didn't want her as his Old Lady, but he also made it clear that no other man could touch her. He treated her like trash, only using her for what suited his needs. When she found out she was pregnant with me, she decided to run. I was told that I was the most important thing to her, and she didn't want me growing up there. He caught her, said he was going to kill her, but she pleaded with him not to, telling him she was pregnant with his kid. So, he kept her locked up and forced her to give birth to me in her room. The moment I was no longer dependent on her to live, she was gone; he shot her. He handed me over to the Old Ladies and told them to raise me. He called my mother a whore and said I could be any one of the club member's sons. They all knew it was bullshit, but they would never call him out on it."

Harlow's eyes are scaring me. There's something she picked up on that I didn't. In a low, dangerous tone, she asks. "Who is your father?"

Seth looks from her to me and back before answering. "Dagger."

My eyes widen, my whole world spinning. Are my ears deceiving me? Or did he just say *Dagger*? As in Harlow's and my birth father.

"How the fuck does that not surprise me?" Harlow starts to laugh like a manic person. My eyes flash to hers, and I grow more confused.

"You believe him? You believe that he's our... our *brother*?" I ask in disbelief. Harlow and I don't have the same hair color, hers being jet black and mine being brown, but we do have similar features that give away that were related. But Seth? The man has blond hair, blue eyes, and looks like he could have been a surfer in another life.

"Emmy, Dagger was a manwhore. He knocked up our mothers and left like it was an everyday thing. Hell, it probably was. We could have fifty siblings out there for all we know. The only way I found out about you was because he acknowledged you as his child even though he abandoned you. If Seth is telling the truth, it makes sense why I couldn't find him before and why I couldn't find anything on him now. To the world outside those gates, he didn't exist."

"So... That's it? We have a brother." I'm still in shock. I mean, am I mad? No, not really. The idea of having an older brother kinda sounds amazing, you know, when I'm not freaking the fuck out about it.

"Well, I'll have to get a DNA test done to be sure. I'm not stupid enough to let something like this go by without checking. But it's really not that far-fetched of an idea." She shrugs, then looks back at Seth. "That's why you helped them? Because you knew who we were? You knew she was your sister? That the baby you were caring for was your niece?" Seth nods but doesn't interrupt Harlow. Smart man. "But, brother or not, I don't trust you. You take one step out of line to fuck any one of us over, and I *will* end you. I don't give second chances when it puts my family at risk, understand?"

"I would never be stupid enough to risk your wrath. But even so, I would never fuck over my family," Seth says, and Harlow raises a brow. "He was no family of mine. Blood doesn't make you family. But I would like to get to know you two more. I thought I was alone my whole life. Knowing I have sisters, well, it gave me something to look forward to."

My face softens, my mind starting to clear a bit, slowly registering the information.

"Fine. If the DNA test shows you are, in fact, our brother, you will move to LA as well. The Savage Hellhound chapter will accept you. They aren't nearly as fucked up as the one here was, but they could use someone like you to help clean it up," Harlow says, leaving no room for discussion. "I would've suggested you join the Phantom Reapers LA chapter with Tyson and Oliver, but the men there would kill you in your sleep."

"Fair point." Seth grins.

So, just like that, I have a brother. What other wonderful surprises is life gonna throw at me? At least, for the first time in God knows how long, the world is not shitting on me like it usually does. I mean, I have always wanted an older brother. This could be a good thing.

We're in the backyard of the clubhouse. Everyone is partying inside. The sounds of laughter, music, and chatter drift through the warm evening air. I'm going to miss this, but we will have something similar over at Harlow's place. I can't believe they have their own mini zoo in the backyard of their place.

"Evie, Harlow, and I talked while you were at the hospital picking up Tyson," Charlie says as she hands Ben a beer.

"Oh boy, that can't be good," Tyson teases, laughing as he dodges the bottle cap Charlie tosses at him while sticking her tongue out.

She sits next to me, and I move so that my legs are draped over her lap. She smiles at me, giving my legs a rub before continuing. "We were talking about jobs. She asked if I wanted to go to college, and after everything that's happened, I said no. I don't want to be wasting hours a day in a room learning when I could be at home with my family."

"So, what are you going to do then? Be a stay-at-home mom with me?" I grin.

"That, aaaaaand" She gives me a mischievous grin. Oh no. "I'm gonna bartend at Queenie's main club with her friend, Roxy."

Tyson chokes on his mouthful of beer. "You're what?" He chokes out between coughs. "You do know what kind of club she runs, right?"

"Oh, chill out, of course, I do. It's not like it's a strip club, but even if it was, there's nothing wrong with that."

"But it's the place she does her..." He looks around like Harlow might be watching, but she's not. They left about twenty minutes ago for the airport, and she took Seth with her. I still can't believe I have a brother. It's crazy. "Playdates."

"Yeah, but they're in a soundproof basement." Charlie rolls her eyes. "I'm not gonna see anything. She has a legitimate business. And she offered to teach me how to pole dance." She wiggles her eyebrows. The idea of Charlie up there dancing with her sexy little body has me shifting in my seat. She looks over at me, giving me a heated look. "Do you like that idea?"

"Hell yeah," I agree.

"Emmy, you should take lessons with her," Talon says.

I look over at him with a raised brow. "Why?"

"Because I gave you a lap dance before, so now you owe me a pole dance." He gives me a sexy grin. Well, if I ever thought I lost my sex drive, I was so wrong. If anything, I want them more than ever.

"Okay, okay, enough of that. We have guests," Tyson says, pointing the tip of his beer bottle in Ethan and Leah's direction.

"Sorry," I say, giving them a sheepish grin.

"We're gonna have to get used to it," Ethan says, with a joking smile. "We're going to be spending lots of time around each other. Our kids will grow up together. I highly doubt you're going to try to be on your best behavior every time we're around."

"Yeah, I don't think that's gonna happen," Talon says. "No way I can keep my hands off her or Ben for that long."

"And I have a feeling being around Queenie and her guys, there's gonna be more than I care to see."

"Oh yeah," Tyson chuckles. "They don't give a single fuck who is around. Warning you right now, Queenie and Neo will fuck in front of people, and you're probably going to see her naked more than you care to. But that's just how it is over there."

"What are we getting ourselves into?" Ben mutters under his breath as he takes my feet into his hands. He slips off my flip-flops and starts to massage my feet. God, that feels amazing. He looks at me, giving me a soft smile that makes my heart melt.

How the fuck did I get so lucky? How did I come to be so madly in love with so many amazing people?

My eyes drift close as my body relaxes while I listen to my loved ones get lost in conversation. Their laughter lulls me to sleep, along with Charlie rubbing circles on my tight muscles and Ben rubbing my feet.

We might have to get creative to make this summer memorable, but I can't wait. For the first time, I can breathe. There's no fear, no anxiety of what's lurking around every corner. Just pure contentment. We might never live a normal life, but it will always be ours and with each other. I wouldn't want it any other way.

CHAPTER 19
Oliver

"EMMY," I CALL out into the almost empty house. We're moving next week, and most of the house is already packed up.

"What's up?" she answers back as she enters the kitchen from the bottom of the stairs.

I smile at my girl as I take in her beauty. This girl has been my world for as long as I can remember, my best friend, my second half.

Her brown hair shines in the sunlight streaming through the kitchen window, tied up into a messy bun. She's wearing workout shorts and one of Tyson's band tees. She's never looked sexier.

"You busy?" I ask, my body humming with excitement.

"No..." she says, a curious smile twitches at her lips as she takes in my body language. "I was gonna read a book while Melody naps and the guys play video games."

"Perfect. You're coming with me," I say, stepping towards her. I pull her into my arms, placing a hard and fast kiss on her, making her laugh when we break apart.

"Ben, Talon," I call down the basement stairs.

"Yeah?" Ben calls back.

"Watch the baby; I'm taking Emmy out."

"Alright, have fun!" Talon answers.

"Let's go," I say, holding out my hand for Emmy to take.

"What's going on?" She asks, her smile so wide.

"You'll see." I wiggle my eyebrows playfully at her.

She giggles in joy as we race outside the house, down the steps, and over to the new bike sitting in the driveway.

"Oh my god." Emmy gasps, looking at the bike than me. "Is this yours?"

"Yup." I grin at her. "Dad got it for me as a farewell gift. I wanna take you for a ride before we have to leave it behind, until they bring it to LA." I hand her a helmet that she eagerly takes and puts on.

Putting my own on, I start it up as Emmy swings her leg over the side, wrapping her arms around and settling in behind me.

"Ready?" I ask, giving the engine a little rev.

"Always." She used to hate riding in the beginning, but we've turned her into a regular biker babe, and she seems to love it almost as much as we do.

We take off down the dirt road, waving to the guys at the gate as we pass by. Knowing we can leave here and not worry if Dagger and his men are lurking nearby, ready to take my girl at any second, is so freeing. Knowing that, from here on, we are free to come and go as we please, to live our lives without always having to look over our shoulders, is an amazing feeling.

Driving down the highway, I feel a rush of adrenaline. I missed the feel of the wind against me. Emmy's grip tightens as we make sharp turns, squealing with laughter as she feels the rush too. It makes my heart swell with happiness.

This is all I ever wanted. To live my life with my best friend. To wake up every day and make her happy, showing her I'm worthy.

Now we're able to do that. We're out of that hellish school, we have a baby of our own, a family started, and a new life to look forward to. We had to go through so much bullshit to get to this point, and although I wish a lot of it didn't have to happen, it led us to thc perfect place in the end.

And because we're moving away from our home and away from any good memories we happened to make in the past, I wanted to do one last special thing for her before we leave.

When we get to our destination, I shut the bike off, and my nerves take hold in my stomach as I wait for her reaction.

"Oliver!" She gasps, taking off her helmet and taking in the sight before her. "What the heck is this?"

"Do you like it?" I ask. Laughter rings out in the distance as we take in the mini golf course.

"How?" she asks, taking a few slow steps towards the sign that says *Firefly Mini golf*. Her eyes fill with emotion as she reads it. My heart pounds as I wait for her to say something. "Did you do this?"

"With help from my dad. Evie was able to recover any money the Hellhounds had, and we put it to good use.

I thought having this place back up and running might help kids growing up like we did have a fun, cheap, safe place to hang out and just be kids."

"You're the fucking best." She sniffs, wiping her eyes before flinging her arms around me, kissing me with so much love and passion my dick perks up. Wrong timing, man, later.

"I love you, Firefly." I mummer against her lips.

"I love you more, Olly." She smiles up at me.

"Never." I nip her lower lip. "Now, how about me and you play some mini golf? I have the sudden urge to win."

"In your dreams, Kingston," she laughs, slipping from my arms and racing towards the entrance.

"Little brat." I laugh to myself as I follow after her. I officially changed my name over the summer. I thought it was about time since we had to get our passports, and it's nice to leave my mother's name as a thing of the past. As for my mother herself, I have no idea if she's dead or alive. I went back to our old trailer to see if she still lived there when Emmy went to her mother's place to clear it out, but there was nothing. My old place was empty and run down, no signs of it being lived in for a long time. As for Emmy's mom's place, there wasn't much in the place, nothing that was worth keeping. She did find some old baby pictures she's never seen before, surprised that her mother even had any.

The next few hours are perfect. I don't think I've smiled or laughed this much in years. But when I'm with Emmy, it's hard not to. And seeing her so carefree and full of joy settles something deep in my soul, something I've been wanting for my girl for so fucking long.

After she beats my ass at mini golf, we take a break to grab something to eat before playing another round.

"Thank you, Olly," she says, burying her face into my chest as she hugs me close. "This has been one of the best dates of my life."

"I'm glad you had fun, baby. But the night's not over yet," I say, then grab a blanket from the side bag on my bike.

"What's that for?" she asks, pointing to the blanket.

"You'll see," I say. "Come." I take her hand, pulling her down the dirt road to the patch of woods at the end.

She says nothing as she follows me. As we walk through the path, we steal glances at each other, both of us smiling like fools when we do.

We pass our old trailer park and end up at the park close by.

"What are we doing here?" she asks, looking over at the hill, the place that started so much heartache.

"I thought we could watch the sunset," I say, guiding her up the hill to the top. I lay out the blanket, and we both sit. Turning to her, I take her hands into mine. "I want to replace the bad memories of this place with some good ones." I bring her hands up, kissing the back of both of them before continuing. "I was young and so fucking dumb back then, Emmy. What I did, it was fucked up and wrong. If I could go back and change it, I would. It killed me knowing I left you like that after something that was meant to be a special time together. But I promise to never hurt you like that again. To never cause you heartache or pain as long as we live."

I want to leave this place with as few tarnished memories as I can. We've been by to say goodbye to our baby boy, promising to always visit when we come back to see his grandpa.

After the mini golf course, this was my last stop before we left all this behind.

"It's in the past. Whatever happened, no matter how messed up, it was meant to happen. All we can do now is look forward and make better choices."

"You're right." I pull her under my arm, snuggling her close as we watch the sunset. We talk about all the good things that happened to us in the past fifteen years, starting with when we first met, right up to our last moments at Emerald Lake Prep.

When the sun has officially set, I watch the field in front of us and wait.

I grin when I see the first little flash of light, followed by the next and then another.

"Emmy," I say, nudging her with my shoulder.

"Yeah?" she asks, looking up from her phone and a photo of Melody the guys sent her. I shake my head and laugh, taking her phone from her, I turn on the camera with the flash off and hit record.

"Look," I say, pointing to her phone.

She cocks a brow at me but turns to watch. When a flash of light shows up on the phone, she sucks in a breath then looks over at the field.

“Fireflies,” she whispers in wonder. “I haven’t seen any in so long.”

We didn’t get to go outside much at night when we were at school, so we haven’t had many opportunities to see them.

“Come on.” I stop the recording and stand up. Holding out my hand to hers, she grabs it, and we both race down the hill until we get to the bottom. We both look at each other, and our faces slip into massive grins as we step into the field. We spend the next little while catching fireflies, and every time she catches one, she lets out that childish giggle that has me falling in love with her all over again.

“Have I mentioned this has been the best date ever?” she says, as we lay back on the blanket, and she cuddles into my side as we watch the stars.

“You may have a few times,” I chuckle.

She moves from my arms until she's straddling my lap.

“Seriously, Oliver, thank you. You brought some of my favorite memories back, even if it’s just for a night, and it means so much to me.”

“I’d do anything for you, baby girl, you know that.” My hands come up to rub her thighs.

“I do. And you know I’d do anything for you too,” she says, leaning over and kissing me. I groan into her mouth as she slips her tongue in and over mine while she simultaneously rocks her hips, making my already hardening cock harder.

“Don’t tease me, Firefly,” I murmur against her lips, before sucking on her bottom one. “Or I just might have to take you right here on this hill.”

She sits back enough so that she can look me in the eyes. “Then do it. Make love to me, here; the same place we had our first time, but let's leave it with better memories.”

With a hungry growl, I pull her down to kiss her again and flip her so that she's flat on her back.

“This time, I’ll make sure you cum.” I grin down at her. She laughs, making me smile wider.

"Well, get to work, big boy. Show me what you got," she sasses back. I love my girl's fire, and moments like this remind me why we were always best friends.

I've never left my girl without her release since the moment we had sex for that first time at Emerald Lake Prep, but last time we were here, I did her dirty. So, I think I'll have a taste of my girl first, make her cum all over my face, before I have her screaming as she cums again on my cock.

My hands find the waistband of her shorts, and I pull them along with her panties, down in one swift tug.

She sucks in a breath as the summer's night air meets with her wet core. I can't see her pretty pussy, but I can smell her desire.

Parting her thighs wide, I lower myself to her core. "You're so fucking wet, baby girl." I lick from bottom to top, loving how much she's dripping for me. "You taste so fucking good."

"Please," she whines, lifting her hips up into my face.

"Greedy little thing," I chuckle, nudging my nose against her clit and making her moan.

"Oliver Kingston, if you don't eat me out like I'm your last meal, I'll punch you in the dick," she growls in frustration, making me grin so fucking wide it hurts.

"Yes, my queen, anything for you," I purr, before doing exactly what she told me to do.

She screams out into the night as I take her by surprise, diving into her sweetness, hungry for my favorite delicacy.

"Oh, god." She pants as I switch back and forth between sucking on her clit and fucking her with my tongue.

"No god here, baby girl, only me." I chuckle as I insert two fingers.

"Fuck!" She bucks her hips making me have to press them down with my free arm, holding her in place.

Emmy is practically speaking in tongues as I work her over with my mouth and fingers.

"I'm gonna cum. Fuck, fuck, please don't stop," she begs, locking her legs around my head. She holds me in place as she uses my mouth to take her pleasure, grinding against me as I do exactly what I was doing to drive her fucking crazy. "Oh, oh, oh yes, right there. Fuck, I'm so close."

Her cries grow louder and louder, before she arches her back off the ground and slaps a hand over her mouth. She lets out a muffled scream that sounds a lot like my name, as she cums hard on my tongue, coating it in her release. I lick her good, making sure I don't miss a drop.

Her body goes slack, her legs losing their strength.

"I love it when you scream my name," I tell her as I crawl my way up her body, until I hover over her, and she gets her breathing under control.

"I bet you do," she says with a huffed laugh.

"I think I wanna hear it again," I say, slipping my hand into my shorts. I grasp my thick cock and give it a few strokes, groaning as I look down at my girl. She looks so stunning in the moonlight, her eyes almost black with lust.

Pulling myself out, I lower myself to line my cock up with her entrance. "Let's see if you have another one in you."

"Oliver," she cries out as I fill her up in one stroke, her pussy gripping me in response.

"Close, but not quite a scream." I pull almost all the way out before thrusting back in. Her hands claw at my back as I start to fuck her into the ground. She feels fucking amazing around me, so wet and warm.

I suck and kiss her neck as she whimpers and whines beneath me.

"You're so fucking perfect, baby," I grunt. "So fucking tight. Always ready for me."

"Olly, fuck, that feels so good," she sobs.

We make love like this for a little while. I'm loving every sound she makes, every claw mark, bite, and hair pull she does. It just turns me on even more. I love it when she marks me as her own.

Her hands find my ass, and she grabs them as she forces me down harder into her.

"Does my girl want me to fuck her raw?" I ask, moving so that I'm on my knees buried deep inside her.

"Please!" She begs, her nails digging into my thighs.

Grabbing her legs, I put them over my shoulder. With one hand, I hold on to her hip, and the other, I hold her legs in place as I start thrusting my hips, driving my cock deep inside her at this new angle.

This drives her crazy, and she starts to thrash under me, the sensations becoming too much for her. I can feel her walls quiver around my cock. She's close, and as I hit her g-spot, making her sob out in pleasure, I know she won't last long.

And it's a good thing because my balls are fucking aching, desperate to empty myself deep inside her.

She screams my name just how I like it, cumming hard, and her pussy grips me so damn tight I can't help but find my release too.

"Emmy!" I roar, my cock twitching as I send jets of warm cum into her, filling her up with my seed and marking my girl how I know she loves it.

When I've got nothing left to give her, I tuck my face into her neck and kiss her damp skin.

"We should get going?" Emmy asks, running her hand up and down my back as we catch our breaths. "I really don't want to be caught with your dick inside me," she laughs.

"Fine, if we must," I pout, making her laugh more. My heart loves that sound too.

I pull out of her and find her shorts. Tucking myself away, she gets dressed, and we grab the blanket before heading back to my bike.

"Oliver," she says, as I swing my leg over the seat of my bike and grab my helmet, putting it on.

"Yes, baby girl?"

"I love you. And this night was perfect."

"Anything for my girl. I live to see you smile."

She gets on the bike, puts on her helmet, and wraps her arms around me. "You're gonna need to wash your seat later," she calls out to me over the roar of the engine.

I grin at the idea of my cum soaking her all the way through as we ride home. The night ended better than I could have imagined, and I'm glad we can leave this place with better memories than the ones of our past.

One thing is for sure, I'll never repeat the mistakes I've made, and I'll never let my girl hurt the way she had before. We will always make sure Emmy is safe, and so I'll keep going to therapy to work on my nightmares and PTSD.

A part of me will never get over the fact that I was unable to protect her so many times over the past year, but I know it wasn't anything I could control. But what we can do is work hard every day to make sure she and Melody are safe, happy, and loved. Because these girls deserve the whole fucking world, and that's exactly what we plan on giving them.

CHAPTER 20
Ben

THE SUMMER PASSED by quickly but was amazing nonetheless, and we took full advantage of making memories. There was hardly a time where we got to sit still, but I don't think any of us minded. After all our years at Emerald Lake Prep, along with everything else that happened, getting to go out and do whatever we want, while spending time together as a family has been so much more than we could have hoped for.

Although, it would have been a lot better if we didn't have to deal with Tyson's constant bitching about having to be in a wheelchair. Although, it was really funny watching him try to use crutches with a broken hand. *Stubborn man.* Emmy loved to point that out any chance she got.

We were able to go camping with Rick and Amy. We rented a trailer for a week for Tyson and Melody to sleep in, while the rest of us stayed in tents. It was a lot of fun. We went swimming, quad riding, and hiking. Tyson stayed back with Melody for those activities, but he didn't mind.

Emmy kept feeling guilty that Tyson was unable to do a lot of things, but he told her to stop worrying, because he was not going to be the one to hold her back from spending time with us and having fun with our families. It took some very fun and sexual ways to convince her not to overthink everything. She still tried to include him in everything she could though.

My parents took us to Drumheller for the weekend. It's a town in Alberta where you can do fun things like look for fossils and other dinosaur related things. It looked like a mini Grand Canyon. I loved seeing how excited Emmy got over everything new she discovered. We came here a lot when I was a kid, but Emmy hasn't been anywhere other than her hometown or the surrounding towns.

"So, you're really moving?" Mom asks me, as she sits at the kitchen island.

"Well, the house is empty, and all of our stuff was shipped to LA, so yeah, Mom, we're really moving," I chuckle.

Her eyes shine with unshed tears, and my heart aches seeing her so sad. "I'm gonna miss you guys so much," she sniffs.

"I know, but remember, we said we'll have you guys down whenever you want, and we will come back to visit too. I know Oliver and Tyson will want to come back to see their dad, and Emmy, to see Rick and Amy. So we're not going to forget about everyone we love and never come back."

"You better not, or I'll move down there, and you will never be rid of me," she says, wiping her eyes.

"We're already planning to come back for Thanksgiving, and you guys will be down for Christmas. I know Abby is excited to visit LA. She's been bugging Emmy to show her around Hollywood. As if Emmy even knows where anything is." I grin, shaking my head.

"You have yourself an amazing woman, Ben. And that man of yours..." she trails off with a sigh before continuing, "I'm just so proud of you." She pulls me into a hug. I love my mom. We've always been close, and seeing how shitty everyone else had it with their parents, it makes me all the more grateful for how amazing and supportive my parents are.

"Well, we better get going if we're going to make it back home before dark," Dad says, stepping into the kitchen.

"Oh, I'm gonna miss you." Mom runs over to Abby, who has Melody in her arms, picking up the baby and smothering her in kisses.

"We will make sure to video chat all the time. And I promise to send you photos of every single cute thing she does," Emmy tells her, giving my mom a soft smile.

"I could never have too many photos of this sweet angel," she says, giving Melody another round of kisses, setting her off into some adorable baby giggles.

"It's true. It's like our house puked up baby photos. They are everywhere!" Abby sarcastically complains, handing Emmy Melody's bunny.

"Oh, it's not that bad." Mom rolls her eyes.

"Honey, there's a photo of Melody on her belly with her butt showing in the bathroom," my dad retorts, trying to hold back a laugh. I look at Emmy, seeing she's trying to do the same.

"I thought it was fitting," Mom huffs.

"Give me that little fireball," Dad requests, taking Melody to say his goodbyes.

"So, I get to come out for Christmas, right?" Abby asks me, cocking a brow with her hands on her hips. I wish the best of luck to whoever she ends up with. *The sass is strong with that one.* "Because you already said I could."

"Yeah, yeah, don't have a cow. You're still coming down," I laugh.

"Good. So, what about next summer? There's so much I wanna do that it can't all be done in one week," she informs me, being completely serious.

"Abby, we haven't even moved yet, and you're already talking about next summer?" I shake my head. "Chill."

"Fine!" she huffs. She's quiet for a moment, before she launches herself at me, wrapping her arms around me in a tight hug. "I'm gonna miss you," she whispers, snuggling her head into my chest. My body relaxes as I hug her back, tears stinging my eyes. I look over at Emmy, who is totally eating up this sweet, big brother shit.

"I'm gonna miss you too. Even though you're a pain in my ass most of the time, I still love you."

"I might not be able to stand you most of the time, but you are the best brother anyone could ask for. I hope Melody gets to have a brother like you."

Well, fuck, I'm gonna start crying for real here soon. The reality of leaving my parents and sister behind is hitting me with all these emotions that I don't really like.

Abby steps away, going over to mom, who has the baby again, and dad comes over.

"Take care of your family like I know you will. I don't care what you do out there, what you chose as your career; just be happy, love hard, and be the man I know you can be."

"I will," I promise, before pulling him into a hug. We hold onto each other a moment, before letting go.

Everyone says their final goodbyes, as I stand on the porch, watching the family I grew up with drive away from me and the family I created. Emmy stands on one side of me, and Talon stands on the other.

"We'll see them again soon," Emmy says, resting her head on my shoulder as the car disappears from our line of sight.

"I know," I sigh.

"Come on, we have one last night in this house, let's make the best of it," Talon says, grabbing both mine and Emmy's hands to pull us back into the house.

Tyson and Oliver are hanging out with their dad and the other MC members, and Charlie is spending time with the Ol' Ladies. So that leaves us home alone with Melody.

"Why do I have a feeling that by you saying *let's make the best of it,* you actually mean *let's have hot, sweaty, dirty sex?*" I chuckle.

"We can't," Emmy protests. "What about the baby?"

"Fast asleep in her playpen," Talon counters, handing over the baby monitor. Looking at the screen, I see her laying on her back; her head tilted to the side with her thumb in her mouth. "We're right across the hall if she needs us," Talon coaxes, pulling her into his arms.

"Fine," Emmy concedes.

Talon smirks, cocking a brow. "What, do you not want to be fucked by me, while our man fucks me in the ass?"

Emmy's eyes light up. "Really?" She breathes, and I can tell Talon has caught her; hook, line, and sinker. My cock jerks to life with his incentive. I love the idea. I love being topped by Talon, and he loves to dominate me. The time in the gym, back at school, was the first time I took his ass, and we only did it once since then, so I'm *very much* looking forward to this.

"Come on, let's go upstairs before I'm dick deep inside your pussy and the daddy life comes-a-calling." Talon grins, scooping Emmy up and flinging her over his shoulder. She lets out a giggled yelp as Talon bounds up the stairs. His concern is valid. It's happened more than once. We'll be in the middle of mind blowing sex, and the baby starts to cry. There's always someone else to get her, but sometimes once you hear her upset, it kills the mood, and you just want to make sure she's okay. Since we got them back, it's been happening more frequently. We used to fight over who got to care for her a lot, but now Charlie has this whole system made up for us. Emmy finds it ridiculous, but it totally works.

I follow, needing to be with them both. We've been so busy this summer that *group activities* are not really a thing anymore, and I miss being with them together. When it's all of us, I feel complete. Also, the sex is hot as Hell, so that's a bonus.

Shutting the door behind us, I watch Talon toss Emmy in the middle of the bed. He doesn't miss a beat as he pulls off her shorts, tossing them behind him, almost hitting me in the face. I bite my lip, holding back my smile as I watch them together. Emmy is in a fit of giggles, as Talon desperately tries to get her naked.

Her shirt goes flying next, leaving her in a sexy black and pink lace bra and panty set. Talon reaches behind her to unhook her bra.

"Stupid bra. Where the fuck is the hook!" Talon growls, and Emmy looks over his shoulder to me with pure glee in her eyes at our eager man.

"It's in the front, babe," Emmy snorts.

"What the fuck?" Talon asks, sitting back on his heels. "Who the fuck puts it in the front?"

Emmy just rolls her eyes, unhooking the bra herself, letting her large breasts spill out. Her nipples are a pretty pink and pebbled. My breathing increases, as I stand there watching them together, my dick begging for attention.

"Fucking finally!" Talon groans, leaning forward to take her nipple into his mouth. She moans, her fingers tangling in his hair, holding him in place. Her eyes close, and she tilts her head back, as she arches into his touch.

He lowers her to the bed, moving to pay the same attention to her other breast. He sucks and massages, getting sexy, breathy sounds of pleasure from our girl.

It's too much. Watching them has me needing to touch myself. Pulling off my shirt, I toss it to the ground, then work on ridding myself of my pants and boxers. When they join my shirt on the floor, I grasp my rigid cock, giving it a few firm strokes. I'm unable to hold back my groan, as I watch Talon kiss a path down Emmy's belly, stopping at each stretch mark to kiss and trace them with his tongue.

"I think our man loves watching us together, baby girl," he murmurs, against the skin right above the strap of her panties.

"Fuck yes," I breathe, walking over to them. Talon moves away to take off his shirt, before moving back down to strip her bare for us and opening her legs wide, putting her dripping pussy on display.

"Look at you, baby, so wet for us. Are you excited?" Talon asks, bending over to kiss the inside of her thigh.

"Yes," she whimpers, her chest rising and falling as her breathing starts to quicken. She waits for Talon to touch her, to lick her, to suck her where she desperately wants to feel him.

Moving behind Talon, I run my hand down his back to grab the band of his shorts, pulling them and his boxers down over his sexy ass. It was just in the air, tempting me.

He moves his knees, allowing me to pull them the rest of the way off, while he gets to work on making our girl come for the first of many times tonight.

I rub gentle circles on his cheek before leaning forward to bite his ass, making him curse against her pussy. I pull away, and with no warning, I bring my palm down, giving it a swift, sharp slap. It leaves a nice red mark, *if I do say so myself.* I move to lay down next to them. I look at his face to see him giving me a heated glare, but I just go to move Emmy's hair out of her face, kissing her cheek. I move along her jaw and then down her neck, leaving open mouth kisses with a smug smile plastered on my face.

"So, I have two brats on my hands tonight?" he growls.

"Maybe." I smirk at him, before going back to kissing Emmy's neck, sucking lightly on the spot where I can feel her pulse beating erratically. She huffs out a laugh that turns into a whimper as Talon gets back to work.

We work as a team; him eating her out while I play with her nipples, plucking and pinching them until our combined touches turn her into a shaking mess below us.

"God!" She mewls with one hand in my hair, the other in Talon's. "Too much. It's too much." She tries to move, but Talon holds her down.

"Let go, Butterfly. Let your body bask in the release it's screaming for. Soak our man's face, as I swallow your cries with my lips." I tempt her. I kiss her, slipping my tongue in and over hers in a dance of passion. She kisses me back with hungry need.

I know she's close. I can feel her body quivering under my hand, while I massage her breast.

The only thing I can hear are the sounds of her harsh breathing as she tries to breathe in air, all while we make out and Talon's fingers fuck her drenched pussy.

Then she shatters. I hold her to me as she screams into my mouth, her back arching off the bed, as her body trembles and shakes out her release.

When she's done, she breaks the kiss, slumping into the pillows.

"I really don't understand how I'm not dead by now." She groans, her breaths choppy. "Orgasms that intense are gonna stop my heart someday; I just know it."

Talon and I chuckle as he crawls up her body, placing a soft kiss on her lips. "We would never let that happen." He looks at me, his eyes hooded. "Want a taste?" he asks. Heat flares throughout my body as I stare at his lips.

"Please." I whisper-beg, before pulling his mouth to mine. I moan into the kiss as I savor the flavor of our girl on his tongue.

"God, you two are so fucking hot," Emmy says. We break apart, looking down at our girl. Her skin is dewy with sweat, her hair's a mess, and her lips are pink and swollen. She's glowing and has never looked more beautiful.

"I *need* you," Talon says, then looks back at me. "Both of you. Fuck me, Ben. Fuck me deep in my ass, as I fuck our girl into this mattress. Let's leave our mark on this house so we'll always remember our last night here. Let's break apart and put each other back together again."

I'm used to his teasing, dirty words; they've always been a part of his personality. But when he says stuff like that? I'm fucking putty in his hands.

"Fuck him, Ben. Make our man cum inside me, marking me as you mark him." Emmy says, cupping my cheek, her thumb grazing my cheek bone.

I lean into her touch, closing my eyes, as I feel the love of these two seep deep into my being.

But my cock brings me back to reality, and the pre cum leaking from the tip is telling me it wants its release. Preferably while buried inside my man's ass.

"I love you, sweet girl," I tell Emmy, snagging a kiss before turning to Talon. "And I love you too. I'm excited to start this new part of our lives together. But right now, I need you too. I'm going to fuck your ass," I grin.

"Hell yeah, you are." Talon's eyes are filled with so much hunger for us, it has my cock twitching, and it fills me with this need to please him with everything I have.

Getting up off the bed, I go to the bag on the floor, grabbing a tube of lube. By the time I'm done lathering up my cock, Talon is already balls deep into our girl, her legs over his shoulders, as he thrusts hard inside her.

"Fucking golden pussy, I swear." He grunts, the muscles on his back rippling as he moves.

I run my hand down his spine, loving the shiver my touch brings him. Squeezing some more lube onto my fingers, I rub it around his hole before dipping a finger in. He groans, his movements faltering.

"Relax, baby." I soothe him verbally, as I prep him to take me. It's still foreign to him. He's tight, and he needs to breathe while letting me get him ready so I don't hurt him.

"Kiss me," Emmy demands, as Talon's body tenses up while I add another finger. He moves her legs so that her feet are on the bed, before leaning over to do as she requested.

He moans into the kiss as I fuck his ass with my fingers. "You like that?" I ask him.

"God, yes!" he groans.

"Are you ready for my cock?"

"Please." I love how desperate he is for me.

Removing my fingers, I replace it with the tip of my cock. Emmy kisses him, her hand rubbing his back to help him relax as I enter him, inch by inch.

When I'm all the way in, he breaks the kiss and curses. "Fuck. I feel so fucking full," he says, hanging his head.

"Do you need time to adjust?" I ask, not moving and waiting for his approval.

"No. Fuck me, Ben. I need you to move so I can move because I'm dying here."

Pulling back, I thrust back in carefully. We start to move together. He fucks Emmy while I fuck him, and it doesn't take long until we find the perfect rhythm.

It feels too good, I need more. I start to thrust into him harder and faster as his cries of pleasure mixes in the air with Emmy's. *Hottest sounds in the world.* It fuels the fire deep within me. I'm lost in the ecstasy that is them. Emmy's eyes are wide with needy desire, her second orgasm coming any second now.

"So... fucking...good," Talon groans. "Now I know how you feel being trapped between us."

"Best thing in the world," I grunt in response, while gripping his hair and forcing his head back as I rut into his ass.

"Sweet god, Ben, yes, keep doing that! I'm gonna cum," Talon shouts.

"Oh, that's good because so am I." Emmy cries, before twisting the sheets in a death grip and locking eyes with me. She slaps a hand over her mouth to smother her scream, as her eyes widen and her body stutters with her climax. The sight of it has my balls drawing up, and I come hard, shooting my cum deep inside Talon.

"Fuckkkk!" Talon lets out a primal growl, before stilling as he fills our girl with his release.

Talon collapses on top of Emmy, tucking his face into her neck, as I drape myself over his back, kissing his sweaty skin. I place my forehead against him, as I give myself a moment to come down from the high.

Pulling out slowly, I watch the cum drip from his ass, making me bite my lip and my cock comes to life again. But I don't push it because I can tell Emmy is on the verge of falling asleep, with Talon still inside her, as the exhaustion of our day takes over her body.

"I'll be right back," I say, kissing Talon's cheek and Emmy's forehead before going into the bathroom. I grab two clean hand towels and head back to clean Talon up first. When I'm done with him, he pulls out of Emmy. "Thank you," he whispers sleepily, snuggling into Emmy's side.

"You never have to thank me for taking care of you, Talon. I love you," I tell him, completely serious.

He gives me a sleepy smile, his eyes closing. “I love you too, baby. So much.”

“Emmy, baby, are you still awake?” I ask.

“Mhhmm.” She blinks her eyes open.

I smile down at her. “Sorry, you can go to sleep soon, baby, but I need your permission. Do you mind if I clean you up?”

She smiles, something soft and sweet that has my heart skipping a beat. “Yes, you can. Thank you.”

“Of course.” I part her legs and get her cleaned up.

“I love you, Ben,” she mumbles sleepily. “Thank you for loving me.”

“Always, my Butterfly,” I say, kissing her knee before leaving them be. I shower and go back to bed, crawling in on Emmy’s other side. We're all gonna need showers again in the morning. Pulling the blankets up over us all, I look over at the baby monitor and see Charlie watching our baby girl sleep. Knowing she's in good hands, I snuggle up to my girl and drape my arm over her. Talon shifts so that his arm is also over her, and we hold our girl between us, safe, happy, and where she belongs.

CHAPTER 21
Tyson

GETTING DRUNK THE night before I have to get my casts off and then catch a fucking flight to LA was not one of my best ideas. My body feels heavy, my head is pounding, and I feel gross all over.

My alarm goes off, doing nothing to help with my situation. "Fucking phone," I groan, smacking at it where it's lying on the side table, until I find the button on the side to shut off the God awful noise.

Sitting up, my head spins, causing me to squeeze my eyes shut as I hold my head, willing the world to stay still. "Never again," I mutter to myself. But I need to get up and get Emmy, so we get these casts off me, before we have to leave.

Oliver and I hung out with dad and the other members, reminiscing about the past. It was nice, and I'm going to miss it, but I'm excited for our new lives waiting for us out in LA. With everything that Emmy has been through, not just in the past two years but her whole life, she deserves this new start. I think being closer to her sister will be good for her. *And* getting to be around my best friend more will be entertaining, to say the least.

Needing to pee badly, I swing my legs over the side of the bed, almost falling back on it when I stand up. At this point, I don't care. I'll walk without any support, hobbling over to the shared bathroom. The only one of us with an ensuite is Emmy, but that made sense seeing how she had more of a need for it.

When I get into the hall, I stop, seeing the door shut. Whoever is in there better hurry because this is fucking painful.

The sounds of someone puking have me cursing. The only other one who was drinking was Oliver, but he was nowhere near as drunk as I was.

"You okay in there?" I ask, tapping my knuckles against the door.

"Just a minute," Emmy's voice answers back. Now I'm concerned.

"Princess, I'm coming in." I give her a warning and time to protest before opening the door. My concern grows to worry, finding her sitting on the floor with her face in the toilet. "Emmy? Baby, what's wrong?"

"Gah." She spits into the toilet, before flushing it and then moves to sit back against the tub. "I think I have food poisoning or something."

Going over to the sink, I fill up the cup that's on the counter with water and bring it over to her, sitting on the edge of the tub myself.

"Thank you." She gives me a weak smile. I frown, not liking how pale she looks.

"We'll get you checked out when we go to the doctor, make sure it's not the flu, so Melody doesn't get sick," I tell her, brushing some sweaty strands of hair away from her face, as she leans her head against my leg.

"Good idea." She sighs. "Bad timing to get sick. The idea of a four hour flight feeling like this sounds like pure Hell."

"What can I do to make you feel better?" I ask, rubbing the top of her back and hating that she feels like this.

"Can you get me a change of clothes and ask the others to help with Melody?" she asks. "I'm gonna take a cold shower and hope it helps me feel better."

"Of course," I tell her, leaning over to give her a kiss on the top of her head. "Holler if you need anyone, okay?"

Leaving her to do her thing, I go to her old room where Talon and Ben are tangled in the sheets together, making out like the world's about to end.

"Don't mind me, just need to take a piss," I say, holding up my hand to block them from my view, as I hobble to the bathroom.

"Why not use the one in the hallway?" Talon questions.

"Emmy is in that one. She's not feeling good, so she's taking a cold shower. When you're done here, can you check on Oliver and make sure he gets up in time to be out of here by one? Our flight is at three pm. We should be there at least an hour earlier. Actually, with a baby, maybe sooner than that."

The airport is only a thirty minute drive, so if they are out on time, we should be fine. Emmy and I are going from the doctor's straight to the airport and will meet everyone there.

"Is she okay? What's wrong with her?" Ben asks, panic clear in his voice.

"She thinks it's food poisoning," I tell him, entering the bathroom.

"Probably the Chinese food we ordered last night," Talon chimes in.

I don't hear anything else they say, closing the door behind me and relieving myself before I burst.

When I get out, Talon and Ben are dressed.

"If you make sure everything is packed in your bag, we'll take it for you. That way, you two don't have to drag anything with you to the doctor's office," Ben says, putting some odds and ends in his bag.

We shipped most of our things ahead in a moving van a few days ago. Harlow called, telling us that it arrived and that she oversaw the movers as they brought everything in. It was mostly just Emmy's room, because she loved it so much that she wanted to keep it the same at the new house. She said it was her dream room set up with all of Melody's things and some personal stuff from each of us. We left the beds here for whoever moves in next. We plan on going furniture shopping when we get there.

Harlow showed us some photos of the place, and it might not be anywhere near as big as her place, but it's still a good size. It looks like a stone cottage only three times its size. She said there's three floors, four rooms upstairs, and two in the basement with room to make more if needed. There's a big open floor plan for the living room and kitchen with a big fenced in backyard that's perfect for family pets and kids to play in. We don't need big and fancy, as long as we have each other. That's all that matters.

"Once I get changed, I'll put the bag outside my door," I tell them, grabbing Emmy a change of clothes. "Make sure all of her stuff is packed too."

"Happy to get that cast off?" Talon chuckles, as he watches me hobble out of the room.

"More than you know," I mutter. As much as I love watching my girl ride me, I'm dying to wrap my hand around her neck and fuck her until she passes out from too many orgasms.

Maybe I'll tie her to the bed and have my way with her once we settle into the new house.

When I get out into the hall, I see that the bathroom door is open, and no one is in there. I can hear Emmy and Charlie talking in Melody's room, so I go into mine. I change into fresh clothes and check the room, making sure nothing is left, before going back into the shared bathroom. Brushing my teeth and then packing my tooth brush, I leave my bag in the hall.

"Hey, Princess, sorry for the wait," I say, walking to Melody's room, handing her a change of clothes.

"Thank you." She leans up to kiss me; her hair wet from her shower and a towel wrapped around her.

"How are you feeling?" I ask her, wrapping my arms around her waist.

"A little better." She smiles softly up at me.

"Get dressed. Then we can go get these stupid things off me." I kiss the tip of her nose and slap her ass as she walks past me. She turns, glaring at me, but I just smirk. I can see the heat in her eyes, and if she was feeling better, I'd have some fun with her one last time in this house. "Give me," I insist, holding my arms out for Melody, who is in Charlie's arms.

"Do you wanna go see Daddy Ty?" Charlie baby talks to Melody, who lets out a high pitched, excited squeal that has me and Charlie laughing. "I'll take that as a yes," Charlie states, handing Melody over to me.

"Hello, my sweet little princess." I pepper kisses on her chubby little cheeks after I have her in my arms. It's crazy that she's almost six months old. She loves to try and walk while we hold her up by her hands. She is a little rollie-pollie and will find her way into another room if we look away too long. And she *loves* baby cereal. Emmy cried the first time we tried it with her, saying it's not fair that she's growing up so fast. I have to agree; it's happening way too quickly. I wish she could stay this tiny forever. I'm dreading the day when she starts talking back and bringing boys home. Not that they would ever make it past the front gate.

"Daddy is gonna miss you," I tell her.

"Dude, you're gonna see her in two hours." Charlie laughs, as she packs up Melody's playpen.

"Yeah, two hours is too long," I answer her, but I'm looking at Melody and responding in the baby talk we have all grown accustomed to doing with her.

Charlie looks over at me, cocking a brow with a smirk on her lips. "You know, I'll never get used to seeing the big, bad, biker dude who goes full softie at the mere mention of her."

"Well, it's only her who can do that to me," I say, passing Melody back over to her. "I'm so glad to get this stupid thing off so I can hold her properly," I grumble.

"You know, I can get you to turn into a teddy bear too," Emmy says, and I turn around to find her standing in the doorway, dressed in a pair of black workout shorts and the top I gave her.

"You didn't want to wear the jean shorts I picked out?" I ask.

She shrugs. "I put them on, but they were a little tight, so I changed into something more comfortable, because we're going to be sitting on a plane for a few hours, and it made sense."

"Yeah, I didn't even think of that." I nod. "Ready to go?"

"Yup." She goes over, giving Melody a kiss, and then Charlie. "You guys have everything under control?"

"Yes," Charlie laughs. "There's four of us; we'll be just fine making sure everything is ready."

We leave the room, and Emmy stops in to check on Oliver on our way downstairs. He's passed out in his bed, on his belly.

"He didn't sleep well last night," Emmy says, sounding worried.

"Another nightmare?" I ask. She nods, before closing the door. He's been having them on and off since we got back from hell. From what the others said, when we were gone, they were really bad. He would wake up screaming every night, and it got to the point where he was staying up as late as he could, sometimes not sleeping for days.

Emmy broke down when they told her, and she had a talk with Oliver. He's been seeing someone here until we move, and Harlow found a therapist for him to see out there. They said that once life settles down and Emmy isn't in harm's way anymore, that the nightmares should stop.

I hope they're right, because I hate seeing my brother's haunted eyes, hearing his screams in the middle of the night when he does have an episode. Emmy is always able to calm him down, getting him back to sleep, but I can see how much it breaks her. She loves us all so much.

"What are you doing here?" Emmy says, smiling as Amy and Rick step into the house.

"You didn't think we would just sit at home and do nothing when we could be here, spending every last minute with Melody?" Amy says, pulling Emmy into a hug. "And because you're going to be at the doctors with Tyson, we're gonna bring everyone to the airport and spend the last few minutes with you there."

"How does that feel?" The doctor asks, tossing my nasty cast into the garbage. I hold my arm out, opening and closing my hand. There's a little stiffness and slight pain, but it's bearable.

"Not bad, a little tender," I tell him.

"It's still healing, and it might take a few more weeks until you can get full use out of it. I want you to still wear this brace on your hand, as well as one on your knee. You need to check up with a doctor down there in a few weeks time , but you'll still be able to do a lot more. Plus, now you can take them off to shower," he chuckles.

"I wasn't really complaining about needing the help." I give Emmy a sly grin, making her eyes go wide, and she slaps my arm.

"Tyson," she hisses, but the doctor just laughs.

"So, how have you been, Emmy?" he asks, turning towards her. "The nurse who checked you in said you wanted to speak to me?"

"She thinks she might have food poisoning," I interrupt, before she can tell him.

His brows furrows in question. "What makes you think that?"

"I got sick this morning, threw up a bit, but I'm fine now. It's making me think that I don't have food poisoning. Maybe it's the heat that's getting to me." She tries to brush it off, but people don't just get sick for no reason.

The doctor nods his head. “How has your birth control been holding up?”

She tilts her head to the side slightly. “Umm, fine, I guess?”

“When was your last period?”

“About a week ago,” she answers with suspicion.

“Can I see your arm? I just wanna make sure your birth control is holding up well.”

“Okay?” she says, as he steps to her side and he starts to examine her arm. What is he going on about?

“Did you know you have a scar here?” he says, pointing to a spot on her arm.

She looks down at it. “Never really noticed it, why?”

“Because that’s where we put your birth control. I’m not feeling it in there.”

“What?” Emmy asks, her voice growing panicked. “What the heck do you mean?”

“It looks like it was cut out. The mark is small, barely noticeable, but it was not done by a professional.”

“Cut out?” She turns to me, a horrified look in her eyes. Then her face falls, growing more pissed. “Jimmy,” she growls.

My blood boils at the mention of that scumbag’s name. “What about him?” I ask.

“He was telling me about how I was gonna have his babies, sounding so sure of himself. He must have taken it out when they took me. Tyson, that must have been his plan all along. He took out my birth control, then the sick fucker was... He was going to rape me and get me pregnant.” Her eyes well with tears, and my heart breaks. I pull her into my arms.

“Shhh,” I soothe her, my eyes finding the doctor. He looks pale, but he doesn't ask questions. “What does this mean?”

He clears his throat. “Have you had intercourse since...since this incident happened?”

Emmy moves away from within my arms to look at him. “Yeah,” she blushes.

He nods his head. “But you’ve been getting your periods.”

“Yeah, haven’t missed one yet. Why, do you...do you think I could be pregnant?” she asks.

"We can run a blood test and send you the results. But, when do you think was the first time you were intimate after your implant was removed?"

"It would have been about a week after we were taken," I answer, my mind wandering to when we fucked in the room she was held in. It was the only time I got to see her in those two fucking weeks. If you don't count the time they tied me to a fucking chair, where I was forced to watch her mother get her brains blown out, and that bastard lay his hands on her. Which I don't. "What was that, about seven weeks ago?" I look at her, and she nods.

"How about we do blood work, but let's do an ultrasound too, okay?" the doctor requests.

"O-okay," Emmy says, sounding shocked.

He tells us he's going to get the machine, then leaves the room.

She could be pregnant. *Holy fuck*, she could be fucking pregnant. Joy replaces the anger, and I try not to get myself too excited, but what if she is? It could be mine. *We could have made a baby!*

"Tyson?" She looks up at me.

"Yes, Princess?"

"I could be pregnant," she says, her eyes watering.

"I know, baby. Are you upset about it?" I ask, holding my breath.

"No." Her voice is small but filled with emotion. "I know we didn't really talk about when we were going to try for the next one, but I've always wanted them close in age so they can grow up together." She puts her hand on her belly. "What if I have a baby brother or sister growing inside me for Melody?"

"Then I'll be the happiest motherfucker to ever exist." I grin.

"Alright, here we go." The doctor comes back, pulling in a cart with a laptop and ultrasound machine attached. "Do you mind switching places with her?"

"Nope," I say, getting off the table. Emmy climbs up, lying back, as I grab a chair and pull it over next to her.

She holds my hand as the doctor inserts a long wand into a spot I really don't want him to. But he said because of how early it would be, doing one vaginally was how he had to do it.

He moves it around, and everything is quiet while we wait. It feels like time is dragging on.

"Well, I don't think we will be needing that blood work for confirmation anymore," he says, a smile taking over his face.

"We won't?" Emmy asks.

"Nope," He turns the laptop to her. "See that little jelly bean looking thing?" he says while pointing to the screen. "That's your baby."

"Baby?" Emmy sniffles, starting to cry. "I'm pregnant?"

"Yes, you are, and the heartbeat seems to be strong. You're measuring around seven weeks, give or take a few days."

Emmy bursts into tears, and I find my eyes stinging too.

"I'll give you two a moment," he says, cleaning up and wheeling the machine away.

"Tyson," she sobs. "Do you know what this means?"

"What, Princess?" I do, but I let her tell me anyway.

"You're next up on the baby train." She lets out a broken laugh. The biggest smile takes over my face. "If I'm seven weeks, then it can't be anyone else's. I haven't been with them until a few weeks after getting back. They wanted to make sure I was in a good place mentally as well as physically. So, Tyson, this is biologically, your baby."

Leaning down, I kiss her, pouring all the love I have deep inside me, before pulling up her top and kissing her belly. Every child she has will always be mine, blood or not. But I didn't get a shot at getting her pregnant last time, so being the next one to give her a baby, fills me with so much pride and joy.

"You know it doesn't matter who the father is, right?" I tell her, helping her into a seated position.

"I know. All of you will always love them no matter what as if they were your own blood. It's a big reason why I adore you all so much."

"We're having a baby," I say. My body is vibrating, and I just want to scream it from the rooftop.

"We're having a baby." She smiles just as wide.

"Now, we get to tell the others."

"Do you think they will be just as happy?" she asks, her expression falling a bit, as worry creeps onto her beautiful face.

I cup her cheeks. “They will be over the moon, Princess. Do you see how they are with Melody?”

“But what if it's too much? Two babies under two is a lot!”

“And there's six of us. And you know your sister, Neo, and Evie will be jumping at the bit to help with both of them any chance they can get.”

She smiles again, letting out a little laugh. “You’re right. This feels right, you know? Us moving, starting over. And now we're having a baby. It’s meant to be,” she says, before sighing happily.

“It is.” I lean in, kissing her again.

We check out, thanking the doctor before leaving.

“I’ll love this baby no matter what gender, but I’m kinda hoping it’s a boy,” she says, as we walk out to the car. “And I hope he’s just like you.”

“Woah there, let’s not go that far,” I chuckle.

“Why not? You’re amazing, Tyson. You are strong, brave, loving, and kind. You’re one of the best dads anyone could ask for. I would love our son to grow up to be just like you, to be like any of you.”

“I love you, Princess,” I tell her, pushing her against the car, grinding my growing ejection against her belly, making her whimper. “I am the luckiest man alive. I don’t deserve you or our kids, but I’m so fucking grateful I have you. I want to always wake up and prove it to you guys every day. You're my everything. My heart and soul.”

“I love you too,” She moans as I kiss her neck. “I know I tell you all that I’d be nothing without you. But that's not true. I know I could be strong enough on my own if I had to. But I’m so glad I don’t have to. I want you by my side, loving me, caring for me and our kids. And I wanna do the same for all of you.”

“Forever, Princess. That’s us. It’s us against the world,” I promise her.

“Forever.”

CHAPTER 22
Emmy

"WHEN DO YOU want to tell them?" Tyson asks me, as we navigate the airport's parking options. Steel is going to have one of his guys come and pick the car up. I text him to let him know exactly where it is as we get out. Taking the hand Tyson holds out for me, I lace my fingers with his, as we head into the parking garage's elevator and make our way up to the top floor to meet the others.

"I don't know. I feel like right now isn't really the best time. We have a lot going on, and as exciting as it is, it's still stressful. So I think I might honestly need a few days to just get settled and relax before dropping a big bomb like this. Especially, after we already made such a big change. Do you think they would be mad if I didn't tell them right away?" I ask, looking up at him. We exit the elevator, and Tyson pulls me to the side.

"This is your body. If you feel like you need some time, then take a few days. It's not like last time where you waited weeks, but you also had a good reason for that back then. I know for a fact it's going to go much smoother this time. None of us would want you stressed, and if waiting until we're moved and settled helps, then wait."

"I love you." I smile up at him, as he pulls me into his arms.

"I love you too, Princess, so fucking much," he growls, nipping my bottom lip, before kissing me hard.

We find everyone waiting by security. Amy is holding Melody as Oliver and Rick talk.

"There's Mama," Amy says to Melody as we approach them.

"Hi, sweet girl," I say, giving Melody a kiss on the cheek. She grabs my hair, holding me there as she lets out one of her high pitched squeals of excitement. I'm glad I started wearing contacts after graduation, because I feel like she would have already broken twenty pairs of glasses by now.

Laughing, I carefully pry her little fingers off my hair.

"Sorry it took us so long," I apologize, as Tyson kisses my cheek and heads over to the others.

"No problem. Just means extra time with this cutie pie," Amy says, handing Melody over to me.

My eyes start to water as reality sinks in. We are *actually* about to get on a plane and move away from home, from the only people who ever loved me enough as their daughter.

"I'm gonna miss you so much," I admit, tears slipping, as my voice cracks.

"Oh, honey," her voice fills with her own emotion, as she pulls me into a hug. "We're gonna miss you too," she weeps.

"I wanna thank you. You never gave up on me when the people who helped create me did. You saw something others didn't. You took in a pre-teen and gave her a home. You loved me, cared for me, and went above and beyond. Not because you had to, but because it's just who you guys are. You two are the best parents I could have ever asked for. You love me, love my sweet girl like your own. You will always be my mom and dad."

She cups my face. "I'm so honored to call you my daughter, Emmy, my sweet, sweet girl. You will always have us, no matter what. I love you," she assures me.

"I love you too," I sniff. I look behind me, making sure there's no one else around. "I need to tell you something. I hate that it's right now, and we won't be able to celebrate, but this isn't something I want to tell you over the phone."

She wipes the tears from her eyes, her face growing into a curious grin. "What's going on?"

"Tyson and I found out something else when we were at the doctor." My face splits into a giant grin. "I'm pregnant."

Her eyes pop wide, before glossing over with tears, her lower lip wobbling. "You're pregnant?"

I nod. "Only Tyson knows. I'm going to tell the others when we get settled into our new place. But I wanted to tell you in person. I'm about seven weeks."

Her brow pinches. "Seven weeks?" She takes a moment to think. "But you were still being held by the Hellhounds."

I bite my lip, holding back a laugh. "Yeah, well... Seth snuck Tyson into my room, and...let's just say we were very happy to see that the other was okay."

Understanding dawns, and she giggles. “Well, I’m so happy for you.” She pulls me into a side hug, careful not to squash Melody.

“Thank you.”

“Hey, babe. We better get going, they're going to start boarding soon, and we still need to go through security,” Oliver says, wrapping his arm around me and kissing my temple.

We say our last goodbyes to Rick and Amy before getting in line.

Once we're on the other side, we find the gate we're departing from just in time to hear the lady say that people with children, or those who need assistance can board first.

“Looks like that's us,” Tyson says, heading towards the front of the line.

“Wait, so after weeks of you putting up a fight and swearing up and down that you don’t need any help getting around, all of a sudden now you're crippled?” Talon asks, and I try to hold back a giggle at the annoyance on his face.

“Umm. Yeah,” Tyson says, looking at him like he's crazy. “Do you know how long it takes to board big planes like this? I wanna sit the fuck down,” he retorts.

“Asshole,” Talon mutters, as Ben takes his hand, a smile creeping onto his lips.

“What matters is our seats are all next to each other. We’ll survive waiting an extra half hour if need be,” Ben reminds us.

“We can wait with you,” I tell him, really not wanting to cause any issues if we go first.

“No, Talon can suck it the fuck up. Plus, Melody is hungry. It would be easier to just feed her in your seat and to have her fall asleep in your arms there,” Tyson explains. He does have a point. Melody is getting more fussy by the second.

“It's fine, Firefly. Like Ben said, we’ll survive.” Oliver gives me a kiss.

“I’ll make sure he smartens up before we get on.” Charlie grins, giving me a kiss too, handing Tyson the diaper bag.

Tyson and I show the lady our tickets, and we board the plane.

Thankfully our seats are at the front and near one of the bathrooms. I’m not sure when my morning sickness is going to act up, so having easy access to a toilet is a good idea.

It still hasn't fully set in that I'm pregnant, and we're going to have *another* baby. I'm so scared, but also really excited. I get to experience this pregnancy properly. Everyone will be able to come to all of our appointments. We can celebrate everything at home with family and friends, and *not* in a school library. Plus, this time, I can give birth in an actual hospital, because I really want the good drugs this time. Like hell, I'll be feeling that pain again.

As Melody feeds, my mind wanders, thinking about what it's going to be like with a new little one. Will we have two little girls? Or will we have one of each? Doesn't matter to me, because no matter the gender or health, I'll be happy, because they will be ours.

"You okay, Princess?" Tyson asks, softly turning my head to look at him, wiping a tear from my eye. I didn't even realize that I was crying.

"Yeah. Better than okay." I smile. "We're having a baby."

He smiles back. "We are." He leans in, placing a sweet kiss to my lips.

The rest of the plane starts to board, and eventually, the rest of my crew makes their way on.

"About time," Talon mutters, taking his seat in the row behind us, followed by Ben and Oliver. I shake my head, and Charlie rolls her eyes, as she sits next to me so that Melody and I are between her and Tyson.

"You're such a drama queen," Charlie says, turning so that she can see him through the gap between the seats.

"I just hate planes, okay," he mutters.

"Then why the hell did you want to get on here so bad?" Oliver questions, his voice filled with confusion.

"Because I knew the moment the doors lock behind us, I couldn't chicken the fuck out and refuse to get on, ruining this trip for everyone," Talon says through gritted teeth.

"Wanna make out? It will take your mind off of everything for a while," Ben asks.

I try to smother a laugh at how quiet Talon goes.

"Fucking hornballs!" Oliver mutters.

A moan has me turning back to look through the crack as well. Ben's tongue is tangled with Talon's as they devour each other.

"Tease," I say to myself, turning back around in my seat.

"Ever wanted to be a part of the mile high club before?" Tyson asks, leaning in to whisper in my ear.

"Never really thought about it," I say back. My body really likes the idea of being locked in a small space while Tyson fucks me, and knowing we need to keep quiet, so we don't get caught.

"We'll have to fix that then." Tyson nips at my earlobe, making me squirm in my seat.

I've always wanted to join a club, and this one sounds like a fun one to be a part of.

CHAPTER 23
Emmy

A RUSH OF nausea washes over me as we step off the plane, making my body sway. Slapping a hand over my mouth, my eyes frantically search for a trash can. Spotting one, I take off from the group and get to it just in time, before bringing back everything I ate this morning.

"You okay?" Tyson asks, rubbing my back.

"Yeah, sorry," I say, taking the bottle of water and napkin he holds out to me. I wipe my mouth and toss the napkin in the trash, before taking a sip from the bottle of water. Cracking off the cap, I take a mouth full. "Thank you."

"You have nothing to be sorry about. And, of course. Do you need anything else?" Tyson asks, looking at me like I'm about to break. Tyson has always been protective of me, but it's gone up a few levels since the moment he found out we were having another baby.

When I was pregnant with Melody, things were new, and we were just starting to work through our feelings. So most of my pregnancy, he acted like a worried best friend in front of the guys, when I knew he wanted to be there for me on the same level the others were. I know he's excited that he gets to go through it with me one-hundred percent this time.

"Firefly, what's wrong?" Oliver asks. His face, a mask of concern as he and the others walk over to where Tyson and I are.

"Just felt sick from the ride, but I'm fine now." I give him a small smile. It's not really a lie, it was the traveling that finally got to me.

"Are you sure?" Charlie asks, shifting Melody from one hip to the other.

"Yes, yes, I'm fine," I tell them, playing it off like it's no big deal. Only a few hours more, and then I'll tell them everything once we've gotten settled in.

"We should get going," Tyson urges us, looking up from his phone. "Your sister is waiting for us by the baggage claim."

"Come on, my Queen," Talon says, hooking his arm in mine, pulling me away from the garbage can.

"What about that?" I say, stopping and looking back over my shoulder. I'd feel bad if we just left it like that.

"I'll find someone who works here and let them know, before I meet you down there," Tyson says, kissing the side of my head and taking off.

"Ready to start our new life, Butterfly?" Ben asks. He laces his fingers with mine, bringing my hand up to his lips and placing a soft kiss, while his eyes bore into mine. I can feel the love and excitement radiating off him.

"More than you will ever know." I beam at him.

We're here, in LA. I've always wanted to visit this place. To be able to put my feet in the warm sand, to walk on the Santa Monica pier, to visit the Hollywood sign, and the Walk of Fame. Now it's my home, and there's so much more at our fingertips. Not that I didn't enjoy Alberta, but Canada's winters are, well...shitty. I hate the snow, the cold, and now I can have sun all year long. Plus, it's not like we can't go back for a visit if I miss it bad enough.

Oliver carries Melody's bag while Charlie holds the baby, and we follow the signs down to the baggage claim. I see Harlow when we get there, and when her eyes find me, I can't help the smile that takes over at her immediate excitement. Neo notices Harlow walking over to me, but he beelines past her and over to us. With no words, he takes my baby from Charlie and walks away.

"Okay then, yeah, sure. Just kidnap my baby from me, that's cool," Charlie grumbles.

"Sorry, babe, get used to it." Harlow laughs, before pulling me into a hug. "I missed you, baby sis."

"I missed you too." I hug her back.

"How was the trip?" She takes a step back to look me over.

"Not bad, Melody slept most of the time, and when she was awake, we all took turns keeping her entertained. So, it was a pretty smooth flight," I explain.

"We grabbed your bags for you already," Harlow says, as we start heading over to where Evie is trying to take Melody from Neo and failing as he glares down at her with a snarl.

But Evie isn't afraid of the crazy man. No, she puts her hands on her hips and glares right back, but she doesn't fight him on it. "Fine," she snaps. "But I get her later."

"Yeah, sure," Neo snorts, before starting in on a baby-talk conversation with my daughter.

"When are you gonna give that man a baby of his own to obsess over?" I ask Harlow with a laugh.

"Soon." She smiles over at me. "We've been together for a few years now, and being pregnant would put a limit on my...career. But I know they want to grow our family. They have been bringing it up more and more lately. So, I told them one more year of playtime and fun, then we can start trying."

"And I get to be first," Neo says, popping up at our side. "I told the others I'd chop off their dicks if they argued, making the choice so much easier." His grin tells me he's serious and would enjoy doing it too.

Harlow rolls her eyes. "Don't worry, babe, we already agreed."

"Good." Neo nods. "Just making sure." He turns around and leaves. As in, he takes my baby and *leaves the building*. Oddly, I'm not worried.

"Ready to go?" Harlow asks us as each guy picks up some bags.

"I think so." I look around, making sure we didn't forget anything.

"Emmy," Charlie says, gaining my attention.

"Yes?" I respond, turning around to see Tyson has caught back up to us and everyone is exiting the building, leaving just me and Charlie standing here.

"I love you." She grins, gripping me by the shirt and kissing me until I feel drunk.

"I love you too," I breathe, giving her a dopey, love struck smile.

"I hope it's a boy." She smirks, raising a brow.

My eyes go wide. "You know?"

She laughs. "Of course. Babe, one of my favorite things about your body, is your amazing tits. Don't you think I'd be able to notice that they started getting bigger? Just like when you were pregnant with Melody."

"Are you mad?" I bite my lip, my eyes welling with emotion.

Her face softens. "Of course not. You know I love Melody, and I'll love any babies we have. They are just as much mine as they are yours, you know that," she affirms.

"You're not worried that having them so close together limits us on being able to do things? You don't feel held back?" My worries spill out of me like the contents of my stomach had when we arrived.

She shakes her head. "No, because it just means more love to give and more happiness to have. *And* a major key point that you keep forgetting...is that there are *six* of us. We are not limited to anything. We just need to make sure that we keep the lines of communication open," she tells me.

"Charlie. I'm really excited." I smile, feeling so much better knowing someone else isn't freaked out about this.

"I am too." She kisses me. "It's Tyson's this time, right?" she asks me.

"Yeah." I sigh. "He's so happy he got to have his hat in the ring this time," I say with a laugh.

Charlie smiles and shakes her head. "Two down, two to go. You know they are not gonna be happy about wearing a condom when you try for baby number three."

"I don't even wanna think about that right now." I giggle as we link fingers and catch up to everyone else waiting outside, where a black hummer limo awaits.

"Is that limo for us?" Charlie gasps, her eyes bugging out. The guys put the bags in the trunk, and I can see Neo holding Melody in the back.

"She needs a car seat," I tell no one in particular. There's no way I'm risking her sitting on someone's lap.

"Already got that covered," Harlow says, climbing out of the limo and revealing a car seat that's already strapped in. "Something to remember about me. I almost always think of everything. It's how I stay on top." She winks.

We all load into the limo and take off. When Neo suggests sticking my head out of the sunroof, I jump at the chance. I stand there like that the whole ride, my eyes wide in fascination as I take in everything for the first time.

The air is warm, there are palm trees everywhere, and there's just something about this place that fills me up with excitement.

Before long, we pull onto a road and up to a gate. “This is our place,” Harlow informs us from inside the limo. “We’ll give you the codes to get in, but under no circumstances can you give them to anyone else. As much as I love to play, I don’t like bringing my work home with me.”

“But, your place is also gated in, and we made some adjustments, so that you can access our backyard from yours,” Neo says, as the limo starts to move again, taking us just a little further down the road before stopping in front of another gate. I can’t see over it, but I really want to get out and explore our new home.

We all exit the limo and stand next to the gate. “Ready to see your new home?” Harlow asks, a wide smile taking over her face.

“Hell yes!” Talon cheers, making me laugh.

Harlow keys in the code, and the gate starts to slide open, but it’s painfully slow. We already know what it looks like, but seeing it in photos is completely different than experiencing it in person.

When the house comes into view, an overwhelming feeling fills me up, and it feels like everything in the world is going to be okay. Talon whoops, racing toward the house. Ben shakes his head and follows after. Harlow and Charlie talk as they start walking with Harlow pointing things out to her, and Tyson heads in with Neo. I stand there, taking it all in.

“How are you doing, Firefly?” Oliver asks me, coming up behind me and wrapping me tight in his arms. He lays his chin on my shoulder.

“We did it, Olly,” I say, trying not to cry. “Remember when we would lay on the little hill next to the mini golf course and look up at the stars, talking about how someday we would leave that town and make a better life than the one we were living? Well...we did it.”

“Yeah, we did.” He kisses my cheek. “I’m so glad that we get to do this together,” he hums.

I turn in his arms so that I can face him. “Thank you for never giving up on me.

For doing everything you did to keep me safe when you weren't around, and for continuing to do so when you were."

He snorts a humorless laugh. "Yeah, I don't think getting you almost killed on more than one occasion would count as *'keeping you safe'.*"

"Olly," I say in a warning tone,

"I know," he chuckles.

"Good. Now let's go explore," I say, giving him a light shove, as we walk towards our family and home.

We ran around the entire place like a bunch of kids, checking out every inch of the space. Our rooms were all set up, thanks to Harlow and her guys, so we really didn't need to do anything. The backyard is gorgeous with a fenced-in waterfall pool, a sandpit, playground set, and lots of space for other things. It's perfect, and I know our family can grow here. I can already see it. And being next to my sister makes it that much better. She showed us the renovations she had made, where our front fence wall was extended to connect with hers. She pointed out where she had two doors installed in both of our backyards, making it easier to come over to each other's places, so we don't have to spend so much unnecessary time walking. It's very convenient.

Harlow and Neo leave for the night so we can get settled in. We're all tired from traveling and all the excitement from the day. Melody is asleep, and we're relaxing in our new living room, watching TV and eating pizza.

"So, I need to talk to you guys about something," I say, sitting up from my cuddled position on Oliver's lap.

"What's up?" Ben asks, pressing pause on the movie.

I bite my lip, nerves fluttering in my belly, but Tyson and Charlie both give me encouraging looks. "When Tyson and I were at the doctor's this morning, and once we explained our concern about me not feeling well, the doctor wanted to check in with me, make sure everything was okay..." I start, dragging it out of myself.

"And is it?" Talon's brow creases in worry.

"Yes, everything is fine. I'm healthy, don't worry," I reassure him. "But he wanted to check on my birth control after we had a little conversation, only to find it wasn't there," I say hesitantly.

"What do you mean it wasn't there? Where did it go?" Ben asks, looking more confused the more I talk.

Charlie snorts a laugh, and Tyson shakes his head.

"My guess is Jimmy removed it when they took me," I tell them.

"Jimmy?" Oliver's chest rumbles, as he lets out a dangerous growl. "I can't wait to watch him die a slow and painful death."

"Guys, you're missing the point," Charlie sighs.

"What's the point?" Ben questions. "I'm so confused."

Taking pity on my poor guys, I take a deep breath in and just blurt it out. "The doctor told me I'm seven weeks pregnant. At least something good came out of being kidnapped, right?" I joke, trying to make light of the situation.

The room goes silent. Oliver doesn't move, just stares at me, blinking. My breathing starts to pick up, and I'm about to have a full blown panic attack when Oliver smashes his lips into mine with a bruising kiss.

I moan into his mouth as his tongue swipes at my lips, before slipping past and in against mine.

"Get off her!" Talon orders, suddenly appearing at my side.

"Give her to me," Ben demands. Hands are on me, and I break apart from Oliver's lips, giggling as my guys try to smother me with their love. *Literally.* They kiss my neck, my face, and my lips.

"I'm taking this as you're happy about it?" I laugh.

"Happy? Baby girl, I'm fucking ecstatic!" Talon says, scooping me up and pulling me onto his lap next to Oliver. Tears of relief slide down my cheeks at his reaction. When I told him I was pregnant with Melody, his reaction crushed me, so seeing him over the moon like this fills my heart with so much happiness it could burst. "Why are you crying?" his brows pitch.

"I'm just happy that you're happy." I wipe at my eyes.

Understanding takes over his face as Ben sits down next to us, pulling me half into his lap as well."I know I was a grade-A asshole last time, but I promise, never again will I react like that.

Bring on all the babies, give me a hundred, and I'll be just as happy." He leans over and kisses me sweetly.

"I think four is good enough. If we're meant to have more, we will deal with it then," I laugh.

"Hi, Butterfly," Ben says, cupping my cheek and guiding my face to look at him.

"Hi," I say softly back.

"So... we're gonna have another baby?"

"Yeah." I smile. "We are."

"I'm so fucking happy." He smiles back. "You are amazing, you know that? A goddess growing all these perfect little meatballs in your belly." He puts his hand on my tummy.

"I wasn't done with her," Oliver growls, putting his hands under my armpits and pulling me back into his lap.

My face hurts so much from smiling, and my heart is overflowing with joy. We sit and talk, everyone squishing on the couch as they drape me across them. The movie is forgotten as they all start talking about baby names, the nursery, finding me the best doctor, and everything else baby related that they can think of. I just lay there with my head on Oliver's lap and my feet in Tyson's while I listen.

Every day I ask myself what I did to deserve the love and support of all these amazing people, but to be honest, I don't really care. I'm just so fucking grateful I have it. I know I could be in this world without them, and I never want to find out what that might be like.

CHAPTER 24
Emmy

"YOU KNOW," TALON says, his fingers tracing little circles around my belly button. "I think now that life is ours for the taking and there's nothing else getting in our way, we can make one of our girl's dreams come true."

I perk up. *One of my dreams?* I think for a moment, and then my eyes widen a bit, excitement starting to fill my body as heat pools in my belly. Does he mean what I think he means?

"And what dream are we talking about?" Charlie asks, her brows pinching.

"You know, that conversation we had at your family's cabin when we spent the weekend there for Emmy's birthday?" Talon reminds her. So, he is talking about what I was hoping for. Charlie agreed then that we would do it someday. Is she still comfortable doing that?

Understanding dawns on her beautiful face. "I kind of forgot about that, to be honest," she says, looking at me, and my heart drops. "But, if that's what you want, I'm down."

"If you're not sure about it, we can do things just you and me, and then the others can have their time with me after." I smile at her, letting her know that I won't be upset if she says no.

"I think I have an idea that I'd be comfortable with," she says, getting up off the chair she ended up in after getting too hot being squashed between all the guys. She leans over, brushing her lips against mine. "How about I ride this gorgeous face while Oliver fucks your sweet pussy?" My pupils dilate as my core clenches.

"I would very much like that," I breathe, making her grin.

"Am I missing something?" Tyson asks. We all look over to him at his place at the end of the couch.

"Right. This was before you joined the merry band of misfits," Charlie says, straightening up. "Well, long story short... Emmy wants, even if it's just once, all her lovers...at the same time."

Tyson looks at me, and I can tell right away he's not down for it. I'm a little disappointed, but I'm not surprised. What we did with Oliver was a big step for him, and he has mentioned more than once that he won't participate in group activities. He loves having me to himself, and that's okay.

"You know where I stand with that," he tells me. "But, when they are done worshipping your body, I'll take you to my room and make you scream louder than they did." He shoots them a cocky grin. I bite my lip and look at the others.

"Are you guys okay with that?"

"Anything you want, Butterfly," Ben says, pulling me onto his lap so that I'm straddling him. "I would love to have our man fuck me while Oliver fucks you." He pulls me in for a kiss, his lips moving slowly against mine. I squirm on his lap as his tongue slips into my mouth, feeling his cock grow hard beneath me. I moan while grinding down on him, needing more friction. I'm really fucking turned on right now, and my body is humming at the idea of having everyone all at once.

And then Melody's cries make their way through the baby monitor. But before I can be disappointed, Tyson gets up from his spot. "I'll make her a bottle and put her back to bed," he tells us, kissing the top of my head before taking off upstairs.

"Told you, babe. There's six of us, and we will be just fine when this little one comes too," Charlie says. Right now, I am very happy that group activities are *not* Tyson's thing.

"Come on, hot stuff, let's try for twins," Talon says, picking me up so that I cling to him like a spider monkey as he starts to carry me up the stairs.

"It doesn't work like that, dummy," Charlie scoffs, making me giggle into Talon's neck as I start to lick and suck it.

"Fuck, baby girl, if you don't stop that, I'm gonna take you right here on the stairs," he groans, as he grips my ass, grinding me against his hard cock.

I ignore him, moving my hips to chase the friction I so desperately need. He slaps my ass.

"Bad girl," he growls, as we enter my new room, where a massive California king bed sits in the middle. Charlie takes off down the hall; I'm assuming she's heading to her room.

Talon tosses me into the middle of the bed. "I can be a *really* bad girl if you want me to," I purr, biting my lip as I move up to lean back on my forearms.

"Enough of that sassy mouth, Firefly," Oliver says, crawling onto the bed. "The only things that should be coming out of your mouth are screams and moans of pleasure, understand?" He grabs the band of my shorts and pulls them clean off, taking my soaked panties with them. I fall back onto the bed, loving the hungry look in his eyes. Talon and Ben move to my sides, pulling up my shirt to reveal my bare breasts. My nipples are pebbled, and I moan when Talon and Ben each take one into their mouths.

Oliver wastes no time as he parts my legs. He kisses down my inner thighs, and my pussy grows slick with every passing second. When he finally has his taste, I moan out his name, and my hips buck wildly as I grab handfuls of Talon and Ben's hair.

The guys work together to drive me mad like they always do. And they do it so well too.

"Fuck," I whimper, my senses are on overload with the pleasure becoming too much.

"Shhh," Talon whispers against my breast, nibbling on my nipple. "Give in, baby girl. Cum all over Oliver's face, and then you can have his cock in your greedy pussy."

I moan at his words, my core squeezing around nothing but air.

Oliver's tongue laps at my pussy, dipping in before sucking and nipping at my swollen clit.

"I can hear how wet you are, baby girl. Your thighs are shaking," Ben says, as he breaks away from my breast to kiss me on the lips...*the ones on my face*. "Cum for us, and we'll give you everything you need."

My body reacts, and my thighs trap Oliver's head right where I need him, as I do exactly what they ask. "Oh god!" I scream, my back arching as I toss my head back. My eyes roll into the back of my head as I shake and writhe around throughout my release.

"So fucking beautiful," Oliver rasps, as I relax my legs, letting him come up for air.

"Sorry," I huff out a laugh, his raven black hair looking like the definition of *'sex hair'* without even having had sex yet.

But he looks so yummy. He crawls up my body, his mouth wet with my juices.

“Nothing to be sorry for, Firefly.” He grins, leaning down to kiss me. I can taste myself, but I don’t care. “If I died, it'd be an honor to go out by making you scream.”

Ben and Talon have moved to one side of the bed, and I can hear Ben moan, which draws my attention. I whimper at the sight I see; Talon has Ben’s cock in his mouth. He bobs his head causing Ben to thrust his hips as he fucks our man’s mouth.

“Don’t mind me,” Charlie says, as she walks into the room in a black silk robe. “Did I miss the party?” She asks, putting her hand up to block out the blow job that’s going on beside us.

“No,” I say, giving her a smile.

Everyone is still wearing clothes but me, so other than Talon gagging on Ben’s cock, there's nothing at risk of being seen.

“Good.” She bites her lower lip, and I can see she's nervous. She looks over at Oliver then down at my naked body. “Well, I was going to taste every inch of her pussy, but I see you already did that,” she chastises, and I can’t help the giggle that slips from my lips as she raises a brow at him, her sass coming out in full force.

Oliver raises a brow right back. “You’ve had this divine meal before. Do you really think I could resist?”

“Good point,” is all she says, while shrugging her shoulders.

“Charlie, baby, I want to please you tonight, seeing how these guys have that covered on my end. Come here,” I demand, holding out my hand for her. We ignore Ben and Talon as they do their thing. I’d normally love to watch, but I want all my attention on my girl. Plus, I don’t need my eyes to hear all the delicious noises they are coaxing from each other. They seriously spur me on, making me want to hear everyone’s satisfaction mixing together.

“I’m gonna play with you a little while you two do your thing, is that okay?” Oliver asks, rubbing his hands up and down the inside of my thighs. "I'll fuck you when you’re done, so Charlie feels more comfortable." I look up at Charlie, seeing what she's okay with. My eyes prick with tears, and my heart soars at how much these guys care for my girl. They've become close friends, and making sure this dynamic works for everyone is one of their top priorities. I absolutely love it.

"Yeah, that's fine, just keep your meat stick away from me," she says, climbing on the bed.

"Yes, ma'am," Oliver laughs. I gasp, as he slips a finger inside me, lazily pumping it.

Charlie rolls her eyes, but the smile she gives me calms my nerves. This might be new, but we've all heard each other have sex, and it's not like we try hard to hide it. Including the times it's just been Charlie and me. I'm sure the guys have heard her more than once. It's just this time, we're all in the same room.

"Where do you want me?" she asks, kneeling next to me on the bed.

"On my face." I give her a sly smile. Her eyes fill with lust as she moves to straddle my face. I can see straight up her robe, and she's not wearing any panties. I can smell her excitement already. My hand comes up, slipping under her robe to squeeze her plump ass cheeks. She bites her lip, opening up the robe for me to see everything underneath. I know I gush around Oliver's fingers at the sight of her.

"So fucking perfect," is all I say, before gripping her hips and forcing her down onto my mouth.

"Fuck," she whimpers, as I start to suck and lick at her dripping core. She rocks her hips, leaning over to grip the headboard as she starts to fuck my face.

Looking up, I can see her lost in her own pleasure, but I'm hypnotized by the swaying of her breasts. I knead her ass, dipping my tongue in and lapping at her flowing juices, before sucking on her clit. All the while, I'm driving her out of her mind.

Charlie takes what she wants from me, and I fucking love it. No longer worried about what's going on around us, she lets loose. Her moans and cries edging me closer to another orgasm of my own, as Oliver slips another finger in and picks up his pace as he fucks me with them.

My fingers press into Charlie's thighs as I try to mold her to my mouth, needing every drop of her that she's willing to give me.

I love the look of pure bliss on her face as she teeters on the edge. "Fuck, fuck, fuck," she pants. "I'm gonna cum." I work harder, flicking my tongue back and forth until she explodes on my face. One of her hands flies to my hair as she grips it so hard it hurts. But it's a good kind of pain.

I lap up her release as she rides out her climax.

"Well..." she says breathlessly. "That wasn't so bad." She grins, as she ties her robe back up, climbing off my face.

"Something you would do again?" Talon asks, releasing Ben's cock with a pop.

Charlie looks over, quickly covering her eyes with her hands. "Nope, nope, sorry. This is a one-time thing. I don't need to be around your footlongs, sorry."

She leans over, kissing me hard. "Have fun, baby. I love you."

"I love you too. And thank you." I smile happily up at her.

"I'll do anything for you once, my love." She gives me a wink, before heading out of the room. "Take care of our girl's needs, you fuckers."

"We always do," Ben calls back, immediately groaning, as Talon starts to pump his cock. "Tease," Ben growls.

"Well, I didn't want you to cum just yet. Don't you want to do that down our girl's throat while I fuck your ass, and Oliver takes her from behind?"

Ben looks over at me, his eyes blazing with need. "Fuck yes."

"On your hands and knees, Firefly. I want that second orgasm to be around my cock," Oliver commands, and a jolt of excitement shoots down my spine.

Quickly, I move into position, sticking my ass in the air and tempting him with a little wiggle. He slaps my ass, making me groan at the slight sting. I feel his lips against the spot he just made contact with, kissing it to soothe me. "You really are being bratty today, aren't you, baby girl?" He bites my ass, before moving back onto his knees. I feel his cock glide across my wetness as he uses my natural juices to lube his cock up.

My chest heaves as my pussy clenches with each brush against my clit. Ben moves until he's on all fours, his face next to mine. "Hi, sweet girl," Ben says, his hand coming up to cup my face, but he doesn't kiss my lips. Instead, he places a soft one on my forehead. "Out of respect to Charlie," he winks.

My heart does funny things at his words. He won't kiss me. He won't taste someone else on his lips, and not just because he doesn't want to, but because he knows Charlie most likely wouldn't like the idea of that. Her sweetness is for me and me only.

This is another reason why we work so well. We have an understanding of each other.

Ben's eyes roll into the back of his head, and Talon grunts as Ben's body moves forward. Talon's inside him, already having prepped him while Charlie and I did our thing.

"Fuck Ben, your ass is so fucking tight," Talon groans.

"How about you, baby girl?" Oliver croons, kissing down my spine. "Is your ass nice and tight?" He damn well knows that it is. But, just to be sure, he dips two fingers into my wet cunt before slipping them past my tight ring and into my ass. I moan, looking up to see Ben now flush up against Talon's chest and Talon's hand wrapped around his neck. They're both looking at me, eyes burning with lust and heat as Talon thrusts up into Ben. Ben's dick is bobbing, slapping against his abs with the movement, and leaving a little smear of pre cum behind. They look so fucking hot that it has my pussy clenching around nothing, and I feel empty.

"Change of plans," I breathe, an idea forming that I hope works. "Talon, on your back with your cock buried deep inside Ben." They both look at me with curiosity, but I can tell they like the idea so far. Talon pulls out of Ben, making him whimper at the loss, and moves to lean back against the pillows and headboard. "Ben, sit on his cock, facing me," I direct.

Ben bites his lip, his eyes lighting up. He hovers over Talon, and I watch as Talon's cock disappears into his ass. "Lay back on him now." Ben does as I ask, and Oliver's fingers leave my ass. I move until I'm hovering over Ben's cock, gripping it tight and making his hips buck.

"Does our dirty girl want to ride Ben while I fuck his ass and Oliver fucks yours?" Talon groans as Ben continues to move with my hand, causing Talon's cock to move in and out of Ben.

"Yes," I breathe, lining Ben's cock up with my entrance before slamming all the way down.

"Fuck yes!" Ben shouts, gripping my hips.

Rocking my hips a little, I close my eyes, loving the feeling of his cock piercings rubbing me in all the right places.

"I fucking love your cocks," I moan, feeling Oliver's hand on my back, urging me to lean over Ben. He moves behind me and starts to slip into my ass.

"Yup, you're just as fucking tight," Oliver curses. "I will never get used to feeling your cock so close to mine." He says to Ben.

I'm deliciously full, but I need them to move. My clit is throbbing, my pussy is aching, and I really want to cum.

"Move. We need to move," I beg. "Fuck me."

"Your wish is our command," Oliver says, before pulling out and thrusting back in. Both he and Ben work me over as they rock with my movement. My eyes close as I concentrate on the feeling of both their cocks moving inside me. I know it won't take long until I explode, the sensation is already too much, and I'm sensitive from before.

When I open my eyes, I lock them with Talon's. His are lidded, and pure bliss is splayed across his face. He's along for the ride, too, as Ben moves up and down his cock, helping with little thrusts from his hips.

"I love fucking our man while he fucks you," Talon says, biting down on Ben's neck, making him curse.

"Same," I pant, my body flushed and humming. Oliver slips his hand over my belly and down to my clit. He starts to rub with determination to get me off. He must be close. They always try to get me to cum first, never wanting to leave me hanging. I have me some *real* gentlemen here.

Our collective moans mingle with the slap of skin, and heavy breathing fills the room.

"I'm gonna cum," I whimper. "Please don't stop," I tell Oliver. The way he's touching me as he and Ben fuck me has me right on the edge. And the way Ben's eyes roll into the back of his head as Talon pinches his nipples while leaving open mouth kisses on his neck in between sucks becomes my undoing.

"Oh, oh, ohhhh!" I cry out, my nails digging into Ben's chest as I cum so fucking hard that my vision goes dark. Like a domino effect, the guys groan out their releases. Oliver grips my hips, sending spurts of cum into my ass. Ben thrusts up into me one last time, filling my pussy full of his. And Talon shoves his face into Ben's neck as he roars out his climax into our man.

None of us move for a moment, heavy breathing filling the room. "Remind me to thank Charlie for agreeing to do this," I say, snuggling into Ben's chest as Oliver carefully pulls out of my ass.

Ben and Talon roll us onto our sides as Talon pulls out of Ben. Oliver and Talon leave for the bathroom.

"She is an amazing girl," Ben says, kissing the top of my head as he rubs my back. "Always so supportive of us in everything we do."

"I love her, and you guys, so much. I can't wait to be able to have a normal pregnancy with each of you involved."

"Same, my love," he murmurs back.

Talon and Oliver come back, cleaning the both of us up. We change the sheets and pile back into bed, snuggling up. I lay here, waiting for Tyson to come for me, worried that maybe something is wrong with Melody. But I know he would ask us for help if there was, so he must be just having a hard time getting her back to sleep. I'd offer to help, but he would just shoo me away. So I lay here, closing my eyes and waiting with a smile on my face. One of the best nights ever. Soon, fun times like this will have to be put on hold once again.

CHAPTER 25
Tyson

THIS MIGHT BE a big house, but I can still clearly hear them all the way from Melody's room. It's not loud enough for it to bother the baby, but it makes it kind of distracting when I'm trying to get our daughter to sleep.

Turning the music up on her light projector, I sit down with her on the rocking chair.

"You know, little Princess, there was a time I didn't know if we would get to live a normal life." I talk to her as she drinks her bottle. My heart is sad that she likes to try and hold it herself now.

We rock as my eyes roam over her little face, taking in every one of her features. Her small chubby cheeks, her tiny dimples, her curly red hair. Her eyes are still blue, but I can see them starting to slowly turn green. My little girl is growing up so fast, and the two weeks I was without her felt more like two months. She changed so much in a blink of an eye. I don't want to miss any more.

This little girl right here, she owns me wholeheartedly just like her mother. I would die for my girls in a heartbeat. I stayed awake in the compound way too many times, wondering if I was ever going to make it back to them alive. To be able to hear her giggles, to see her smile again. I will never take advantage of the time I have with my family.

And now our little family is growing. "Did you hear the news, sweet girl?" I kiss the top of her head as her eyes start to drift close. "You're gonna be a big sister soon. You two are going to be so spoiled and loved."

"Luckiest kids to ever be born." Charlie's soft voice has me looking up to the doorway.

"Done already?" I ask, raising a brow as my lip twitches.

She rolls her eyes. "Not much for me to be involved with. My part is done, but I'm sure they have only just begun."

"I know she wanted all of her lovers, but I wasn't a part of that deal when you made it.

I'm okay with her doing whatever she wants with everyone else. It's her body, her choice, and no one has the right to tell her what to do with it, but that's just not something I can handle. I like having her all to myself, you know?"

"I know." She laughs, taking a seat on the chair next to me. "It's one of my favorite things about our relationship. The guys, they're close, they love to share her all at once, but I love my 'Emmy' time. I don't want others around when we're getting close like that. So I get how you feel."

"Sharing with Oliver is probably the furthest I'd go."

"I don't think she's bothered by that. She gets to have her group fun; her needs are being met as well as ours. What we all have, it works and will continue to work."

"So, you ready for another one of these?" I ask, looking down at Melody.

"Fuck yeah," Charlie says, and I smile at her excitement. "I mean, if it was just me and Emmy, I think I'd be happier with just one right now. But with there being so many of us, I think we can handle a few more without feeling too overwhelmed."

"I don't think we will ever have to worry about not getting a break when needed. I have a feeling we're gonna wake up a few times with notes in their cribs from Harlow saying they took our babies and to come over if we want them back," I say with a quiet chuckle.

"I have a good feeling about this, Tyson. I haven't felt so sure about anything in my whole life. But this move, these changes, it's our time. The storm is over, and all I can see is bright, sunny skies. I know we will have our ups and downs, but I don't think it will ever get as bad as all the bullshit we just waded through."

I look up at her, "I agree."

Charlie takes Melody from me, insisting on some cuddle time before bed.

Heading down the hall to Emmy's room, I don't hear anything. Pushing the door open, I see her in the middle of the guys. Oliver on one side, Ben on her other, with Talon cuddled into him.

"She's asleep," Oliver whispers. "She tried to stay up, but we kind of wore her out."

"Let her sleep. I'll get my time with her tomorrow. Goodnight."

Shutting the door, I head to my room to take a shower before getting a good night's rest.

"Good morning, Princess," I say, kissing her cheek. She slowly blinks her eyes open, giving me a beautiful smile when she sees me.

"Hi." Her voice has a sexy rasp, and my dick jolts to life. I've been horny as fuck since waking up from a *very* sexy dream that she was the star of, like always.

"Thought we could spend the morning together since we didn't get to have any alone time last night."

Her eyes widen. "Shit, I'm sorry, I fell asleep."

"That's okay." I pull back the blanket. "You needed your rest." Looking down at her naked body, I decide I need to be inside her...like right now.

"What are you doing?" She starts to laugh as I scoop her up.

"We're gonna have a morning shower. I'm gonna get you all fresh and clean, then I'm gonna make you a healthy breakfast before we go over to Harlow's for the day."

I carry her from her room over to mine, ignoring my brother's cocky smirk as we pass him.

"Give him all the sass, Firefly," Oliver calls out.

"Count on it," she calls back with a giggle.

"So we woke up and chose to be naughty?" I growl.

Her eyes flash with excitement and lust. "You like it when I'm naughty."

"I also like it when you do exactly what you're told," I tell her, putting her down on her feet. I turn on the shower and strip my clothes off, loving the way she bites her lip, as her eyes roam over my body, stopping at my stone hard cock that's pointing right at her.

"You're so fucking sexy," she breathes, her eyes moving back up to meet mine.

"And you're so damn stunning, it hurts to look at you for too long," I shoot back at her.

She rolls her eyes, but her lip twitches. "You're full of shit."

"I never lie when it comes to how beautiful you are," I tell her, cupping her face.

"Every scar and stretch mark is like a stroke from a paintbrush on a masterpiece of art." I kiss her lips softly. "Every curve and dip of your body is a wonderland to explore." I kiss her jaw before running my lips down her neck. Her breathing hitches and her breaths comes out in short pants. I dip my fingers into her wet heat. "And I really love to explore this body, over and over again."

"Tyson," she whimpers.

"Yes, Princess?" I ask, pulling back to look in her eyes. They're filled with tears of emotion. We're always open with how she makes us feel and what we love about her. But I know deep down she will always have a small part of insecurity that tries to fight its way to the top of her mind. So, if it takes us telling her how perfect she is in our eyes every day, all day, then we will gladly do so.

"I love you," she says, and I bring her lips to mine in a crushing kiss. Her arms come up and around my neck. My hands grip her thighs, and I lift her up, her legs locking her to my body.

Carrying her under the warm spray of the water, I place her back against the tile wall. We kiss like it's our last, like we're the air the other needs to survive.

"I'm going to fuck you now," I say, against her lips, as I break the kiss. Her chest heaves, her breasts rising and falling.

"Please," she pleads.

A grin takes over my lips. "I love it when you beg for my cock, Princess."

"Fuck me, Tyson," she whimpers. "I wanna feel your thick cock inside me."

Growling, I trap her body between mine and the wall, before grabbing her arms from around my neck and pinning them against the wall above her head. Her eyes widen, and I give her a shit-eating grin as I shift my hips, feeling the tip of my cock finding her entrance. Her scream of pleasure as I thrust into her is music to my ears.

"Oh fuck," she cries out. "Yes, Tyson. God, please, fuck me!"

She doesn't have to ask me twice. I fuck her like a mad man, biting my lip as I thrust up into her. Her cunt feels so fucking perfect around me that I want to live inside her.

"Your pussy grips me so tight, Princess. Do you love my big cock filling you up?"

"Yes!" she screams, her eyes rolling into the back of her head, as I place both wrists in one hand and use the other to play with her clit.

"Let them hear how good I fuck you," I growl. "Let them know I make you cum just as hard as they do."

She starts to chant my name as I work her into a frenzy. "I'm gonna cum," she sobs in need.

"I know, baby girl, I can feel you quivering around my dick." I groan, feeling my balls start to draw up. I could last all day if I really wanted to, but I'll have her again tonight. Right now, she needs to cum, then eat. And *I* need to take care of my girl in every way possible.

"Cum with me," she pants. "Fill me up, mark me as yours."

"I think I've already done that," I tell her, biting her nipple. She cries out, her pussy strangling me. "But I'll gladly do it again and again."

Releasing her hands, I grab a hold of her plump ass cheeks, using my grip on them to help me fuck her with my cock. She holds on to me, digging her nails into my back.

"Tyson!" She cries out against my neck as she cums, her pussy spasming around my cock.

"That's it, baby girl." I praise her, as I pump into her a few more times before roaring out my own release. My cock twitches inside her, jets of cum filling her up, just like she asked.

"I will never get tired of this," Emmy breathes against my neck.

"Of what? Shower sex?" I ask, confused and breathless.

"Yes, but I meant orgasms." She laughs, making me chuckle too.

"Don't worry, Princess, there's never a shortage of that."

"I know, and I fucking love it." She sighs in contentment.

I wash her hair and body, sad that my scent is no longer on her skin. I'll fix that later. When we're done, I dry her off and wrap her in a big fluffy robe, before bringing her down to the kitchen. Everyone is in there, and they stop talking when we walk in.

"Hell yeah." Harlow walks up to me, high fiving me. "You made my baby sis scream this whole house down."

Emmy's face turns bright red, and I smirk. She has no idea what she's gotten herself into by moving next door to Harlow. She's her own brand of crazy, but I love her. This is the life I never knew I wanted, but so fucking glad I got it. I never want to lose it. I will always fight for this family, and I'll take down anyone who dares to try to come between us again. It's us against the world, and we will always come out on top.

Ben

We're hanging out at Harlow's place, celebrating our move and now the news of our newest addition.

Rosie has Melody on her hip as she shows her the pet goat they have named Bob. Bob licks the bottom of Melody's feet, causing her to burst into an adorable fit of laughter, the sound filling my heart with love.

Relaxing in the lawn chair with a cold beer in my hand, I have never felt so happy. I watch my family interact with each other, and I know for a fact this was all meant to be.

That everything that happened for the past few years, no matter how messed up and heartbreaking it was, was meant to happen the way it did. If even one thing was changed, we may not have gotten to this point. And yes, that includes the kidnapping. If that didn't happen, she wouldn't have had her birth control removed and gotten pregnant with our future son or daughter.

Now we're happy, in love, content, and have no one out to get us. We can build a new life with no restrictions.

Emmy is talking to Harlow and Evie about the baby news. Tyson and Oliver are chatting with Axel, Cass, and Dean. And Talon is with Neo. I have a stupid grin on my face, as I watch my man get excited over Neo's alpaca, Susie. This place *really* is a mini farm. All morning, Neo has been carrying a pig in a tutu in his arms. There's a duck quacking as it waddles around the backyard like it's just a normal thing. But, it works for them. And I'm not at all surprised by it.

"What has you smiling like an idiot?" Charlie questions in an amusing tone, as she sits down next to me.

"Just enjoying being truly happy with no stress or worry for the first time...ever." I take a sip of the beer, looking over at her.

"It's nice, isn't it? But sometimes, I can't help the feeling that something is gonna pull the rug right out from under us and slap us with another shit storm. I think I just need time to get used to everything."

"I know how you feel. It's in the back of my mind too. But I try not to let it take over my thoughts because I want to focus on the positive things in life. Like our daughter, my man, and our beautiful Butterfly."

"I've been meaning to ask you. What is up with all the nicknames? And why haven't you just stuck with one?"

Smiling, I look over at my girl, who looks like a glowing angel under the setting sun as she laughs, her smile is heart stopping. "When she first came to school, she was just starting out in life, finding who she was. She was always a strong woman, but being there with us, she started to grow, finding pieces of herself. She was my little caterpillar. Then everything happened with Mad Dog, and it changed her. With each thing that happened, she slowly morphed into the woman she was meant to be. She was halfway there, my little cocoon. Also, it helped that she was growing our little someone inside her too," I chuckle.

"Then after the shooting, giving birth in the middle of all that, she came out like the warrior she is. She became a bright, beautiful butterfly. She knows who she is now. She knows what she can handle and when to lean on us. She is bright and stunning, something that anyone would be lucky to hold in their hands, even for just the smallest moment in time. Emmy is more than anyone could ever hope for. A rare beauty, and she's all ours."

We will wake up every day and show her we are worthy of the love she blesses us with. We will stand by her side and help her continue to be her best self as she does with us. We will grow, learn, and thrive together as a family. Like it was always meant to be.

We had our second chance at happiness after being tossed into the unknown. We picked up the shattered pieces of ourselves, and redemption was found in the end.

This might be the ending of that chapter in our lives, but it's only the beginning of the next. The start of a glorious future, and I can't wait to see what comes our way.

The end. Thank you for coming along on Emmy and the gang's journey through Emerald Lake Prep and the start of their happily ever after. I hope you enjoyed reading their love story as much as I enjoyed writing it.

Want to read more about Queenie and her lovers? Check out my Blood Empire series.

WARNING!

This is a bonus chapter in Queenie's point of view. There is graphically described murder and torture like there is in my Blood Empire series.

If this is not something you like to read or think you can handle, please skip this.

Thank you for reading my Emerald Lake Prep series.

Bonus Chapter
Queenie/Harlow

"HELLO, HELLO, HELLO, all my lovely people!" I greet my waiting audience, my knee-high boots clicking with each step I take. "We have some extra special guests today! As well as playmates." I grin, my body humming with giddy excitement. I've been waiting months for these kills, and now that my sister and her guys are here, I can give these fuckers what they deserve.

"My sister and her guys, as well as her father-in-law, were awesome enough to be here with us tonight. These playmates have done some naughty things, and now they must be punished. So, without further ado, let's get the show on the road."

The curtain that is blocking them drops, revealing Dagger and Jimmy hanging from the roof, chains wrapped around their wrists.

"Now, I was going to strap them to chairs, but Neo wants to have some fun with this one." I hike a thumb over my shoulder to Jimmy. "So this was our solution, and this way, we can be a little more creative." I wiggle my eyebrows.

Charlie isn't here to watch, so she's upstairs with Roxy. Emmy and her guys only want to watch to get their pound of flesh, then she's going upstairs with them. With her being pregnant, watching what we're going to do to them probably won't sit well with her stomach.

"Let's start with daddy dearest," I say, and each of Emmy's guys stand up and get in a line in front of Dagger. Tyson takes his first swing, hitting Dagger in the stomach, making him grunt. Dagger screams in anger against his gag, but they all ignore him. Tyson punches him in the face, the ribs, the junk, over and over until he is a heaving mess. Tyson takes a step back, letting Oliver have a turn next. One by one, they take out their anger on Dagger for what he did to my sister and them for the past few years.

For what he did to Oliver, taking him away from his best friend and the love of his life.

When they're done, I'm surprised to see Emmy step in front of him. She looks up and down at his bloody and bruised body before sneering. "I hope the devil takes a special interest in you. I hope you suffer every single moment in Hell. You won't be missed. No one will shed a tear at your loss. I will sleep peacefully every night knowing you're rotting in the ground." She spits in his face, before Tyson wraps an arm around her and guides her out of the room, her guys following after.

"Well, that was fun," I laugh, looking at Steel. "I'm guessing you want to do the honors of ending his life?"

"Don't you want that?" he asks me.

"Nah, if anyone deserves that, it's Emmy, but that's not who she is. This man might share my DNA, but he's done more to hurt you than me. So with these two kills, I'm willing to let others have fun… Just this once." I wink. However, I do plan on having Neo by my side when we play with Mr. Perv sleeping next to Dagger.

Steel walks up to Dagger, a fun little evil smile taking over his face. "Looks like the better man won. You fucked with the wrong guys, and now all your men are dead. And you're about to join them." Steel takes a switchblade from his pocket. The blade flicks out, and he wastes no time stabbing Dagger with it. And he really goes to town, riddling Dagger's body with gashes. Tilting my head to the side, I watch with fascination as blood flows from the cuts down his bare chest and belly until he's a pretty shade of red. The life starts to fade from Dagger's eyes from the blood loss, and his screams die out. Steel pulls the blade out of his ribs, walking around Dagger's body. He grabs him by the hair, tilting his head up to reveal his neck. Steel brings the blade up, and Dagger looks right at me as Steel swipes the blade across Dagger's neck, ending his suffering.

Not like he didn't get a lot of that while he was here. We enjoyed taunting him in his cell alongside Jimmy. We made them go hungry for days, before giving them the most random combination of food. Neo really enjoyed coming up with bizarre meals. One time he fed them a mushed up bowl of Oreos, pickles, mayo, and sardines. It smelled nasty and watching them eat it was fucking hilarious.

Steel nods his head at me, not giving a single fuck that he's covered in blood, before turning around and walking out. He got what he came here for.

“I’m next!” Neo shouts, making his way to the table of goodies. He looks everything over, biting his lower lip in concentration as he figures out what he's gonna use. My eyes are wide with excitement as I watch, but my face drops when he only picks up a dagger.

I watch him walk over to Jimmy, back-handing him across the face. I snort as the slap echoes around the room. Jimmy’s eyes fly open in panic, taking in the room before him. He quickly realizes what's going on. He starts to shout, thrashing about.

“Please, no. Please don’t do this. I’ll do anything, please don’t kill me,” Neo mocks Jimmy’s pleas.

“Did you listen to Emmy when she told you no? How about every other person you raped? No? Well then, sorry dude, we don’t want to hear it from you,” I tell him, rolling my eyes when I see the patch of piss growing in his jeans. “Really? How much can one man pee? We haven't even given you that much water.”

Neo pretends like nothing is happening, whistling, *‘She'll be coming around the mountain’* as he starts to cut Jimmy’s clothes off until he's naked.

“No fucking way.” I roar with laughter when I get the sight of his micro penis. “Dude, like how? How do you jerk off?” I hold up my thumb and pointer finger. “Even that seems like it’s too big.”

“Well, that's disappointing. I was gonna cut it off, but there's nothing to cut off,” Neo says, genuinely sounding disappointed. “Oh well. I can still do the other things I have planned,” he shrugs, stepping forward. I don’t see what he's doing, only hearing the wailing cries of Jimmy’s pain. When he turns around, he holds up two pieces of flesh. “Look, pepperoni nipples!” He starts to cackle, as he takes them and randomly sticks them to Jimmy’s face. This man always does the oddest, most random things, but there's never a dull moment.

Grinning, I shake my head as I go over to the table, my brows furrow as I look down at a cactus plant. “Pet, what is this for?” I ask, holding it up.

He looks over at me, blood splattered on his cheeks, and his eyes light up. “Well, he seems to like to shove his sad little dick into places it doesn't belong, so why not return the favor?” he asks.

“I fucking love you.” My eyes go wide when it clicks in my head what he means.

"Come here, my Queen," he tells me, and I walk over with the cactus. Neo grabs a small table from behind the guys and drags it over. He lifts Jimmy up so that it looks like he's on his knees, his ass sticking out like he's begging for someone to fill him. "Give this man a fun and exciting way to go out of this world."

"With pleasure." I give him an evil villain grin, as I take the cactus in one hand, holding my arm out as far as I can. Neo steps back, taking his gun out, leveling it with Jimmy's head. With all my might, I ram that cactus right up his ass. I love the blood curdling scream that rips from his mouth before the bang rings out in the room, cutting off his screams.

There are two less sick fucks in this world. And what a fucking way to go.

BOOKS BY ALISHA WILLIAMS

Emerald Lake Prep – Series:

Book One: Second Chances (February 2021)

Book Two: Into The Unknown (May 2021)

Book Three: Shattered Pieces (September 2021)

Book Four: Redemption Found (March 2022)

Blood Empire – Series:

Book One: Rising Queen (July 2021)

Book Two: Crowned Queen (December 2021)

Book Three: Savage Queen (Coming 2022)

Silver Valley University – Series:

Book One: Hidden Secrets (January 2022)

Book Two: Secrets Revealed (May 2022)

Angelic Academy – Series:

Book One: Tainted Wings (Summer 2022)

Standalones

We Are Worthy- A sweet and steamy omegaverse. (2022)

ACKNOWLEDGEMENTS

I would love to give a big thank you to anyone who has supported me on this journey. A big thank you to all my amazing readers both who have been with me from the start and new ones who gave my first series a chance. Without each one of you, this series would not have been possible.

I'm also beyond grateful for Jessica Pollio-Napoles, Jennifer Storke Felderman, and Amy Waayers. You ladies are more than just my Alphas, you're family now! Thank you for all the time and energy you put into Redemption Found and for helping it become the awesome book that it is! I don't think I would have had as much fun writing it without you three! Can't wait to make way more books with you!

And a big shout out to Tamara Bui. Thanks for being there for me, and helping me with everything you do, you're the best wifey!

ABOUT ALISHA

Writer, Alisha Williams, lives in Alberta, Canada, with her husband and her two headstrong kids, and three kitties. When she isn't writing or creating her own graphic content, she loves to read books by her favorite authors.

Writing has been a lifelong dream of hers, and this book was made despite the people who prayed for it to fail, but because Alisha is not afraid to go for what she wants, she has proven that dreams do come true.

Wanna see what all her characters look like, hear all the latest gossip about her new books or even get a chance to become a part of one of her teams? Join her readers group on Facebook here - **Naughty Queens.** Or find her author's page here - **Alisha Williams Author**

Of course, she also has an Instagram account to show all her cool graphics, videos and more book related goodies - **alishawilliamsauthor**

Got TikTok? Follow **alishawilliamsauthor**

Printed in Great Britain
by Amazon

10642311R00116